Children, Development and Training

Theological and Sociological Challenges for Mission

Children, Development and Training

Theological and Sociological Challenges for Mission

Jesudason Baskar Jeyaraj

Jubilee Institute
2018

CHILDREN, DEVELOPMENT AND TRAINING: Theological and Sociological Challenges for Mission—jointly published by the Rev. Dr. Ashish Amos of the Indian Society for Promoting Christian Knowledge (ISPCK), Post Box 1585, 1654, Madarsa Road, Kashmere Gate, Delhi-110006 and Jubilee Institute, Madurai, Tamilnadu.

ISBN: 978-81-8465-667-1

Copies available:
Jubilee Institute
30/31 Ananda Raj Nagar
K. Pundur, Madurai, Tamilnadu-625007
Email: jubileeinstitute70@gmail.com

Laser typeset by
ISPCK, Post Box 1585, 1654, Madarsa Road, Kashmere Gate, Delhi-110006
• *Tel:* 23866322/23

e-mail: ashish@ispck.org.in • ella@ispck.org.in
website: www.ispck.org.in

Contents

Abbreviations

AIDS	Acquired Immune Deficiency Syndrome
ATA	Asia Theological Association
BPL	Below Poverty Line
CAR	Children at Risk
CCM	Child, Church and Mission
CFCD	Christian Forum for Child Development -India
CIC	Children in Crisis
CRC	Convention on the Rights of the Child
CT	Child Theology
GA	Global Alliance for HCD
HCD	Holistic Child Development
HIV	Human Immunodeficiency Virus
ILO	International Labour Organization
JJA	Juvenile Justice Act
NCPCR	National Commission for Protection of Child Rights
NGO	Non-Governmental Organization
NHRC	National Human Rights Commission
SSC	Senate of Serampore College, West Bengal
TAFTEE	The Association for Theological Education by Extension

TD   Transformational Development
UDHR   Universal Declaration of Human Rights
UNHCR   United Nations High Commissioner for Refugees
4/14 Window   Children between the age group of 4-14
10/40 Window   Regions between 10 degree and 40 degree in the globe
                            (Africa to South East Asia)

Introduction

Many books are written on children by psychologists, sociologists and medical professionals discussing their problems, prospects and development from their perspectives. Stories and novels written for children are flooding the market. Parents are interested to buy them for their children. Some of the stories are included in the curriculum in schools. Leaders of Christian ministry or missionaries involved in social work or theologians in seminaries are not showing much attention to produce books for the development of children. Most of the scholarly books in the theological education do not discuss the problems and development of children. However, there is an awakening among leaders to write books and articles on different aspects of the development of children. Yet, not enough importance is given to train parents, teachers and pastors with proper curriculum and approaches to develop children to enjoy welfare, justice and empowerment.

This book comes with the collection of essays I presented in conferences and published in books and journals. Now, they are revised to be published by ISPCK, Delhi. I am thankful to the Publisher. The first part with four essays discusses the insights of the Bible and the need of Child Theology for each context in the world to provide a basis for theological reflection and action. The Second Part having another four essays discusses the social problems of children. Some of the problems such as poverty, child labour, street children, orphans and trafficking are common in many countries. These issues are discussed by churches and NGOs. Nevertheless, the issue of female infanticide, foeticide and abortion is a special one in the Indian context. So it is included here. India is one of the few countries where many children could not have proper education due to various reasons. They have the right to education is discussed as a key social problem in this book. The mission of churches should include children and their development is emphasized. This agenda cannot be ignored anymore. The last part of the book is presenting the need of shift in theological education and training with new programmes such as HCD.

Any reader in the West or East can notice the urgency of working for and with the children drawing some insights and challenges from this book. In this age of global net-working today, people concerned with the development of children can join hands in partnership and make our world child-friendly. Let us raise new generation of children committed to divine values.

Jesudason Baskar Jeyaraj
Hon. Director, Jubilee Institute
Madurai -625007 India.
2017

THEOLOGICAL PERSPECTIVE

CHAPTER - 1

Biblical Perspectives on Children and their Protection

Children are loved and valued in all societies. They attract us by their innocent look and smile. It is estimated that India had 298 million children below the age of 14 out of 827 million in 1990[1]. The children population has increased since 1990 from 36 percent to 40 percent in 2004 and estimated to be appx. 400 million. Many of them, between day one to 14 years old, are at risk due to famine, drought, unclean environment, infected virus of HIV/AIDS, ethnic conflicts, violence, discrimination, war, lack of care and protection. According to a report, the children between the age of 5-14 involved in labour are 73 million. However this estimate is low because of the difference of opinion regarding defining 'Child Labour' and 'Child Work'. Questioning this data, another report points out that the children between the age of 5-14 out of school in India alone are 100 million. What are they doing is another question leading to the suspicion that they are involved in child labour[2]. More than 3,00,000 children under the age of 18 are in armed forces of the rebel groups in different parts of the world. Approximately 10 million children die due to under nutrition in poor countries and 5,15,000 women die every year as a result of poor care during pregnancy and child birth[3]. In India, 60 million children are underweight[4]. Female children are at greater risk more than the male children due to the prevailing gender bias in our societies. They are discriminated over against male children in getting enough food and care at home, assigning more domestic work of cooking, fetching water and cleaning and priority in getting educated. Teenage girls are in danger of being abducted and raped or sold to prostitution if they come from poor families seeking jobs in towns and cities. The survey published by THE HINDU News Paper (dated 8th Nov. 2005) on the abuse of children particularly female children is alarming. Out of the total child abuse in India, the most affected are female children (75%) compared to male children (6%). Children from poor families are the most affected to the tune of 44% compared to the children of middle class (34%) and the rich families (22%). The culprits are people known to the child (53%), relatives of the child (22%) and people unknown to the child (25%). Reports, articles and books written on children and the news items of TV expose the serious problem children are facing in the world and challenge us to protect them[5].

The Bible values children highly and pays attention to take care of them. As we give importance to protect the environment through our Eco-theology and projects, we need to give importance to protect the children and build future generation in health, literacy, value orientation and fullness of life. A child could be defined from the perspective of physiology, psychology, social relationship, economic status, caste, race, religion, culture and age limit. Many scholars and UNO regard 18 years is the upper limit to consider a person as a child. The Bible, quite often, speaks of children without defining their age limit. I prefer to bring different biblical references on children under various sub-headings and articulate the theological dimension of children towards a child theology. This paper deals briefly with the theological, sociological, legal and ethical dimensions related to children and lists a few challenges. It is my wish that this paper will be of some help to the theological students as well as people involved in the ministry to children through their churches, missions and NGOs and lead them to explore Child Theology.

I. THEOLOGICAL DIMENSION

Theological dimension of children is an important basis to value the children and fulfill the responsibility towards them. Different theologies such as 'Child Theology', 'Theology of Childhood' and 'Theology of Children' have emerged emphasizing certain aspects of children. Many books on these theologies related to children published in the West are not available for us at an affordable price in India. I have to concentrate on the Bible and our context in understanding both male and female children and suggest a Child Theology for the holistic child development[6]. One can notice a number of terms used in Hebrew and Greek to refer to children[7]. These words mean different stages of the growth of a child or the status as a son or daughter or a virgin rather than their age. Instead of taking up terminological study of these words, my interest here is to find out the way the Old Testament and New Testament define children and summarize the portrayals in terms of Child Theology. Theological dimension of children becomes the basis for formulating or evaluating or modifying sociological, legal and ethnical dimensions. The interactions of these dimensions are important for the care and empowerment of children.

Children are God's Gift

The Bible affirms that all children are God's gift to the families. God pronounced the blessing to Adam and Eve to 'multiply and fill the earth' (Gen. 1:28). On commenting on this blessing, Claus Westermann says, "The blessing given to humanity in Genesis 1:28 means that as long as humankind exists, God will remain effectively at work in them because of this action at creation"[8]. Procreation of human generation is God's plan in creation. Humanity must not end with Adam and Eve. God could have easily made again thousands of children out of the dust and given to Adam and Eve to bring them up as their children. Adam and Eve would have reared them up not as their own children but as an entrusted responsibility. Their affection towards such a ready-made children outside their own blood cannot be biological. But God chose a plan to increase the descendants of human race through Adam and Eve allowing them to be involved in the creative activity of bringing forth children out of their own flesh and blood. God did not take away the creativity of Adam and Eve. The blessing and the power of creativity given by God to humanity to have children is appreciated in Ps. 104:30. The same verb *yaled* used to denote 'bring forth' refers to 'offspring' or a 'child' when used as a noun. The action of bringing forth and the outcome of a child referred to by one root *yeled* indicate that the text emphasizes the creativity of human beings. Getting children is regarded as receiving an inheritance from God (Ps. 127:3). We need to take into consideration the problem of infertility among many people today and the growing interest in adopting and adding children to the family. It could be by a biological process of conceiving and delivering a child or using the medical techniques of fertility or implanting embryo or hiring a surrogate mother or even adopting a child as their own. Children standing around the parents, as stated in Ps. 128:3-4, is viewed as a blessed family.

Children are created in God's image

Although children are biological descendants of parents, they are created in the image of God[9]. For, they inherit the image of God from Adam and Eve who were created in God's image. The 'likeness of God' is translated through procreation. Creating both male and female in his own image means that the sexuality is a gift of God and God's will for his creation. Speaking on the sexual distinction, Gerhard von Rad remarks that " ... the idea of man finds its full meaning not in the male alone but in man and woman"[10]. Both sexes are created in the image of God is repeatedly emphasized in Gen. 1:26-27:

> Then God said, 'Let us make man in our image, in our likeness
> ....
> So God created man in his own image,
> In the image of God he created him;
> Male and female he created them. (NIV)

God has given the same image to a girl child that he has given to a male child. She is equal to a boy in all respects. It is the society that makes the girls to feel inferior to boys through gender bias. The identity of a child is not his or her own caste or tribe or race or sex but the image of God. The image of God seen in children is important that the inherent image should not be destroyed by using violence against them or denying their rights. Wounding, hurting, depriving, oppressing, denying the rights of a child means affecting the image of God.

Giving birth to a child is not a curse

The blessing of 'being fruitful and multiplying children' is inclusive of labour pain. Labour pain was part of the process of delivering the child even before the fall. 'In pain you will deliver children' is an indication that God has granted the gift of children to human beings and did not pronounce the curse of infertility (Gen. 3:16). Many assume that the pain at the time of delivering the child is a curse introduced as a new element by God. Work at home, labour pain and feeding children were already a part of woman's life. What happened due to disobedience is that the burden of work (labour in household in the case of women and field in the case of men) is increased can be understood from the use of the word *'eseb* (labour, toil, pain, work) in both v. 16 and v.17. The phrase 'I will multiply' is directly linked to the direct object of 'your work' and 'pregnancy' and indirectly with the following clause 'in labour you will deliver children' (3:16). Carol Meyers points out that the same word *'eseb* (meaning 'toil' or 'labour') is used in 3.17 to refer to the toil of Adam. Therefore the punishment is the increasing of Eve's work at home, and the pain at the time of delivering the child. Since the same word *eseb* is used in the clause 'in pain you will give birth to children' which stands closer to the previous clause in v.16, we may say that the pain which is an unavoidable component in delivering the child also will be increased. The development of household by bearing more children who were needed for the economy in the early agrarian society that had high mortality rate and by investing more labour to take care of the domestic work and rearing of the children on the part of Eve is not a curse but an increase of duties and responsibilities. If so, then we need not regard v. 16, the increase in the toil and pain as a curse but an additional burden[11]. The better translation of 3:16 suggested by Carol Meyers is as follows

> I will greatly increase your toil and pregnancies
>
> (along) with travail shall you beget children. _ (Page 29)

The pain and difficulties a mother goes through at the time of giving birth to a child is biological. Medical science discusses it from biological perspective and sees a positive element in it. Conceiving, carrying the baby for 9 months in womb and the labour pain give the value of the child[12]. If we give birth to children without any difficulty or pain, then it seems like machines are producing products without any emotion or feeling. The product may have a commercial value and not any value for the machine that produced them. Women are not machines to produce children but human beings with their feelings and emotions attached to what they do. Their lives are at risk in delivering each child. That is why each child is of value for humanity. Machines do not attach their feelings with their products. But the feelings of the mother are so intrinsically attached to her child that she loves the baby, cares for the child and sacrifices herself for the growth of her son or daughter and deeply mourns at the death of her children. Men can only see it and understand it. But the mother experiences it. If so the labour pain is not merely a curse but a blessing in disguise. It tells the humanity that the birth of human being is painful but so valuable. Can we say that God did not curse the women who are his own creation but included a meaningful blessing to the life of human beings? Puberty, menstruation, marriage and bearing the child and labour pain must not be considered a curse or pollution for women. Women should not look at their biological functions as a curse of God but a blessing special to them.

Children signify Fatherhood and Motherhood

Parenthood is possible because of having children. A husband and wife married for long without a child cannot experience the fatherhood and motherhood respectively. Having a child of their own blood or by adoption makes them to be proud of their parenthood and realize the significance of the status and role of parenthood. Love and affection flow naturally towards their children. A father and mother are prepared to adjust their lives, share their resources and sacrifice their comforts and convenience for the sake of their child. Children create new relationship in the family and enable the father and mother to realize the meaning of fatherhood and motherhood of God portrayed in the Bible. God is not bisexual but God is like a Father and a Mother. God created both male and female sex but God is beyond sexual difference. People of Israel are called as 'children of God' or 'daughters of Zion' in metaphorical language. They have a special relationship with God as a chosen people to serve God (Ex.4:22-23; Dt. 1:31; 8:5). Ex. 19:5-6 describes them as a 'kingdom of priest' and a 'Holy nation' for the ministry of God. God, as a father, disciplines those whom He has chosen to be in special relationship for the special task (Dt. 7:7-11). Psalms 103:13 speaks of God's compassion is like that of a father to a child. A child could be abandoned by his or her father and mother but God as a Heavenly Father would not desert a child (Ps. 27:10). Even a mother may forget her child but God as a heavenly mother will not forget the child (Isa. 49:15-16). As a mother comforts her baby, God comforts his children (Isa. 66:13). The important aspect in the Child theology is the fatherhood and motherhood that God is the heavenly father and mother for all the children. However, God is concerned more about the fatherless and motherless children who are at more risk (Ex.22:22; Isa. 10:1-2). So God on behalf of orphans demands the society to take care of and render justice to them. His love towards the fatherless and motherless child is more than towards the children with parents. Our experience as children to our parents and as parents to our children helps us to understand God's role as father and mother and enlightens the parenthood of God.

Children are ministers of God

Priesthood of all believers includes children too. Children are not only worshippers of God but also part of God's ministry. The prevalent notion is that God selects only the adults for his ministry and the children have to wait till they become adults to serve God. Till then children have to be at the receiving end of getting instructions in the churches or Sunday Schools or VBS. We treat them as consumers rather than contributors. But God has selected Samuel and revealed His word to him. Eli, the well-experienced and senior minister could not get the divine revelation. God used Samuel at his childhood to open the eyes of Eli and to minister to the people at Shiloh. God used David, the young boy to challenge Goliath, the warrior of the Philistines (1 Sam. 17:31-34). David was taken for granted and laughed at because he was a young boy to challenge Goliath. Furthermore, using the sling to drive away wolf and fox trying to harm the flock was regarded as the toy of the children. What has been regarded as a childish tool brought victory to the Israelites because the sling was used to defeat Goliath who cursed the name of the living God of Israel. As children, both Samuel and David had the zeal for God and commitment to glorify His name. They praised God and led others to praise God through their actions. Another example is the guidance of the young servant girl from Israel leading Naaman to Elisha for healing and understanding the greatness of the God of Israel (2 Kings 5:2-4). Keeping their lives in front of us, could help us to understand the meaning of Ps. 8:1. Children use naturally their lips, voice and hands to praise God. On commenting on this verse, Peter Craigie says that the babies symbolize human weakness and humility but they reveal the 'strength' when they pronounce the name of God in their praises. God uses the weak even the child to show the strength of His name and to question the oppositions of the enemies[13]. Sometimes, innocently, they repeat what we sing and dance to the songs in worship. Jesus made a reference to children praising God (Hosanna) was a challenge to the adults of Jerusalem. Their shouting of 'Hosanna' with the crowd at the time of Jesus entering into Jerusalem implies their demand for freedom of their nation (Matt. 21:1-11; Jn. 12:12-19)[14]. They are regarded as more spiritual and moral than the Pharisees, Saducees and Priests. Children without any age bar or a special call for ministry are partners in the ministry of God. God accepts their praises and contributions in glorifying the name of God.

Children are leaders and contributors

Many of us assume that children cannot be leaders till they become youths or adults. But we notice that the children play a major role of leading in the most difficult and dangerous situation of natural calamities, ethnic violence and bombing. We have evidences of children rescuing children and adults. Bravery awards are given to such children each year for alarming the coming dangers or rescuing the victims or leading the people to safety. Manasseh and Josiah became kings of Judah at the age of 12 years and 8 years respectively and contributed for political stability with the help of their mothers and royal court (2 Kings 21-22). Isa. 11:6-8 says:

> The wolf will live with the lamb,
> The leopard will lie down with the goat,
> The calf and the lion and the yearling together;
> And a little child will lead them.
> The cow will feed with the bear,
> Their young will lie down together,
> And the lion will eat straw like the ox,
> The infant will play near the hole of the cobra
> And the young child put his hand into the viper's nest
> They will neither harm nor destroy on all my Holy Mountain,
> For the earth will be full of the knowledge of the Lord
> As the waters cover the sea - (NIV)

What is the relevance of this text for children? The basic thrust is that peace and harmony can be created between the powerful and powerless only when the powerful becomes powerless. In other words, they should share their powers, riches and authority with the powerless. They restrain themselves to use the powers and authority to oppress the weak. The powerful wolf and lion, metaphorically symbolizing the rich and powerful, voluntarily relinquish their powers and aggressiveness and relate cordially with the lambs. They do not harm the lambs which are by their nature harmless and powerless. A child can put forth his or her hand innocently into the pit of a poisonous snake and yet not being bitten or harmed by it. A child cannot lead the powerful and harmful lion and wolf. These ferocious animals can kill the child. The children are at risk in the midst of the powerful. However, when the danger of misuse of power and authority is averted, the children are no more at risk and can lead the powerful that were a threat to their lives. This text demands to create the situation of peace and harmony on earth that a child can feel free from dangers and enjoy security of life. Sharing of powers with the powerless and insignificant can empower them to take up leadership and contribute for the good of others. Children can be leaders not necessarily in heaven but even now on earth if the ruling class and powerful can change their attitude and approaches towards the poor and marginalized. John Watts believes that this is possible if the righteousness and knowledge of God controls the society, the predators are tamed and the reptiles are no threat[15].

Child, the incarnated Saviour

The focus of the New Testament is more on Jesus, the incarnated child to save the people. We cannot ignore him as a child or his teachings about children.

Represent the Weak

God entering into the world through the birth of Jesus was predicted by the angel to Mary and Joseph. This is narrated in Luke 2. Simeon's prayer and blessing highlight the importance of the child. Anna, the prophetess speaks about this child as the redeemer (Lk. 2:38). Mathew links the birth of Jesus to the fulfillment of the prophecy of Isa. 7:11-14. Most of the scholarly discussions focus on the issue of historicity of Jesus, prediction of the prophecy, doctrine of virgin birth and the theory of kenosis rather than on the representative function of the incarnation. Why should God appear in the form of a human being particularly to be a child than an adult to fulfill his mission. How can God represent the weak, marginalized and the poor? The best representation is a child because a child is small, weak, illiterate, dependent, powerless and vulnerable. Baby Jesus represents the weak and the oppressed section of the society to God on the one side and to the rich and powerful on the other side to challenge them not to take advantage of the weak and exploit them.

Represent the values of the kingdom of God

In the preaching and teachings of Jesus, children were appreciated for their child-likeness and used as illustration to teach the values of the kingdom of God such as love, sharing, innocence, justice and equality. Jesus pointed out the important requirement to enter into the kingdom is to become like a child (Mt. 18:3; 19:13-15) by placing the child at the centre.[16] The identity of this child is not clear but the little boy in the midst of them is the focal point to stimulate theological reflection on the Kingdom of God and practical issues of becoming like a child. Douglas Hare suggests three possible meaning for 'becoming like a child' viz. to become as teachable as children and learn God's ways, as to depend totally on the sovereign God as a child depends on parents or to assume the lowest status of a child in the society signifying the humility. If so, becoming like a child means to have the nature and quality of a child. It means to 'born again' as told to Nicademus (Jn. 3:1-10)[17]. It is to abandon all the corrupt nature of adulthood and restart the life again like a new born child. It is a new birth revealing the innocence, dependency and vulnerability of a child. Greatness in God's kingdom has nothing to do with status, power and wealth but becoming like a child is a tremendous challenge from Jesus to his followers.

Represent the hope of salvation

The incarnated baby became the Saviour of the world. The apostles preached this message on the basis of the fulfillment of messianic prophecies and self understanding and acclamation of Jesus. Isaiah, the prophet, predicted the birth of a child and called the child Immanuel (God with us) in the context of Syrio-Ephramite war. The message gave hope to the king Ahaz and the people of Israel that God is with them and will deliver them from the attack of Syrians. God as a deliverer is symbolized by the birth of Immanuel. The same prophecy is used by Matthew (1:23) to refer to the birth of Jesus. He points out that the prophecy of Isaiah is fulfilled in Jesus. Jesus will deliver and save the nation from the hands of the Romans. Luke also acknowledges that this child is the Messiah (Lk. 2: 8-20, 48-51). The presence of the incarnated child in the midst of people gave them the hope of salvation. Jesus also proclaimed himself as the Messiah in various ways in the later period of his life, namely, through his teachings (Lk. 4:16-21), dialogue with people (Jn 1:35-42; 4:16-26) and actions of healing the sick, feeding the hungry, delivering the people from evil spirit and reconciling communities (Jn.4).

Death which creates a permanent separation in human relationship teaches us to realize the value of the presence of our beloved ones. No one likes to lose a child or a youth or even an old person in a family. By giving his only begotton child to die for us, God not only showed the magnitude of his love but also the value of the child. God has taught the divine values and the need to protect lives particularly the children. The death of God's only son on the cross has brought reconciliation between God and the fallen humanity (Rom. 5:8-11)[18]. If so, as a peace making son, Jesus brought peace to humanity. The vicarious death and resurrection of this child at his later period had created a new humanity (Col. 1:15-20).

Children of God is a special relationship and responsibility

All the children created on this earth are children of God in general. Since the fallen humanity is redeemed by the death and resurrection of Jesus Christ, the relationship between God and humanity is restored (Rom. 5:8-11). However, the Bible speaks of a special relationship between those who accept the redemptive act of God through Jesus Christ. These people are bestowed with a special status of being called "Children of God". John 1:11-12 says that all those people irrespective of age limit, race, culture and geographical jurisdiction who received Jesus and believed in his name, Jesus gave the right to become children of God. Matt. 5:9 speaks of those peacemakers as blessed and shall be called sons of God. Another condition to qualify to be the children of God is to love enemies and pray for the persecutors (Matt. 5:44-45). St. Paul points out those whom God foreknew, he has predestined to be confirmed to the image of his Son (Rom. 8:29). The special relationship is for a special responsibility and does not make God to show favoritism to this group of children and nepotism to the rest of the children outside the special status. The people who received the special status of 'children of God' have special responsibility to work for the welfare and development of all the children.

II. SOCIOLOGICAL DIMENSION

Societies do not remain unchanged. Society like ancient Israel came into existence because God called Abraham and Sarah. He gave them promises to have descendants to become a separate society. They came from the society of shepherding sheep and possibly were existing as a tribal group in Mesopotamia. The tribal group consisting of Abraham, his family and servants grew to be a confederation of twelve tribes in the settlement period (1300-1050 BC) and went through further development to become a political nation with kings, army, court and trade (1050-587 BC). Although the structure of the society changed from the tribal family of Abraham to a powerful political nation under David, the basic understanding of the status of children as the property of the parents remained the same in Israel. The relationship of children to the family and their responsibilities grew at different levels in accordance to the changes in the structure of the society. The concern to protect the rights of children gained importance as the civilization of Israel made a progress and the children faced new threats and problems. The sociological perspective leads us to notice a number of violations of their rights in different periods of their history. A few cases of vulnerability of children and youths and the response of God and society towards such violations are listed briefly below.

Abel, the slained brother

Where is your brother? is the question raised by God invites Cain to be accountable for his brother and reveals God's concern for the lives of sons and daughters (Gen. 4:1-16). The story of Cain and Abel does not tell the exact age of them. They could be in their teenage to bring their offerings from their labour. One cannot believe that an elder brother killing his own younger brother on the issue of offering in worship. Abel has every right to bring an offering of his own choice to Yahweh and worship him the way he wanted. It is God's decision to accept the worship and offering of the people. Cain has no authority or right to question the worship of Abel or the decision of God to accept his offering[19]. But Cain has every right to ask God to accept his worship and offering too. Cain can plead and struggle with God to be accepted. Instead of pleading to God or be happy with his brother's offering being accepted by God, Cain became jealous and committed this cruelty of murdering Abel. We sympathize with Abel and try to give different answers for God accepting the offerings of Abel and rejecting the other. Cain should not have committed this murder and responded as if he has no responsibility towards his brother saying 'Am I my brother's keeper'? This is precisely the point here. 'To keep' means to watch, protect and redeem (Lev. 25:48; Num. 36:12-28). God is holding him responsible for not taking care of his brother. The word 'brother' refers to Abel in this story. However, Abel represents similar brothers who are despised and ill-treated by other brothers in the same family or community.

Hagar, the driven out pregnant

Hagar a servant maid of Sarah was given as a wife of Abraham since Sarah was childless. This is not unusual in the early nomadic society. Sarah gave Hagar to Abraham with an intention of getting a child for Abraham. When Hagar became pregnant, she started looking down Sarah, her mistress. We do not know exactly what went on between Sarah and Hagar. But the problem could be the pride and assertiveness on the side of Hagar and jealousy, insecurity and inferiority feeling on the side of Sarah. So Sarah forced Abraham to send Hagar away from the family and severe all relationship with Hagar and the forthcoming child of her. Listening to Sarah, Abraham drove Hagar out of the family. As Hagar was in the desert looking for water and struggling to save her life and the child in her womb, God appeared to her, shown a pool of water for drinking and asked her to go back to Abraham (Gen. 16:7-16). It is important to note here that God took the side of Hagar and vindicated the ordinary maidservant. God is on the side of the oppressed and victims. God saved the life of her and the child. Abraham has to accept her again and take care of her. This kind of ill-treatment to second wife is seen in many Indian families. Some women of this situation in pregnancy go through cruelties meted out by the first wives or mother-in laws or sister-in laws or husband and experience depression. They are driven out of the families before or after giving birth to a child. Often, the mother and child are left at risk to take care of themselves or commit suicide or throw themselves to begging or bonded slavery.

Jacob, the Fugitive

The story of Jacob tells us that he cheated his brother Esau and inherited the birthright belonging to the first born so that he could enjoy all the possessions of his father as the sole heir. He cheated again and obtained the blessing of his father at the instruction of his mother (Gen. 25:29-34; 27:1-28:5). What Jacob did to his brother was wrong. He had to flee from his home to a far away place to escape the fury of Esau. He was at risk on his journey to Paddan-Aram. His prayer and vows in Gen. 28:10-22 reveal the difficulties he went through as a fugitive. His feeling of uncertain future can be noticed. Taking advantage of his situation, Laban exploited him to serve for a long period. Fugitives are always at risk on their journey and at work place. Alienation from their family, native place and the feeling of uncertain future affect their personality. Many young boys and girls are running away from their houses every day for various reasons and end up as cheap labour or in prostitution or take up dangerous jobs. Their masters know that there is none on the side of the fugitive to question their cruelty.

Joseph, the sold out slave

Joseph born to Jacob and Rachel was despised by his step-brothers because he was born to Rachel and loved too much by Jacob. The eleven brothers of Joseph were waiting for an opportunity to kill Joseph. When Jacob sent Joseph to find out the welfare of the rest of his sons who went on pasturing the sheep to a far away place, the brothers of Joseph saw him coming towards them. They plotted against Joseph and decided to kill him and inform Jacob that Joseph had been attacked by wild animals. But they were stopped from murdering Joseph by one of their brothers and earn the guilt of killing their own brother. They sold Joseph to the Caravan traders to be a slave (Gen.

37:12-36)[20]. His life was at risk when his brothers plotted to kill him and later left in deep down the pit to die of thirst and hunger. Joseph was taken by the traders to the Egyptian market to be sold as a slave. The story in Genesis does not tell how much cruelty he faced from the traders when he resisted. But it is clear to us that a slave is always at risk. No brother or sister in a family has the right to sell another brother or sister as a commercial product either to make money or to meet out their vengeance. Blood relationship is not for misusing the right over the rest of brothers and sisters but demands the obligation of protecting and caring them.

Moses, deprived of Family

Political governments in different parts of the world tried to eliminate ethnic groups in their nations due to racial hatred or for economic or political reasons. Hitler killed millions of Jews because of his anti-Semitic policy. Pharaoh of Egypt, as we notice in the book of Exodus (Ch. 1-3), implemented racial discrimination towards Jews who settled in Egypt. His policy of killing the male children born to the bonded Israelites was combined with economic, political and cultural reasons. Moses, born at his period of rule was at risk of being killed at his birth and thereafter. But taking the risk, his family placed him in the basket to be floated in the river to be picked up by the daughter of Pharaoh. The family of Moses did not float him willingly. They were not sure that the child will be picked up the daughter of Pharaoh. Moses was a fortunate child to survive but many other male children born to the Israelites could not survive for long. When the male infanticide plan was failed by the midwives, Pharaoh ordered to throw every boy born to the Israelites into the Nile river (Ex.1:22)[21]. They lost their lives although the nurses saved them at their birth. Moses escaped the genocide happened in his period. Although his mother was paid to bring him up, Moses was alienated from his family and lacked the love and care of the rest of the members of his family. Adoption of child can save the child but cannot provide the relationship of parents, brothers and sisters of his or her family. Alienation from family causes emotional imbalance in a child and the alienation itself puts the child at risk.

Dead and Living Child

The case of a quarrel between two women on a living child is recorded in 1 Kings 3:16-28. These two women were sex workers and lived in the same house. Both were pregnant and about to deliver the babies. One gave birth to a baby earlier than the other one. The other woman who gave birth to a baby after three days laid her hand by mistake on the baby during her deep sleep in the night. When she found her son died on that night, she took the child of another woman and replaced the dead child to her. The mother of the living child complained that the living child is her own and not the dead one. But the other woman who had stolen the living child argued that the living child belongs to her. The mother of the living child has the right to own her child. The living child has every right to be with the mother. It is their biological right. The mother who gave birth to the child only can show real love for her baby and maintain true relationship. She was not willing to lose her baby and so approached the court of the king. Solomon, in his wisdom, found out the real mother and handed over the baby to her and solved the dispute. Similar incident happen in hospitals today either by mistake or deliberately exchanging the dead baby for the living one. Sometimes, the stolen babies from the hospitals are sold outside for a price either for adoption or as a future labour force in the families.

Sons under Mortgaging

A wife of the prophet who died leaving the family in debt cries to Elisha to help her. Because of the unpayable debt, the creditors came to take away the children of the widow to be slaves and work for them. The creditors want the money borrowed to be paid to them. In order to redeem the two children from the hands of these creditors, Elisha did a miracle of multiplying oil (2 Kings 4:1-7). The widow could sell the oil and clear the loan. She was able to stop the money-lenders taking away her children to bonded slavery. Similar situation exists in many places in India. The money lenders take the children of their debtors and sell them for money to others or use them as their bonded slaves in their farms, shops, sex business and industries. Many parents who could not redeem their children live in a trauma of losing their children. The children who have gone into the oppression of the money lenders too go through trauma and long to be restored to their parents.

Mortgaging human beings for the loan and selling them as slaves are social evils. Neither God nor the society approves of this evil.

Children, political victims

Children suffer and die at times of ethnic conflicts, tribal war or during the attack and invading another nation. Moments of political changes had placed children at risk in different parts of the world. Biblical history narrates the death of the first born of Egypt due to the hard heartedness of Pharaoh. The exact number of children died is not mentioned in Ex. 12. The political decision of the Pharaoh's government refusing the Israelites to go out of bondage caused the death of hundreds of the first born male children in the land of Egypt[22]. The political revenge of Jehu forced the rulers of Jezreel to kill all the seventy sons of Ahab (2 Kings 10:1-11). It was possible that there could have been children, youths and grown up adults among the seventy sons of Ahab's family. Children pay the price for what their father had done during his political rule. They could be denied succession to the thrown of their father but not their rights to live. Emerging potential leader in a nation is regarded often as a threat to the existing ruler. Killing such a leader is one of the political strategies. The words of the wise men about Jesus as the rising king of Israel threatened Herod. He massacred all the male children below two years in and around Bethlehem (Matt. 2:16-18). Random killing of children for political reasons goes on even today that place many other children at risk in nations.

The above cases indicate that both male and female children are vulnerable. Some social, economic, political and religious factors contribute to the oppression of children and violation of their rights. Such factors need to be challenged in order to protect the lives of children and mothers.

III. LEGAL DIMENSION

The Bible contains some laws relating to the protection of children. The Old Testament has three major codes of laws called Covenant Code-C (Ex. 20-23), Holiness Code-H (Lev.17-26) and Deuteronomic Code-D (Dt.12-26) and instructions in the wisdom and poetic literature demanding the Israelites to obey the laws for the sake of smooth functioning of their society and achieve progress in socio-political and economic areas and promote peace and harmony among people. The laws were developed over a long period of time, possibly from the period of Exodus to the post-exilic return and restoration (1300 B.C-520 BC). It is, therefore, difficult to locate the exact period and context in which each law is developed and implemented. Those laws appearing in the Covenant Code could have been enacted from the time of Exodus (1300 BC), to the middle of monarchy (1050-900 BC) particularly during the settlement in Canaan and developing their agrarian society. The laws appearing in the Deuteronomic Code could have been a repetition of some of the existing laws or a modified version of them. Or they might have been introduced newly during the middle and later monarchical period (900 – 600 BC). Similarly some of the laws in the Holiness Code are repetition of the existing laws or modified version of them or introduced newly during the exilic and post-exilic period (587-400 BC).

Scholarly studies of the laws and law codes in the Old Testament focus their attention on the literary style and form of each law as Casuistic or Apodictic, comparison to the Code of Hammurabi and the place of the laws in different law codes[23]. A number of questions can be raised on the nature and validity of the laws particularly related to slaves and servants. My interest in this section is to highlight the meaning and usefulness of a few laws in the Bible.

Protection from selling a girl as slave (Ex. 21:7-11)

Buying and selling men and women to be slaves or servants was practiced in the Ancient Near East. The nomadic society of Abraham, Isaac and Jacob had slaves. Hagar, an Egyptian girl was purchased to be maid to Sarah. But in the later period of Israel, this practice was not cherished because the Israelites experienced slavery in Egypt. They knew the pain of losing freedom, identity, dignity and welfare by being slaves to another person or a government. Their liberation theology condemns enslavement of people. Their God is their master and lord and not another human being. Yet, circumstances such as drought, famine, debts and poverty forced some families to sell their children to be servants to another family within their own community. Instead of the entire family committing suicide or die of starvation or forced to prostitution, the provision of selling the children to be servants or slaves saved the life of their sons and daughters. There were two kinds of slaves namely slave in general for household duties and slave as bride or concubine[24].

Ex. 21:7-11 tells us the practice of selling female child to be adopted as a bride or concubine to the master and the danger of being reduced to mere slave girl breaking the marriage contract:

> If a man sells his daughter as a servant, she is not to go free as menservants do. If she does not please the master who has selected her for himself, he must let her be redeemed. He has no right to sell her to foreigners, because he has broken faith with her. If he selects her for his son, he must grant her the rights of a daughter. If he marries another woman, he must not deprive the first one of her food, clothing and marital rights. If he does not provide her with these three things, she is to go free, without any payment of money (NIV)

The case in this law is selling the daughter to become a wife or concubine after puberty to the buyer and become part of his family. The buyer should marry her and give her the rights of food, clothing, shelter, sexual relationship and bearing the children even if he takes another woman as his wife. If he violates the sale contract and fails to grant her these rights, then she can go free. But this law prohibits the trading of the servant bride by the master to another party. The term 'foreigner' could mean anyone outside her nuclear family or the master's nuclear family or outside the community of Israel. She can be returned to her own parents. This prohibition of selling her to another person and bestowing of the right to return to her nuclear family is noticed as distinct in Israelite law from the similar marriage contract law in ANE[25]. Human beings cannot be traded as a commodity in the market. If this prohibition is not in their legal system, many girls could end up in the sexual abuse of their master or remain unwanted or could have become a tradable commodity. These risks were minimized through the law.

Protection from physical injuries (Ex. 21:20-21)

Having male or female slaves whether they are teenage youths or middle aged persons, does not mean that the master can ill-treat the slaves and injure them. Purchasing of a slave to work in his house or farm does not give rights to beat or kill the slaves. Many servants who worked for their masters in their farms and homes were beaten up, wounded badly and even burnt alive in different parts of the world because of the notion that the servants are their properties. The employer forgets that he has a great responsibility to take care of the servants. Ex. 21:21-22 prohibits the cruelty done to the male or female slave[26]. The master can be punished for killing the slaves (v. 20) or the slaves can go free for losing an eye or a tooth as a compensation for the cruelty.

> If a man beats his male or female slave with a rod and the slave dies as a direct result, he must be punished, but he is not to be punished if the slave gets up after a day or two, since the slave is his property (NIV)

What we can infer from this law of bodily injuries is that the male and female young people, sold as slaves are at risk in their master's place. Scholars notice difficulties in interpreting the second part of the law 'he is not to be punished if the slave gets up after a day or two since the slave is his property' and point out that this law is dealing with two different cases of slaves, one died and the other injured. According to Martin Noth, in the case of deliberate or intentional murder, the master must be punished. A concession of not to be punished is granted if it is an accidental or unintentional attack and the slave recovered from injuries after a few days of sickness[27]. It is difficult for us to accept the concept of ownership granting the master a right to beat and injure and a concession of not be punished. This concession can give undue advantage to the master to beat and injure cruelly as long as the slave is not dead. Gregory Chirichigno rightly points out after studying this text that this law is not dealing with two different cases of intentional and unintentional punishment and concession to the master. According to him, if the slave dies because of beating with the stick then the master is punishable but if the slave survives then the master is responsible to take care of the injured slave because the slave was a fellow member of the community. This is emphasized by the motivational clause 'the slave is his property' underlining the responsibility to treat the slave properly and not that ownership gives undue authority to kill or injure a slave[28]. In both the situation, the master is accountable and had great responsibility to slaves. Similar to this situation is the cruelty faced by many boys and girls who work as servants in agricultural farms, chemical industries, workshops and in homes as servants in many parts of India.

Protection from Rape (Ex. 22:16; Dt. 22:23)

Rape is a crime in all the societies whether they are traditional or modern[29]. Raping a woman causes an injury to her and creating a permanent psychological upset in her mind. She carries the hurt in her conscience throughout her life. Raping is violence and the woman can be at a risk of conceiving a child or going for abortion or die on the spot or could commit suicide. The Israelite society takes the crime of rape seriously and created different laws against seducing a girl. One of the laws narrated in Ex. 22:16 speaks of protection for a virgin seduced by a man for his own sexual pleasure[30].

> If a man seduces a virgin who is not pledged to be married and sleeps with her, he must pay the bride price and she shall be his wife. If her father absolutely refuses to give her to him, he must still pay the bride price for virgin.-(NIV)

This law demands that such a man should marry and take the virgin he seduced as his wife and pay the bride-price to her family. It implies that a virgin cannot be seduced before the marriage and a man cannot misuse a girl's virginity for his own sexual pleasure and sends her away. It is a warning to men folk that they had to marry the virgin girls they had seduced unless their fathers object the marriage for some valid reasons. Paying the bridal price of fifty pieces of silver to her father is compulsory whether the father is willing to give his daughter in marriage or not[31]. This penalty charge belonged to the family and not to her because she was part of the household's economic assets.

Another law in Dt. 22:23 prohibit a man from seducing a virgin already pledged to another man to be his wife either in a town or country side:

> If a man happens to meet in a town a virgin pledged to be married and he sleeps with her, you shall take both of them to the gate of that town and stone them to death — the girl because she was in a town and did not scream for help, and the man because he violated another man's wife. You must purge the evil from among you - (NIV).

Indulging in the activity of raping means violating the right of the man who had pledged the virgin to be his wife and paid already the bride-price to her family. In the event of abducting her for seducing, she should raise the alarm for help whether she is taken to a place in the town or remote village side. She should not keep silence or allow him to seduce her. The man is responsible for death penalty because he has done a double crime of raping and damaging the betrothed property of another man. Although these laws provide security to the wronged women, Joseph Blenkinsopp understands that they were more concerned about the economic interest of the household rather than the interest of the victims[32]. However, these laws prohibit seducing girls and protect their virginity and help them to safeguard their marriage in the near future.

Protection from Prostitution (Lev. 19:29)

Prostitution is regarded as wrong and a social evil in all societies. Yet, it goes on in societies either illegally or legally. Lev. 19:29 prohibits the father from selling his daughter to prostitution either due to debt or poverty. He can sell her as a servant or even as a slave to another Israelite family but not to be a sex – worker to raise money or dedicate to be a temple prostitute (Dt. 23:17-18) to involve in cult prostitution as part of the fertility cult[33]. Both practices are prohibited.

> Do not degrade your daughter by making her a prostitute, or the land will turn to prostitution and be filled with wickedness - (NIV)

This practice of prostitution was regarded as profaning the honour of his daughter and the name of God. Israelites believed that selling a daughter to prostitution defiled the land and lead to lose God's blessing of rain and fertility and earn the punishment of famine, drought and plague which can force the people to leave the land and lose it for ever. Another belief is that sin breeds sin. So the sexual perversion can pollute the land by multiplying various sociological crimes (Dt. 23:18-19; Amos 2:7; Hos. 4:14, Ezek. 33:37-39)[34]. Women whether young or old come under the risk of catching and spreading various diseases or facing the cruelty of men. The society that promotes prostitution supports crimes. This law controlled many parents from selling their daughters to prostitution in ancient Israel.

Protection from Divorce (Dt. 22:13-19)

Virginity of a girl and loyalty of wife were given importance in ancient Israel. The sexuality of women was under male control, first by fathers or brothers and then by husbands in Israel[35]. Divorce was rare in the early period but was allowed in the later period on two grounds. If a wife has a relationship with another man after the marriage, then she can be divorced. Another case is that a girl should remain a virgin till her marriage as stated in Dt. 22:13-19:

> If a man takes a wife and after lying with her, dislikes her and slanders her and gives her a bad name, saying, 'I married this woman, but when I approached her, I did not find proof of her virginity'. Then the girl's father and mother shall bring proof that she was a virgin to the town elders at the gate. The girl's father will say to the elders, 'I gave my daughter in marriage to this man but he dislikes her. Now he has slandered her and said, 'I did not find your daughter to be a virgin'. But here is the proof of my daughter's virginity.' Then her parents shall display the cloth before the elders of the town and the elders shall take the man and punish him. They shall fine him a hundred shekels of silver and give them to the girl's father, because this man has given an Israelite virgin a bad name. She shall continue to be his wife, he must not divorce her as long as he lives. (NIV)

According to this law, if her husband finds after the marriage that his wife was not a virgin at the time of marriage, he has the right to divorce her. But he cannot divorce her for some other reasons of his own interest. The father of the girl can prove that his daughter was a virgin till the marriage and challenge the intention of her husband seeking divorce. If her father proves the truth, then, divorce is not possible. Her husband has to accept her and continue to live with her. Newly married girls were protected from this kind of husbands seeking divorce and go on marrying other girls. The law regards the marriage as sacred and did not allow those men who disregard marriage and seek divorce easily. On the other hand, a girl who lacks virginity is a shame to her father. If proved that she lost her virginity before the marriage, she be stoned to death after the wedding night (vv. 20-21). This law controls the young girls to remain virgin and protects them from indulging in sexual relationship with men and risking their marriage in future.

Protection from sacrifice and sorcery (Lev. 18:21)

Sacrificing children was practiced in Canaan because the religion of Baal promoted fertility cult which demanded human sacrifice to get rain and harvest. The Israelites settled in Canaan were warned against the religious practices of the Canaanites particularly worshipping nature and devoting and offering their offspring, male or female, to Molech (cf. Dt. 12:2).

> Do not give any of your children to be sacrificed to Molech, for you must
> not profane the name of your God. I am the Lord - (NIV)

The exact form of sacrifice is not clear but could have burnt the children to death on altars than cutting them to pieces for sacrifice. But the belief and practice of human sacrifice which was foreign to the ritual of Israel became part of their worship and it was criticized as inhumanitarian[36]. The Israelites cannot worship nature except the Lord of creation who grants them prosperity. Human sacrifice is a violation of the rights of young children and destroying their image of God. It profanes God's Holy name. It is an unethical practice equivalent to murder. So the above law was introduced to prohibit human sacrifice and thus the killing of young children in the name of false worship and religion (Lev. 18:21; 20:1-4).

Another law in Ex. 22:18 - "Do not allow a sorcerer to live" (NIV) prohibits parents dedicating male or female children to be the medium of evil spirits and promoting sorcery in Israelite society (cf. Dt. 18:9-13). We do not know how the initiation ritual to sorcery was performed[37]. But it could have demanded the female children to worship Canaanite gods and goddess and possessed by their spirits. Anyone involved in sorcery or approach a sorcerer was criticized as doing prostitution (Lev. 20:6-7) and punished:

> I will set my face against the person who turns to mediums and spiritists
> to prostitute himself by following them, and I will cut him off from his
> people. - (NIV)

The girls involved in the practice of sorcery were led to follow false worship and even might have been abused by the priests. The God of the Israelites does not reveal his plans through such mediums dedicated to false gods. The belief that the medium can foretell their future is wrong because the God of Israel is controlling the history of the nations (Isa. 48:48). Sorcery misleads the people and can influence the listeners to commit mistakes. Children particularly female children are at risk even today to be misused by magicians and sorcerers to be mediums or an offering for sacrifice to gods and goddesses.

Protection from discrimination (Gal. 3:26-29)

Women are discriminated in every society and they face inequality. Female children are not wanted and regarded as a burden. Different kinds of discrimination are done to women irrespective of their age. One of the reasons for female infanticide and foeticide in India is the attitude towards female child as inferior and unwanted arose from some religious teachings and socio-economic factors. Some of the discriminations are dangerous and leaves women folk in risk. Paul brings out the message of equality between men and women in his letter to the Galatians (3:28).

> There is neither Jew nor Greek, slave nor free, male or female, for you are all one in Christ Jesus.- (NIV)

He repudiates gender discrimination and tries to promote equality and welfare for all human beings irrespective of their class, caste, race and gender. Commenting on this text, Charles Cousar says that Paul reveals his Jewish self-consciousness to treat Jews and Gentiles as ethnic units and regards slaves, masters, men and women as distinct groups. However, 'the unity, he declares is not one, in the first instance, in which ethnic, social and sexual differences vanish but one in which the barriers, the hostility, the chauvinism, and the sense of superiority and inferiority between respective categories are destroyed'[38].

From the above selected texts of the Old Testament and New Testament, we can say that children in ancient Israel particularly female children were at more risk. The implementation of the law and the administration of justice were taken care by the fathers at homes, priests in cultic centres, elders at the city-gate and later by the royal court and local churches.

IV. ETHICAL DIMENSION

The theological, sociological and legal dimensions of protecting the children lead us to ethical dimension. I like to highlight ethical dimension as a separate section in terms of instructing children about the values of God and protecting them from unethical teachings. The study of perspectives on children should include their rights to have knowledge about values and dangers of the world and responsibilities to follow the valuable instructions to lead a good life. One can notice instructions in different books of the Bible (Dt. 6:1-9; 11:18-21) particularly in the Wisdom literature of the Old Testament and epistles of the New Testament. Giving birth to children is not enough. Unless we educate them on the ethical aspects of life, we cannot expect the future society to provide them welfare and security of life.

The book of Proverbs speaks of the role of parents instructing their children. It emphasizes that the children should be taught to listen and obey the teachings of their fathers and mothers[39]. They need to avoid the company of friends and peer groups who can mislead them to wrong values and end up in criminal activities (Prov. 1:8). Children need to be guided to seek God and divine values (4:1-4). Children were called to gain wisdom and prudence to analyze what is evil and good in life (5:1-6).

Paul writes about the rights and responsibilities of children and parents in Eph. 6:1-4. He is asking the fathers not to provoke their children to anger and react negatively[40]. He points out that the children have their own rights and freedom and the parents have to recognize and instruct them in such a way that the children could accept the guidance of their parents. Reminding one of the Ten Commandments (Ex. 20:12), Paul asks children to obey and honour their parents. In instructing Titus, Paul urges him to teach youths to have self control, integrity and involve in good works (Titus 2:6-8).

Peter instructs the members of the churches particularly younger people to accept the authority of the elders and their teachings (1 Pet. 5:5). John addresses the Christians as children in his letter and instructs them to be righteous and avoid all injustices of the world (I Jn 2:1; 3:7-10; 4:4-16). These writings of the apostles indicate that churches are concerned about each generation whether young or old and called to play on important role in shaping the ethical thinking and living of Christians.

Three major kinds of Christian institutions are the Christian families, churches and organizations and educational institutions in addition to other social service agencies. As a concluding remark, let me point-out a few initiatives these institutions can take up. Families should teach the biblical values to children, educate their sons and daughters in gender equality and develop the critical skill of analyzing mass media and the values promoted by them. Churches and Missionary organizations should develop biblical perspectives on children and teach their congregations. Rarely series of preachings and teachings are given on children to adults in churches. Children in Sunday schools and VBS are told biblical stories or taught doctrines rather than their rights and responsibilities. Churches should organize seminars to discuss the problems and difficulties faced by children in our society and work out plans for involvement with the children at risk. Establishing orphanages and primary health centres are not enough. Ministry should go beyond social service to social action of rescuing children from poverty, slavery, prostitutions and illiteracy and empowering them to regain their identity, self-respect and right to study and prosper. Schools and colleges managed by churches as well as trusts of Christian families cannot ignore the problem of children. Children cannot be treated like customers for their institutions and commercialization of education. Cruelty in terms of using abusive language against children, threatening, them with severe punishments and penalty charges and allowing gender discrimination in these institutions should be stopped. Educational reforms should include introducing Gender-Equality and Holistic Child Development courses for all the students and practical involvement with NGOs working among children.[41]

Endnotes

[1] Ram Ahuja, *Social Problems in India* (Jaipur: Rawat Publications, 2002), p. 218.

[2] Neera Burra,'Crusading for Children in India's Informal Economy' *Economic and Political Weekly* (EPW), 3rd Dec. 2005, p. 5199.

[3] Manu N. Kulkarni, 'Child Survival Programmes Revisited', *EPW*, 7th Jan. 2006, pp. 28-30.

[4] Michele Gragnolati, et.al., 'Integrated Child Development Services (ICDS) and Persistent Under-nutrition: Strategies to enhance the impact, *EPW*, 25th March, 2006, p. 1193.

[5] Ram Ahuja, *op.cit.*, pp. 218-242.

[6] Various movements use different phrases and definitions for Child theology. The international Child Theology Movement, a registered agency in UK uses the phrase 'Child Theology'. The reports of their seven consultations (24-28 June 2002, 25-27 Feb, 2004, 6-8 May, 2004, 28 June- 3 July, 2004, 8-10 Sept, 2004, 1-6 April, 2005 and 2-17 June 2006) are valuable resource on Child Theology. A number of books are published on Child Theology within the last one decade in the West.

[7] Some of the Hebrew terms are viz. *yeled, zera, na'ar, bahur, betula, gamul, elem, yonek and olal* and the Greek terms are viz. *pais, huios, paidion, teknon, brephos, etc.*

Refer to *TDOT* , Vol. VI, 1990, pp. 76-81, *IDB,* Vol. I, pp. 558-561 and *TDNT* for details on these words.

[8] C. Westermann, *Genesis 1-11: A Commentary* (Vol. 1, tr. J.J. Scullion, Menneapolis: Augsburg Publication, 1984), p. 161, G.J. Wenham, *Genesis 1-15* (Vol. 1, WBC, Waco: Word Books, 1987), p. 33.

[9] Scholars have given different interpretations for the phrase 'image of God' and 'likeness of God'. Refer to C. Westermann, *op.cit.,* pp. 146-158 lists the views of scholars and speaks of it as relationship with God. Henri Blocher, *In the Beginning: The Opening Chapters of Genesis* (Leicester: IVP, 1984), pp. 79-94. G. J. Wenham, *Genesis 1-15,* pp. 29-32, David Atkinson, *The Message of Genesis 1-11* (Leicester: IVP, 1990), pp. 36-38 emphasizes the relationship between God and humans that 'God places himself with human beings, a relationship in which we become God's counterpart, his representative and his glory on the earth'. Derek Kidner, *Genesis* (TOTC, Leicester: IVP, 1967), p. 50f- warns that the words 'image' and 'likeness' are not two distinctive terms but used to reinforce the same idea that humans are created by God in his own image.

[10] G. von Rad, *Genesis: A Commentary* (tr. J.H. Marks, London: SCM, 1984), p. 160, C. Westermann, *op.cit.,* p. 160.

[11] Victor P. Hamilton, *The Book of Genesis: Chapters 1-17* (NICOT, Michigan: Eerdmans, 1990), p. 200f, Carol Meyers, 'The Family in Early Israel', *Families in Ancient Israel (FAI)* Written by Leo G. Perdue, et. al. (Louisville: Westminister John Knox Press, 1997), pp. 22-30.

[12] G. von Rad, *Genesis,* p. 93 – warns against the opinion that woman and man are cursed but interprets Gen. 3:16 saying that the several afflictions and contradictions have emerged due to the fall. E.A. Speiser, *Genesis: Introduction, Translation and Notes* (Vol.1, Anchor Bible, New York: Doubleday, 1962), pp. 22-24 suggests that the pain at child birth becomes intense and not that the pain itself is the result of the Fall. J.B. Jeyaraj, 'Lesson 3- Primal History in Genesis 1-11', *An Introduction to Christian Studies* (New Delhi: AIACHE, 2001), pp. 21-35.

[13] Peter Craigie, *Psalms 1-50* (Vol. 19, WBC, Waco: Word Books, 1983), p. 107f. Mitchell Dahood, *Psalms 1-50* (Vol. 16, AB, New York: Doubleday, 1966), pp. 49-50 points out that some scholars have identified the babies in v. 2 as divine beings or angelic powers and rejects this view.

[14] D.A. Carson, *The Gospel According to John* (Grand Rapids: Eerdmans, 1991), pp. 432-434. Cornelis Bennema, *Excavating John's Gospel: A Commentary for Today* (Delhi: ISPCK, 2005), P. 131. Andreas J. Kostenberger, *John* (BECONT, Grand Rapids: Baker Academic, 2004), pp. 367-370. J.B. Jeyaraj , *Meeting The Messiah: Expository Studies from St. John's Gospel* (Madurai: Vacation Institute Publication, 1999), p. 45f.

[15] Many Christians assume that the peace and harmony will happen only after the coming of Messiah as in Isa. 11:1 and understand this text is referring to the situation after the second coming of Jesus Christ. But the prophetic message has significance either to the current context of the prophet or to the near future. John D. W Watts, *Isaiah 1-33* (Vol. 24, WBC, Waco: Word Books, 1985), p. 175.

[16] Douglas R.A. Hare, *Matthew* (Interpretation Series, Louisville: John Knox Press, 1993), pp. 208-210 and 224-225. What is the thrust of the text in its context? Some think that it is speaking about the kingdom of God and the requirement to enter the Kingdom in line with the main thrust of the Gospel of Matthew on the Kingdom of God. Some others emphasize the child placed in the midst of them.. For example Keith White emphasized the 'child at the centre' during the Child Theology Movement Penang Consultation III in June 12-17th, 2006 and made this text as one of the key texts for Child Theology. Instead of depending on one or two texts in NT, we need to explore the holistic dimension of children from different texts in the Bible.

[17] Most of the Christians think that the phrase 'born again' refers to the spiritual birth of being born of the Spirit (e.g. C. Bennema, *op.cit.*, pp. 44-45 argues for spiritual birth in contrast to physical birth which is not possible) Definitely, it is not speaking of transmigration of atman (soul) being born again in different forms as believed by some Hindus. Reading from the perspective of children, it means to become like a child not in terms of Childishness and immaturity but in the nature and quality of a child. Also see: "Churches and Kingdom of God: Relationship and Development of Children", pp.60-64.

[18] Matthew Black, *Romans* (NCB, Grand Rapids: Eerdmans, 1981), pp. 81-84, C. K. Barrett, *The Epistle to the Romans* (London: Adam and Charles Black, 1977), pp. 106-109, Ernst Kasemann, *Commentary on Romans* (tr. G.W. Bromiley, Grand Rapids: Eerdmans, 1994), pp. 136-139.

[19] G.J. Wenham, *Genesis 1-15*, p. 104 – lists a few different types of explanation for accepting the offering of Abel and rejecting the offering of Cain. V.P Hamilton, *op.cit.*, p. 224.

[20] G.J. Wenham, *Genesis 1-15*, p. 356 points out the use of the word 'child' by Reuben in vv. 29-30 is to emphasize the vulnerability of a child, referring here to the vulnerability of Joseph, the youth.

[21] C.F. Keil and F. Delitzsch, *The Pentateuch* (Vol. I, COTTV, Grand Rapids: Eerdmans, 1983), p. 425.

[22] Male children include the one newly born to the adult in Egypt. Why this death of the first-born *enmass?* Various reasons are stated. One of the reasons is to reaffirm Israel as God's first born and show the difference between them and the first born of Egypt (Ref. G.A.F. Knight, *Theology as Narration: A Commentary on the*

Book of Exodus (Grand Rapids: Eerdmans, 1976), p. 83f. Another reason to justify the killing of the first-born in Egypt is that they were the ruling class and held responsible for bonded slavery and denying the freedom of Israel.

[23] For example, Hans Jochen Boecker, *Law and the Administration of Justice in the Old Testament and Ancient East* (tr. Jeremy Moiser, London: SPCK, 1980), Martin Noth, *The Laws in the Pentateuch and other Studies* (tr. D.R.Ap-Thomas, London: SCM Press Ltd, 1984), pp. 1-107, Frank Crusemann, *The Torah: Theology and Social History of Old Testament Law* (tr. A.W.Mahuke, Edinburgh: T & T. Clark, 1996)..

[24] I. Mendelsohn, 'Slavery in the Old Testament' *IDB*, (Vol. 4, Nashville: Abingdon Press, 1982), pp. 383-391, Cornelis Houtman, *Exodus* (Vol. 3, tr. Sierd Woudstia, HCOOT, Leuven: Peeters, 2000), p. 123 suggests that Ex. 21:7 refers to a women intended for work but also to be concubine. But commentators vary in their opinions.

[25] Gregory C. Chirichigno, *Debt-Slavery in Israel and the Ancient Near East* (Sup. No. 141, Sheffield: JSOT Press, 1993), pp. 244-255. Gershon Brin, *Studies in Biblical Law: From the Hebrew Bible to the Dead Sea Scrolls* (Sup. No. 176, tr. J. Chipman, Sheffield: JSOT Press, 1994), pp. 62-63, H.J. Boecker, *op.cit.*, p. 160.

[26] H.J. Boecker, *op.cit.*, p. 161f, B.S. Childs, *Exodus: A Commentary* (London: SCM, 1982), p. 471, Alan Cole, *Exodus* (TOTC, Leicester: IVP, 1979), p. 168f.

[27] Gershon Brin, *op.cit.*, p. 96 – studying the Hebrew 'if' clause as a 'formula of option' points out the purpose of the formula of opition here is to show some concession.

[28] This phrase is usually interpreted as a loss if the slave dies and it is a punishment to the owner. e.g. J.P. Hyatt, *Exodus* (NCB, Grand Rapids: Eerdmans, 1971), p. 233. If the owner is rich, he may not mind about the loss of investing on a slave and beating him to death. Another interpretation lays its emphasis on the responsibility of the owner to take care of the slave and his limitation in ill-treating the slaves. e.g. Gregory Chirichigno, *op.cit.*, pp. 169-177.

[29] For details on the reasons and consequences of child abuse, refer to Ram Ahuja, *op.cit.*, pp. 219-230.

[30] Joseph Blenkinsopp, 'The Family in the First Temple Israel', *FAI*, p. 60.

[31] Gershon Brin, *op.cit.*, p. 68.

[32] H.J. Boecker, *op.cit.*, p. 50f, J. Blenkinsopp, *op.cit.*, p. 63.

[33] It is possible that Lev. 19:29 means prostitution outside the temple since it is not qualified as in Dt. 23:17-18 which refers to cult prostitution in the temple.

[34] John E. Hartley, *Leviticus* (WBC 4, Waco: Word Books, 1992), p. 298 and p. 321.

[35] H.J. Boecker, *op.cit.*, p. 111f. Ilona N. Rashkow, *Taboo or not Taboo: Sexuality and Family in the Hebrew Bible* (Minneapolis: Fortress Press, 2000), pp. 34-36. Phyllis A Bird, 'Images of Women in the Old Testament' *The Bible and Liberation: Political and Social Hermeneutics* (ed. N. Gottwald, New York: Orbis Books, 1989), p. 260f.

[36] Roland de Vaux, *Ancient Israel: Its Life and Institutions* (London: DLT, 1980), p. 446.

[37] J. Blenkinsopp, *op.cit.*, p. 89- suggests that the intention of necromancy using the medium could be to loosen the spiritual bond of kinship in general and to remove the inalienation of the ancestral land. Another view is that this practice is lined with magic aimed at obtaining fertility or victory of life over death is pointed out by C. Houtman, *op.cit.*, (Vol. 3), p. 213. This practice of having relationship with departed spirits or ghosts was regarded as leaving Yahweh and doing prostitution. J.E. Hartley, *op.cit.*, p. 338.

[38] Charles B Cousar, *Galatians* (Interpretation Series, Louisville: John Know Press, 1982), pp. 85-89, G. Walter Hansen, *Galatians* (Leicester: IVP, 1994), p. 112f.

[39] On educating the children in Israel, refer to Roland de Vaux, *op.cit.*, pp. 48-50.

[40] Harold W. Hoehner, *Ephesians: An Exegetical Commentary* (Grand Rapids: Baker Academic, 2002), pp. 794-796, Walter L. Liefeld, *Ephesians* (Leicester: IVP, 1997), p. 151f, Ralph P. Martin, *Ephesians, Colossians and Philemon* (Interpretation Series, Louisville: John Knox Press, 1991), p. 72.

[41] UGC-India is encouraging Universities and Colleges to offer Gender Justice Courses. Women Study's Programme (WSP) is becoming a special discipline of study in some colleges and universities. However, Holistic Child Development (HCD) as a special discipline in these institutions is not given importance but the awareness started spreading at present. Some secular and theological institutions will soon establish a department of study for HCD.

Chapter - 2

Theology of Development and Transformation of Children

Reading the Bible from different perspectives and contextualizing biblical messages gained importance in the past few decades. New hermeneutical approaches bring fresh insights on biblical texts. One of the areas neglected often is reading and interpreting the text for the development of children. The prevalent opinion is that the study of developing children belongs to the discipline of psychology or sociology. Scholars have discussed social and psychological theories of development of children. Children are God's creation and they are important members of the society. Children belonging to Christian families are part of the church. We need to develop theological basis for developing children. This article is not an extensive study of principles and theories of psychology or sociology but an initial exploration for a theology of development and then relating to the development of children in churches and society.

I.   TERMS, IDEOLOGIES AND THE BIBLE

The term 'Development' is used commonly to refer to economic or social development of a community or nation. There is not a single universally accepted definition since it depends on the person who defines it. Prof. C.T. Kurien pointed out that the term 'development itself is a developing concept which needs to be re-examined and evaluated from time to time.'[1] Often, the word 'development' is spoken of as 'growth'. But the word 'growth' usually refers to quantitative changes such as increase in size and structure or in number.

'Development' by contrast refers to qualitative and quantitative changes.[2] Development of a community cannot be said as reaching an end point but it is a continuing process. The definition, concept, goal and means vary according to the perspectives of economists, sociologists and psychologists depending on their ideological basis. For example, Capitalistic ideology promotes development in terms of profit, free market economy, multiplication of money, investment and accumulation of wealth by the rich people. One of the key consequences of such a development is exploitation of natural resources and labourers for business and widening the gap between the rich and poor. On the other hand, Marxist ideology is to control the mode of production and distribution. Privatization is opposed in the State- owned economy promoted by Communism. In such a state- owned economy, labourers lose interest in work since they cannot own properties and gain prosperity. Lack of money hinders the modernization of industry and development of economy as we noticed in the old USSR. Gandhian ideology of development is *Sarvodaya* (welfare of all) and *Swaraj* (indigenisation and self-reliance). It emphasizes sustainable development. Although it has a lot of merits over Capitalistic and Marxist models of development, the implementation through *Trusteeship* fails often due to lack of able leadership and co-operation of the mass. The modernization of industries cannot happen fast and stand against the competition of capitalistic model of development. Democratic socialism envisaged at the time of Independence of India tries to combine part of Capitalistic, Marxist and Gandhian ideals promoted by the National Congress Party but fails to strike a balance since the practice and implementation depend on the ruling party, majority strength and political stability in the Parliament.

Some others talk about Sustainable Development, People-Centred-Development in contrast to economic-growth-centred development, Alternative Development and Transformational Development.[3] Sustainability is to do with developing and doing justice to environment and other resources. Alternative Development emphasizes more power for household and members of the community to promote local decision making, self-reliance and participatory democracy. People-centred Development emphasizes human wellbeing. Each ideology has some advantages and disadvantages.

Can our Bible be a basis for development?

What is the understanding of Jesus Christ about development even before these personalities proposed their theories? Can our Bible be a basis for development in a pluralistic context? Yes. The Bible reveals God's plan for humanity. First, it speaks of God as well as society. It emphasizes the value of human life and wellbeing of society. Often Christians failed to look at the dimension of community as the arena of God's action. Blessing for individuals is over emphasized by the preachers of prosperity theology. But individuals are part of the community and they exist in relation to society. Asian society is basically a society of communities. Individuals contribute to the welfare of the community and the community contributes to the individuals. Both are mutually inter-dependent for their wellbeing. Second, God is interested in involving with human beings promoting welfare, demanding justice and peace to be established and requiring each person to use his or her own power and authority for the development of the community. If community concept in terms of socially and theologically (i.e. Body of Christ as a community), is recovered again and re-emphasized, then individualism in the church and society will not be over emphasized. The Bible shows us that the incarnated Jesus involved directly in the human affairs and stood for their justice and progress. Third, the Bible pictures the Israelite community as a model for development with divine values, rules and regulations and an instrument to be used for the welfare of other nations (Ex. 19:5-6; Dt.28:9-14; Isa.49:6). I will discuss the above aspects more in the following sections. The theology of development can challenge our mission for the development of communities.

Did the churches in India develop a biblical ideology of development? We can notice a number of articles on poverty, poor, injustice and human rights are written by Christian leaders.[4]   These jargons are repeated with some statistics on poverty and violation of human rights. In the past, leaders emphasized the 'Theology of Poor' which helped us to use the critical analysis of economic policies based on the insights drawn from Marxism and Liberation theology. Such an attempt suggested a few proposals for reform rather than having a positive perspective of biblical teachings on development.

Shalom

The term 'development' comes from the western society having its own secular values.[5] The Bible does not use the term 'Development' but it is expressed through the concept of creativity, welfare and stewardship in the Bible. The concept of *'Shalom'* in the OT is an important ideological basis for the theology of development. The meaning of the word 'Shalom' cannot be brought out by one word but in a general sense it is translated as 'peace' in English. However, its meaning is more deeper referring to 'completeness', 'soundness', 'welfare', 'progress' or 'well-being'. In the context of Joseph asking the welfare of his brothers and their father, the word Shalom is used to refer to being alive as well as having a life of health and soundness (Gen. 43:27). When Moses wanted to return to Egypt to see the situation of the people of Israel, Jethro wished him and said, 'Go and I wish you well' (Ex.4:18). Jethro did not cause any problem to the relationship between them. Rather, he gave Moses permission and also wished him safety on his travel, protection and security while in Egypt. The emphasises of harmony and peaceful relationship with others can be noticed in the concept of Shalom eventhough the Gibeonites deceived the Israelites by asking for an oath. The Leaders of Israel wanted to maintain the agreement of peace and be honest to the oath given by them to the Gibeonites because it is related to the life and death of the Gibeonites (Jos.9:16-21). Their well being is in the hands of the Israelites and so allowed the Gibeonites to live among themselves. The Psalmist links peace (*shalom*) and security (*shalah-progress, at ease, secure*) to mean a secured life in the city of Jerusalem. All sorts of progress in the society are possible only when the city or the nation can enjoy peace from all the external and internal threats (Ps. 122:6). Jeremiah asked the exiled Israelites not to rebel and cause problem to peaceful situation in Babylon but to pray for and seek the welfare of that nation. Only when there is peace, the exiled Israelites can make a progress in Babylon and return alive to Israel after the exile (Jer. 29:7). A peaceful situation existed between Hiram and Solomon through the treaty they made (1 Kings 5:12). The peace is not only a good relationship between them but also enhancing the welfare of both parties through trade. The development plans of Solomon were achieved through the treaty of trade. Good plans of development can fail if trust and peaceful relationship are lacking between two nations. Shalom means material prosperity such as land, houses, labourers, money, gold and silver jewels (Ps. 73:3). It includes spiritual well being also. The Psalmist is clear that shalom cannot be merely secular and materialistic. He links the concept of shalom with three important aspects of spiritual life viz. steadfast love *(hesed)*, truthfulness *(ameth)* and righteousness *(sedeka)* in Ps. 85:10. In his beautiful literary style he describes the integration of peace with righteousness by saying, 'Love and faithfulness meet together; righteousness and peace kiss each other'. The spiritual qualities of love, faithfulness, truth and righteousness and peace are integrated. The wellbeing or prosperity of a family or community or society depends on accepting this spiritual dimension and practicing it. The theology of development based on biblical ideology of Shalom includes spiritual and materialistic dimension of a nation.

Kingdom of God

In the NT, the Greek word *eirene* is translated as 'peace' but it means wellbeing. The Shalom concept is emphasized in the preaching, teaching and healing ministry of Jesus Christ. It is linked to key words such as 'grace' (Rom.1:7), 'life' (Rom.8:6) and 'righteousness' (Rom. 14:17). All the aspects of material prosperity, security, peace, relationship, spiritual development are linked to the concept of the Kingdom of God. Jesus summarized all his teachings in the values and benefits of the Kingdom. He integrated seeking the kingdom of God and wellbeing of the people by saying, 'But seek first his kingdom and his righteousness and all these things will be given to you as well' (Mt. 6:33). The phrase 'all these things' refers to what Jesus was mentioning in the previous verses of 30-33 about the food, clothes, shelter, safety and water which point to the basic need of human life and the necessities for the development of society. The Kingdom of God is the content of the good news of Jesus because it brings welfare and development to human beings.

As in the teachings of the OT, the NT also points out that God is the bestower and withdrawer (cf. Isa. 45:7; Hos. 2:9-13; Mt.6:32-33, 7:7-12) of the blessing and the development of a nation depends on practicing the values of God (cf.Dt.28:1-7; Rom.1:18-20; Rev. 1:6). The Messiah is the Prince of Peace and has authority to bring peace to humanity (Isa. 9:6, Lk.2:12-14). God revealing himself through Jesus Christ is the source of the blessing.

God bestows the blessing of wellbeing because he knows that we need the life of wellbeing (Mt. 6:33; 7:9-11). For example, Jesus healed the sick woman and affirmed peace to her by saying, 'Go in peace and be free from your suffering' (Mk. 5:34). Freedom from guilt feeling and sense of being forgiven are necessary for a peace in mind and heart of a person to progress further than being paralyzed by the guilt. Jesus said to the sinful woman, 'Your faith has saved you, go in peace' (Lk. 7:50). Many preachers over emphasize that the NT is only about salvation of soul and eternal life in heaven. But the message of Jesus Christ is the well being of a person in all respect of physical, social, spiritual, economically and psychologically. Although Jesus did not use the term 'development', he used the phrase 'eternal life' enjoyable in Christ, here on earth as well as in future. He often emphasized the wholesome life of people. That is why he emphasized feeding the hungry, giving water to the thirsty, consoling the people in trauma (Mt. 25:35-46), caring the orphans and widows, providing shelter for the homeless, delivering the people bonded by powers of authority and evil spirits, promoting freedom with responsibility, growing spiritually and guided by the Holy Spirit (Lk:4:18-19). He was concerned about the political freedom and socio-economic development of the nation of Israel (Lk.19:41-44; Jn.18:20,37). His teachings and actions together revealed his holistic approach to the life of human beings.

The messengers of shalom, in modern terms 'Agents of Change', are the disciples of Jesus Christ. Jesus asked his disciples to greet the families with a word of peace unto them (Lk.10:5-6). If the man of the house is of peace, then the greetings will be a blessing to him. Later, the early church was expected to be the instrument of promoting peace among the people (Acts 10:36; Eph.4:3; Heb.12:14). Offering the peace of God that passes all the understanding and receiving peace of God are the responsibility of human beings. God is willing to develop humanity but humans are to be partners in his mission of development. But many Christians lost hope in developing this world and struggling against the principalities and powers of corruption and are looking for the second coming of Jesus and going to heaven. This hope is good but makes people passive and inactive to contribute for the welfare of our society. We try to limit our mission to preaching the good news and not doing the development till the Lord Jesus Christ comes again.[6]

The mission history of colonial period and the modern indigenous missionary work in the remote rural and tribal villages prove that Christian missionaries have developed that area and people with schools, hospitals and infrastructure. Many poor people suffering under the bondage of money lenders were liberated in the midst of severe opposition from the oppressors. It could be in a small level, but their achievement is a significant one for those communities to come out of their sufferings, superstitions and bondage.

II.   BIBLICAL BASIS FOR THE THEOLOGY OF DEVELOPMENT

To me, the term and concept of shalom could be used as an ideology for development. But the shalom theology of development needs more support from the bible besides the above explanation of the term. So let me discuss below the biblical basis for developing the theology of development

The academic circles have created various theologies based on the Bible or Context. Biblical theology is written by scholars from the point of doctrines, themes, concepts and contextual issues. What I am trying to do here is to look into the theological reflections on biblical texts and some of the insights brought out so far to articulate them from the perspective of development. I quote some articles and commentaries in footnotes rather than doing exegesis of each text.

1.   God's Creation is for the development of humanity

Creation in the Bible is studied to discuss the issue of God creating the world out of nothing (*ex-nihilo*) and disprove the theory of evolution or preached to encourage the congregation to trust God's power to bless or solve their problems. But we paid little attention to see the whole action of creation is for the development of humanity. Development needs planning, shaping of the plans and implementing the plans. God in his wisdom had a wonderful plan of creating the planets, earth and human beings. God accomplished it not only by speaking the powerful word (*dabar-to speak*) which created whatever God wanted but also shaped it (*asa-to make*) by his effort.[7] God developed the heavens and earth by his powerful word as well as by his careful shaping, setting the planets (Gen. 1-2; cf. Job 38:4-7; Jer.31:35-37), separating and assigning water in a particular place, making the first man Adam by his hand out of the clay. The trees, plants, animals and birds are for balancing the eco-system that human beings can enjoy a good life on the earth. Whenever God said, 'It is good', God not only admired his creation but acknowledged the need of such a created item and its usefulness. God blessed them saying, 'be fruitful and multiply' that the human generation will continue through their procreative power.[8]

What is the use of creation without making it for the use of human beings? God can take pleasure and pride in creating planets but he created the world for the sake of human lives. Genesis chapter 1 should not be limited to see the entire creation by orderly approach or seven-day-scheme of creation but also the utility of the Sun, Moon, Stars and earth for the existence of humanity.[9] The Sun and Moon provided light and the cycle of day and night. Trees and plants supplied food. The land and air helped humans to live. The purpose of placing the people on this earth is to till and take care of the land and develop agriculture. Creating the humanity in the image of God is unique.[10] This image does not make human beings divine but gave the capacity of reasoning to see what is right and wrong and to develop their cognitive abilities. The skill of farming, making tools, building cities and musical instruments developed (Gen. 4:17-22). The gift of blessing for procreation continued the human generation to live and take care of the creation. If the functional aspect is emphasized from the point of science and economics, then we will realize the need of environmental care and develop the nature with accountability. Trusting the human beings, God gave them the authority to control and use it in a responsible way (Gen. 1:26-28).[11] As a partner with God, human beings are expected to develop the creation and not to exploit it.

2.   God's liberation is for the development of freedom and dignity

Amartya Sen regards freedom is the most important aspect in human life and development should promote freedom and not bondage. Calling development as freedom, he writes, 'Development requires the removal of major source of unfreedom: poverty, as well as tyranny, poor economic opportunities as well systematic social deprivation, neglect of public facilities as well as intolerance or over-activity of repressive states'.[12] Keeping the citizens under bondage, as in Communist and some Islamic countries, they can make a progress to a certain extent but it cannot be a real development because people have lost their freedom and dignity and are treated like slaves. Economists with proper understanding of development believe that freedom is 'to be understood in the sense of emancipation from alienating material conditions of life and from social servitude to nature, ignorance, other people, misery, institutions, and dogmatic beliefs, especially that one's poverty is one's predestination'.[13]   One of the important ingredients for development, therefore, is the freedom of people. Liberation theology has explained Ex.2:23-25 and 3:7-10 that the Lord took the side of the oppressed and delivered them. One can emphasize the suffering and pain of the Israelites. God seeing their plight and hearing their cry and groaning, remembering the covenant, sent Moses. Nevertheless equally important is the purpose of deliverance. The reason God liberated the Israelites from bondage in Egypt is to enjoy freedom and dignity and develop their own nation. Liberation theology should not be looked only from the point of justice and human rights but also as a basis for further development of the liberated community. Emphasizing liberation as the most important for any development, Gustavo Gutierrez says, 'Only in the context of such a process can a policy of development be effectively implemented, have any real meaning and avoid misleading formulations'[14] Freedom enabled them to think about their pathetic situation in the past, internalize their history, analyze their needs, abilities and potentials to invest in developing the promised land and the process of administration. [15]

Self-governing of a nation and developing their society are not possible without the freedom of the people. People may misuse their freedom or may use it enough to develop their land. But the theological principle in the liberation event is that God created each human being to enjoy freedom and rights. God is the Creator and lord of all human beings. No other person can be a master of another person enslaving and exploiting the other. St. Paul pleaded Philemon for the freedom of Onesimus and willing to pay the ransom to the master on behalf of the run-away slave and reinstate his dignity that the slave can develop himself.[16]

Freedom is not only from slavery or servitude. Jesus brought another dimension to the development of human beings in terms of freedom from physical disabilities and the power of evil spirits. He knew that an individual or a family cannot develop if a person is sick, disable or mentally affected. He healed the sick, enabled the disabled to see, hear, walk, made the lepers wholesome to enjoy again contacts with others without discrimination and delivered people possessed by the evil spirit. Helping to enjoy good health and normal life in the society is an aspect in the holistic development of humanity. It is also another basis for the theology of development.

3. God's covenantal relationship is for the development of governing the community

Administration of a society includes self-governance, that is, managing the day to day affair of their society and developing it economically, socially and culturally with good values.[17] For which, each society needs rules and regulations, law and order, a proper Constitution, decision making institutions and implementing instruments. Usually it is known as Government. God knew this need when the Israelites left Egypt as liberated community with the freedom to govern themselves in the promised land. They needed laws and leaders to administer. God gave them Ten commandments and stipulations (Ex20-24) as a Constitution to govern themselves. He raised leaders such as Moses, elders, kings, Nehemiah and Ezra to administer the society on the basis of the divine principles of the Law *(torah* -to instruct). Different laws such as Protection of slaves and his family, girl children, betrothed women, wife of another man, widows, orphans, poor, animals, servants, land and birds are for the development of the community.[18] These laws were constituted for the physical protection, social and economic development, spiritual welfare and sustainability of nature. They provide holistic development for the community of Israel. While the principle of loving and being faithful to God, honouring parents, not committing adultery, theft, false witnessing, murder and observing sabbath rest mentioned in the Ten Commandments, remained same for generations. Some of the laws needed modification as their society progressed from the settlement period to monarchical period. Some laws can be static and other laws need changes for further development of the community as the civilization progressed. However, the core of the laws of governing is welfare of the people. All the laws and administrative structures should be based on Shalom ideology.

Why did God make a covenant with the Israelites at Sinai and link the governance to the covenantal relationship? First, the covenant with the Israelites made them to commit themselves for the divine principles of governance. They agreed to accept and practice the Laws given by entering into covenantal relationship with God. Second, it created a mutual responsibility. While they obey the Laws, God is to bless their land and life. The community of Israelites unlike other communities is a community of faith and to be loyal to God who selected them as his special possession and acts continuously in their history. Third, the Shalom ideology for the development is not a secular ideology but a religious ideology based on the attributes of God. That is why it can be called as shalom 'theology' of development.

4.   God's incarnation is to redeem and restore the creation to make further development

Any development can suffer due to human error or lack of proper planning or implementation. If the humanity has inherited the sinful nature due to the fall of Adam and Eve and estranged relationship with the created world, then the first thing they need is forgiveness and redemption. Humanity cannot make a progress without realizing the sinful nature and the need for forgiveness. Mere *karma or ideology* is not enough. They need to be set right with God and the world. When they cannot redeem themselves, they need the help of God. Incarnation is an important aspect in the theology of development. God so loved the world that he gave his only begotten son to forgive humanity and redeem people and world. God did not alienate himself from the world after created it. Nor he visits the world now and then taking an avatar and then disappears. God loves the world and wants the world to be safe, peaceful and make a progress and all the people in the world to enjoy good life. The birth, teaching and ministry of Jesus Christ are not limited to saving the soul but to reform the sinful world with his kingdom values. These values include love, forgiveness, sharing, justice, equality, welfare, deliverance from sickness and the possession of evil spirits, freedom from political, social and economic oppression and exploitation.[19] The Shalom concept is reinstated in the teachings of the Kingdom of God. These two ideas are integrated and reveal the same goal of well being of all people.

The death and resurrection of Jesus Christ show the power of God to transform this world. The death of Jesus on the cross is not a defeat of the son of God but a victory over the powers of darkness that tries to keep the world in its clutches and not providing a wholesome life for humanity (1 Cor. 15:55-57). As Jesus defeated the evil powers on the cross, the cross is a symbol of victory. Furthermore, the resurrection of Jesus revealed God's power over death and the evil forces that crucified Jesus. We notice three important events of God's super power in the Bible. One is the event of creating the world and the other is healing the disabled and resurrecting the dead persons (Lazarus - Jn.11:33-37; Son of a widow in Nain - Lk.7:11-15). The third event is the power of God resurrecting Jesus. How is the power of God particularly the resurrection of Jesus connected to the theology of development? First, the death and resurrection of Jesus gives us a hope and encouragement that the evil powers hindering the wellbeing of humanity are defeated. So we can work for the development of the society. Secondly, the resurrection of Jesus gives us power and strength to struggle against oppression and establish justice and welfare for humanity. Christian theology of development is not merely based on the ideology of shalom and kingdom of God but also on the power of resurrection.

Transformational Development

Development will not be over when the present plans and goals are reached. It is a continuous process because the world is changing and the future is uncertain. Each generation needs welfare. Christian eschatology is challenging us to continue the process of development till the second coming of Jesus, fulfilment of the values of the Kingdom and enjoying eternal life with Christ in heaven.

Christian theology of development, in summary, needs to be holistic and it should contribute welfare for all the aspects of human life. It should include all the sections of people including children in the society. M.A. Oommen elaborates this idea of inclusiveness in terms of integrated approach and strategy, genuine participation in social production, enhancing human dignity and freedom, etc.[20] Wayne Bragg, after analyzing the assumptions and weakness of four major development theories such as Modernization, Dependency and Under-development, Globalization as new economic order, Self-reliance as alternative development, prefers the term 'Transformation' than 'development' because it is a Christian concept emphasizing holistic development of spiritual and material of a society.[21] The six characteristics of transformation, he emphasizes, are life-sustenance meeting basic needs like food, clothes and shelter, equitable distribution of material good and opportunities for progress, justice, dignity and self-worth, freedom, participation, reciprocity and transformation appropriate to the culture which it penetrates.[22] However, the same term 'Transformation' is used today by sociologists, economists and religious leaders of other faiths with above six charateristics to mean transformation of society. But Christian understanding of 'Transformational Development'[23] is unique because of the following reasons:

First, it acknowledges that God is the creator and developer. He blesses the entire creation. God redeemed the fallen humanity through the incarnation of Jesus Christ and reconciled the humanity with him. He is transforming human beings through the work of the Holy Spirit. Although the goal of development is wellbeing, Christian theology of development is God centred as well as people oriented. Unlike other ideologies of development that is based on material wellbeing only, it includes spiritual side of human beings. Second, the development is based on divine values of the Shalom and Kingdom of God. Third, human beings are only partners to act responsibly. People are the objects of transformation as well as agents of transformation. Fourth, the work of transformational development began with the incarnation of Jesus and commissioning the disciples should continue till it will be completed at the second coming of Jesus.

III. HOLISTIC CHILD DEVELOPMENT: BIBLICAL FORMULA

Many Psychologists relate the concept of development to the development of a child. They explain various kinds of development viz. physical, emotional, cognitive, social, moral, personality, speech and skill of a child. Freud, Erickson, Maslow, Piaget and other Psychologists have created theories to discuss the development of a child. I am not repeating the theories of psychologists here. Nevertheless, we need to raise an important question of theological foundation of development of a child. I have already discussed in another article the various theological dimension of children from the biblical texts viz. Children are God's gift, created in the image of God, signify Fatherhood and Motherhood, leaders and ministers of God. [24] This article has brought out the value of children as theological basis for their development. Another article complementing the previous one too contributed for the theological basis for HCD.[25] What I discussed above on the theology of development particularly the Christian 'Transformational Development' is applicable to the development of children. Yet, in order to strengthen the theological basis, we need to explore the biblical understanding of holistic child development.

Although the welfare and growth of children are mentioned in the OT, we cannot find one particular text to refer to various developments of children in the OT. The Jewish tradition uses a *formula* to speak of the growth of a child. 1 Samuel 2:26 says, 'Now the boy Samuel continued to grow both in stature and in favour with the Lord and with men'. The Hebrew word *gadal* means ' to grow' or 'to become great' and the word '*tow*' means 'good' or 'goodness' or 'favour'. Similar formula is repeated with a slight variation to describe the growth of John the Baptist. 'And the child grew and became strong in the spirit… '(Lk.1:80). Both of them are described as growing physically in stature. Samuel found favour with God and men since he needed it to do his ministry as a small lad in the midst of grown up people in the society. Without the favour of God and people in the society, continuing the ministry will be difficult. John became strong in his spirit. Being strong in spirit means growing steadily in the faith of God implying his spiritual development (cf. Ps. 27:14; 1 Cor. 16:13). The purpose of his birth is to witness for Christ facing reactions of the religious leaders and preparing the people to identify and accept Jesus the Savour of the World. So the formula emphasizes his growth in his religious tradition and faith. Each child has to grow physically and spiritually. It is a long process. The individuals and the various institutions like family and community contribute for the development.

St. Luke describes the growth and development of Jesus saying, 'And Jesus increased in wisdom and stature and in favour with God and men'

(2:52). Luke has expanded the usual formula of child development by adding the aspect of growing in wisdom. The Greek word *prokopten* means to progress or advance or increase. Luke uses this verb to describe the development of Jesus in three areas viz. progressed in wisdom, stature and in favour with God and men. The Greek word *sophia*, translated as Wisdom is used in different sense by Greek philosophers, NT writers and Early Church Fathers[26]. The Jewish Tradition using the Greek word *Sophia*, translating the Hebrew word *hokma* (to be wise, wisdom) meant knowledge of God. It does not refer to academic knowledge earned in a school. Wisdom is personified in the Book of Proverbs. The fear of the Lord is the beginning of wisdom (Prov. 1:7). The Israelites believed that the knowledge of God can be gained through the reading and understanding of Torah, Prophets and the books in the Writings, instruction and interpretation of elders and personal experience with God. The knowledge of God gave them insights for their ethical living and governing of their families and society. The Book of Proverbs, Job and Ecclesiastes in the collection of Wisdom Literature emphasize practical knowledge for day to day living coming out of knowing God. People regarded a person as a wise person not because of his or her educational qualification but on the basis of his/her knowledge of God and the way he or she conducts in this society. A school teaches information and analytical skill to contribute to gain the knowledge of the world. The content and teaching methods need not necessarily be in accordance with the teaching of God in the Scripture. In Israel, synagogues, temple, Rabbinic schools added cognitive aspect in religious matters. Families too played an important role in the development of the child. The fathers taught the occupational skill to children and youths. Mothers instructed the children to know their scripture. Jesus grew in the knowledge of his occupation as a carpenter as well as grew in religious knowledge that he was able to answer the questions of the leaders during his visit to the Temple in Jerusalem with his family to take part in the festival. The emphasis in Verse 52 is growing in the knowledge of God from his childhood. Luke speaks of the spiritual growth of Jesus rather than the practical skill in his occupation which Jesus gained at a later period of his life. The wisdom he was gaining is not mere theoretical knowledge but also personal experience with God.

The second aspect is growing in 'stature' (Gk. *Helikia*). It is usually understood as growing in age. The child does not remain as a baby forever but grows each year and gains the age. However, it is not limited to growing in age only. What is the use of surviving each year without physical growth? Is it worth remaining as a tiny baby for ten or twenty years without physical and mental growth proportionate to the years completed? So we can infer that Luke is speaking of Jesus growing in stature which includes mental growth also. Bodily growth should be related to the age and years completed. Not that one part of the body like a hand or leg or head is growing out of proportion. Jesus as a normal child was growing without any defect or disability and the parts of his body developed proportionately to the years he was completing. His personality development including physical, mental and emotional was perfect like any male child.[27]

The third aspect is growing in favour (GK. *Chariti*) of God and men. The word 'favour' could mean goodness, grace, support and blessing. Jesus was growing in the goodness of God and people. It implies, the child is accepted by God and society. Today, some children do not get the acceptance of the family and community if they are born female or disabled or HIV infected or as transgender. They are regarded as unwanted children and they are looked down without the favour of the people. But God loves each and every child whether the child is male or female, poor or rich, healthy or disabled. God's favour is more for the marginalized children and neglected by the society. Favour strengthens relationship between the child and society. The child can enjoy support and all the blessings of the family and neighbourhood. If the child is not accepted, he or she cannot enjoy the relationship and support of the society. The child can feel it and the social development of the child would be affected. The child may show reactions towards people or withdraw from others and lead a depressed life. Both the favour of God and human beings is needed for a child to grow socially, economically and psychologically well balanced in thinking and behaving. It brings shalom, a wellbeing life to a child. Jesus had the privilege of growing in favour with God and community. Only a small section of leaders hated Jesus at the later period of his ministry due to his challenging messages and actions of healing the disabled and sick.

IV.   AGENTS OF DEVELOPMENT AND PRINCIPLES OF ACTION

Transformation of children, local communities and the larger society is an important task of our time. The reasons for the need of trained agents to transform the lives of children are many. To mention a few we can list the problems of children from the context.[28] Some problems of children are global such as the influence of mass media and pornography. Hooked to internet and free telecasting of sexual material in internet, children in different countries are addicted to watching and involving in violence and sexual abuse of children. Other problems such as poverty, child labour, street children, poor health, drop out of school, child marriage, divorce and separation of children, Juvenile criminal activities vary in degree from country to country. Today, children have no safety and security and are at risk. Each child whether rich or poor, upper caste or lower caste, tribal or elite is looking for love of others, empathy and empowerment.

Ideologies and theologies alone cannot bring development of children. We need some agents to implement the theology of development. I have already pointed out above that the disciples of Christ were asked to be the practioners to proclaim shalom and implement it according to the need of the local communities they visit. In this section, I will mention a few principles that the agents should follow rather than giving a blue print of their plans and actions. The goal of development is shalom of all the people including children and the agents cannot use any means to achieve it. Means to be used by the agents count a lot when we base our development on biblical ideology. Jesus Christ is our role model to follow whatever we try to do.

Institutions to involve as Agents

One of the major agents of development is the government of each nation. As we pointed out earlier, the development programmes and implementations depend on the policies of the ruling party in each nation. After casting the vote and electing the ruling party, the public may not have much power to direct them to use the correct policies and proper means. But other agents such as family, schools , churches and missions can play the role of agents of development and transformation.

In my opinion, all the agents of development especially Christian agents need some principles for their action. Some of them are listed below.

i. Love of God and Love for Children

Usually, all the fathers and mothers have love for their children because they are born out of their blood and biological relationship. However, if anyone wants to work for other children, that person should have love for children. Although the disciples were around Jesus, they did not express their love for children coming to Jesus. But Jesus asked the children to be with him and placed his arms around them, listening to their words and answering their questions showed his love for the children (Mark 10: 13-16). Jesus warned those who abuse children to be punished severely (Mt. 18:1-6). Love is the basic principle for service to children. It should flow naturally out of one's heart revealing the heart of God for children.

ii. Knowing biblical theology of development

It is always good to have some knowledge of biblical basis of development. Shalom theology of development emphasizes holistic development of children. Pastors, Evangelists, Missionaries and Social workers need to be trained in the content, principles, methods, goals and means of Christian theology of development. A basic course on Development can be offered to them.[29] This kind of knowledge reforms the doctrines on children, liturgies, approaches to them and revise the budget for the ministry of children.

iii. Understanding the problems of children

Parents, teachers, pastors and social workers are aware of the problems of children because they meet them at home, schools or in churches. But they may not know how to analyze their problems. They lack critical skill to have socio-political analysis to see the factors, people and policies causing problems. Some spiritualize to put the blame on Satan or peer-group or their own children. They need to identify the oppressive forces in the society. One of the key problems of children is being hooked to cyber-net and pornography. Churches are unable to train the children to overcome this problem or to have critical analysis of mass media. Understanding of the problem is not merely knowing their struggles but also the causes and consequences and using remedial actions.

iv. Awareness about the Rights of Children

Each one of us should know the Rights of Children promoted by the UNO through the Convention on the Rights of Children (CRC) and other documents of their own country. The Articles of CRC should be made known to those involved in the development of children. In the process of developing children, they need to be partners in the decision making committee. Their participation in the discussion, planning and implementation is an important principle for development.

v. Periodical evaluation of policies and approaches

Creating suitable plans, budget and strategies to implement need to be done carefully. Once they are implemented as short-term or long-term development plan, periodical evaluation of the way the plans are implemented, success and failures need to be done by the agents. The Agents of Change should be willing to correct their policies, budget and approaches for empowering children on the basis of their periodic evaluation. They can also invite specialized consultancy service to help them in evaluation and revising their strategic plans and methodologies of functioning.

As a concluding comment, I like to suggest that churches should recover its vision and reform their action plans for the development of society particularly children. Each agent can plan for co-operation with other agents to promote integrated approaches for the holistic development of children and the society in which they live. Raising up a new generation to transform the world is a task before of us.

Endnotes

[1] Quoted from the article of Gnana Robinson, 'Challenge to Theological Education in the context of the Poor and Development' *Theological Education and Development* (eds. G. Robinson, H. Wilson, C. Duraisingh, Bangalore: ATTI, 1984), p.9. He quoted it from the book of C.T. Kurien, *Poverty and Development.* CISRS, Bangalore, 1974, p.40.

[2] Elizabeth B Hurlock, *Child Development* (New Delhi: Tata McGraw Hill Publishing Co. Ltd., 1999), p. 23.

[3] Bryant L Myers, *Walking with the Poor: Principles and Practices of Transformational Development* (New York; Orbis Books, 1999), pp. 90-110 discusses the merits and demerits of various development theories.

[4] Articles on development deal with the issues of injustice and human rights. See: *Religion and Society* (Bangalore: CISRS), issues -Vol. 27,3, Sept 1980 and 28,7, June 1981.

[5] Tom Sine analyzes the secular origin of the concept of development and contrasts its values with the biblical values in his article, 'Development: Its Secular Past and Its Uncertain Future' *The Church in Response to Human Need* (Papers of Wheaton '83 Consultation, Monrovia: MARC Centre, 1983), pp.22-33.

[6] Forth coming article of mine titled ,' Holistic Child Development: A Mission Agenda that cannot be ignored today' in *ACTS Journal*, Korea, 2012/13 and the extended version in the book (eds. J.N.Manoharan, Dasan Jeyaraj, Peter Pothan, Bangalore: CFCC, 2012/13).

[7] Claus Westermann, *Genesis 1-11: A Commentary* (Minneapolis: Augsburg Publishing House, 1984), p. 115; David Atkinson, *The Message of Genesis 1-11* (Leicester: IVP, 1990), pp.20-22.

[8] J.B.Jeyaraj, *Biblical Perspectives on Children and their Protection* (Madurai: Jubilee Institute, 2007) Revised 2011. Reprinted in the book *Children at Risk: Issues and Challenges* (ed. J.B. Jeyaraj and others, Delhi: ISPCK-CFCD, 2009), pp. 1-31.

[9] See my *Commentary on the Book of Genesis* (One Volume ,South Asia Bible Commentary, ed. Brian Wintle -forthcoming in 2014).

[10] For the discussions on the issue of creating human beings in 'image of God' refer to various commentaries.

[11] J.B. Jeyaraj, 'Church and Environment' *TBT Journal* (Bangalore: TBT, 1999), pp. 77-90.

[12] Amartya Sen, *Development as Freedom* (New Delhi: Oxford University Press, 2004), pp. 3-11. For M.A. Oommen's recent comment on Sen's views refer to 'The Meaning of Development: Reflections of an Octogenarian Teacher of Economics' *Religion and Society* (Bangalore: CISRS), vol. 57, 3, Sept 2012, pp. 17-19.

[13] Michael P Todaro and Stephen C. Smith, *Economic Development* (New Delhi: Pearson Education, 2004), p. 22.

[14] Gustavo Gutierrez, *A Theology of Liberation: History, Politics and Salvation* (London: SCM Press Ltd, 1988), p. 17, 21.

[15] See: 'Liberation Model' in my book *Christian Ministry: Models of Ministry and Training* (Bangalore: TBT, 2006), pp.88-100.

[16] Peter T. O'Brien, *Colossians , Philemon* (WBC 44; Waco:Word Books, 1982), pp. 286-292.

[17] See the chapter on 'Administrative Model' of ministry in my book *Christian Ministry: Models of Ministry* (Bangalore: TBT, 2007, pp.100-112.

[18] See: 'Legal Dimension' section in my article 'Biblical Perspectives on Children and their Protection' in *CAR* Book, pp. 20-29.

[19] J.B. Jeyaraj, *Christian Ministry* (Bangalore: TBT, 2007) p. 158.-159, discussion on the Kingdom of God.

[20] M.A. Oommen, 'The Meaning of Development' *Religion and Society*, (Bangalore: CISRS, vol.57, 3, 2012), pp. 22-24.

[21] Wayne Bragg, 'Beyond Development', *The Church in Response to Human Need* (ed. Tom Sine, Monrovia: MARC, 1983), pp.39-82.

[22] Wayne Bragg, pp. 72-79.

[23] The term 'Transformational Development' is discussed by Bryant L. Myers in his book, *Walking with the Poor: Principles and Practices of Transformational Development,(* New York: Orbis, 1999), pp. 91-234.

[24] J.B. Jeyaraj, 'Biblical Perspectives on Children and their Protection', *CAR Book* (ISPCK-CFCD-India, 2009), pp.1-32.

[25] J.B. Jeyaraj, 'Child in the Midst: Incarnation and Child Theology' in CAR Book, pp. 49-72. In the West, Keith White, Haddon Wilmer, Marcia Bunge and Dan Brewster are contributing through their Child theology. Their work is listed in the above article, 'Child in the Midst'.

[26] William Barclay, *New Testament Words* (London: SCM Press, 1971), pp. 258-267. See: *Sophia, Phronesis, Sunesis*.

[27] I. Howard Marshall, *The Gospel of Luke: A Commentary on the Greek Text* (Grand Rapids: Eerdmans, 1978), p. 130.

[28] The contributors of articles to the book, *Children at Risk: Issues and Challenges* (CAR) highlight more than 30 problems of children and the role of churches in contemporary society.

[29] *HCD Curriculum book* (Bangalore: CFCD-India, 2010) has listed syllabus of two subjects on Development. One is 'Foundation for HCD' and another is 'Holistic Child Development' - discussing theories and ideologies of development and connecting it to child development.

CHAPTER - 3

Churches and Kingdom of God: Relationship and Development of Children

The recent news about the child sexual abuse in Delhi (TV News in 2013-2015) and other parts of India, death of children due to poverty, trafficking, using children as cheap labour, kidnapping children for kidneys, sacrificing children for religious reasons (e.g. recent child sacrifice happened in Chennai in April 2013 and condemned by DMK Party leadership) and hooking them to watch pornography in cyber-net café indicate clearly that we are losing our children[1]. The policies of one-child-per family deprive the child to enjoy relationship with kith and kin in the future. Ignoring homosexuality and lesbianism which are going on under the surface at present among our youths in schools and colleges and legalizing and multiplying bars to enjoy alcohol are destroying families and communities. The mushrooming of hospitals for Fertility treatment and Invirto –method is a warning that many of our younger generations are losing the procreation capacity due to various reasons. The increase in divorce point out that parenting of the children and youths is not enough. If these problems and issues continue, how can we say that our churches are having quality growth and our Indian society is healthy. The time has come to think about quality growth of churches and communities. I am writing this brief article to emphasize the fact that the future growth of churches depends on the development of children and parenting. Raising up a new generation is important not only for the families, churches but also for our society and nation

I.   NEED OF QUALITY RELATED GROWTH

The term 'quality' is very much used in industrial and commercial sector. Importance to quality enhancement is given by secular companies and institutions by having Quality-Control Cell and getting ISO certification. This term is not very much used to speak of quality of a theology whether it is created in the West or East. It is used to refer to the growth of spirituality. It was first applied by the School of Church Growth with the interest to measure the growth of the church. Church growth is not merely quantity growth or numerical growth. It also includes the other side of quality growth. These two dimensions have been emphasized by the Church Growth School of Dr. Donald McGavran. Although many of us disagreed with his concession of planting caste churches due to ethnic and sociological factors and enhancing numbers through mass conversion, Church Growth School has certainly awakened the churches to think about their quantity and quality growth and the global Ecumenical movement to re-think of their theology of evangelism and mission[2]. It motivated many churches to develop their own national missions and send national missionaries crossing the culture to plant churches. While IMS and NMS, the two early missionary movements have contributed a lot in the field of mission, the concept of Church Growth brought revival to multiply missions and churches in unreached areas of India. More than 4000 national missions were born after 1960s and 40,000 nationals are doing missionary work in India. Some missions e.g. Church Growth Missionary Movement (CGMM) named their organizations using the concept of church growth to shake the stagnant churches to plan for growth.

Multiplying churches is not only a historical reality of the Apostle's period but also even today in India, Africa, Korea and other nations. But the churches planted cannot grow and be a witness unless their quality is strengthened particularly the faith and life of members in families. Special attention is needed to the children in the families since they are the future members and leaders of the churches and society. Where children were neglected, churches lost the generations as happened in the West and continue with a few elderly people. They lost the sustainability by the presence of human resource of younger generation and are now slowly getting closed and their buildings are sold to be Hindu temples or Mosques or Bingo bars.

Many churches in India are not evaluating periodically the quality aspect of their pastors, members, programmes, ministries, administration and infrastructure. In fact, they do not have a scale or tool to evaluate the quality growth of their churches except auditing the accounts and renewing the FCRA number to receive funds continuously. Most of the churches are satisfied if they conduct worship service on Sundays, weekly bible studies, annual convention or retreats and support some missionary organizations. They assume, spiritual growth is the only aspect of quality and ignore relating quality to other areas of churches. Some pastors are satisfied with the increasing number in membership but ignore to find out the ethical life of such members. Quantity and quality are inter-related. They are two sides of a coin. If a church needs to be healthy, then the families inside should be spiritual and ethical in accordance with the biblical teachings.

II.   CHURCH, KINGDOM OF GOD AND CHILDREN

Before listing the characteristics of child-friendly church for the holistic growth of children, we need to revisit the theological nature of Church and Kingdom of God and their relationship with children. Each of these three entities are discussed over a period and a number of books are written by scholars but not explaining in detail the relationship between children and church and the kingdom of God. So my focus is on a few key texts in the Synoptic Gospels speaking of the relationship between Church, Kingdom of God and children.

1.   Church and Children - Relationship

First, Church is not established as an organization or commercial institution but is a fellowship of believers. The term 'church' is today understood as an institution for adults with full of rituals to perform, election for position, getting appointments in mission schools and colleges and for marriage and burial. The basic nature of the Church is a community of believers in Christ and exists visibly as local churches. Because we failed to emphasize the nature of the church is a community for sharing and service, we forget that children are part of that community. Members in spite of their caste, race, geographical location are united with Christ that the universal church is called the 'Body of Christ'. Unlike the hierarchical structure in the 'Body of Bhrama' in Hinduism promoting *varna* and caste system, the Body of Christ emphasizes unity, dignity and equality of all believers and fellowship in serving God and humanity[3]. Children are also part of the Body of Christ when born to Christian parents through faith in Jesus and expressed outwardly by baptism. Whether they received infant baptism or adult baptism after understanding the Christian faith, they are members of the church. In the tradition of mainline churches, the children who received infant baptism with the guarantee of the god-parents to nurture the child in Christian faith till they grow to understand the faith, receive *Confirmation*. This is to confirm their faith in Christ on their own and accept to be members of the Body of Christ. Therefore, their biological as well as theological connection with the local church continue whether their parents continue to be the members of the church or not. The mainline churches based on liturgical worship have very meaningful *Order of Service* for birth of a child, parental responsibility, baptism of children and confirmation.[4] This inclusive nature of the liturgy and worship is an outward evidence for the integrated relationship between children and church.

2.   Kingdom of God and Children - Relationship

Second, the concept of the Kingdom of God developed in the monarchical period of the OT became a messianic expectation and fulfilled in Jesus Christ. The Apostles proclaimed Jesus Christ who inaugurated the Kingdom of God through his coming as Son of God, preaching, ministering, dying on the Cross and rising up again as the Gospel, good news of salvation for the entire humanity. Jesus and his values are so integrated in the theology of the Kingdom of God that it is not an *ism* or *ideology* like Capitalism, Marxism or Socialism. It is neither a political kingdom where Jesus is the king nor a political system. It is centered on the person and work of Jesus Christ and his values to be practiced in each country whatever the political system practiced. Practicing the kingdom values is expected of each family. The message of the Kingdom of God as Jesus preached is to love God and love our neighbour. All those who believe in Christ are members of the Kingdom of God. To make people to believe Jesus Christ and enjoy eternal life, the church has a role to proclaim the Kingdom of God and practice its values. G.E. Ladd discusses the relationship between the Kingdom of God and the Church.[5]   Can all children be part of the Kingdom of God? Although the bible makes thousands of references to children, Jesus makes a few explicit references to the relationship between children and the Kingdom of God. Let us study Mark 9:35-37, 10:13-16 and Matt.18:1-6.

Mark 9:33-37 (cf. Matt.18:1-6) and 10:10-16: An Exposition from Child Perspective

It is good to make a detailed exegetical study of the above three texts dealing with little children but the space is limited. Mathew 18:1-6 and Mark 9:35-37 narrate with some variations a similar context of disciples quarrelling about being greatest. Another incident about children is recorded in Mark 10:10-16. One can notice three issues lying in these texts viz. adults receiving the kingdom of God, welcoming the children in a literal sense and the question of the kingdom of God belonging to children.

1.   Bringing for blessing

First, the context of Mark 10:10-16 is people bringing children to Jesus to touch them. Children were usually brought by mothers may be accompanied by their husbands. However, some of the children brought to Jesus could be from divorced or separated families because Mark places this incident after the issue of divorce raised by Pharisees (vv.1-9).[6] Having a high opinion about Jesus as a divine leader of their religion or a man of power to do miracles, they want Jesus to touch their children. 'Touching' is to express Jesus' love to the children and show that each child is recognized. It could be regarded as equivalent to laying on hands with a purpose. Their belief could be that their children will have the blessing of Jesus. We do not know the content of Jesus' blessing but his blessing could include enjoying good health, physical and spiritual development, grace and favour of God and people in society. There is a biblical formula of blessing for the holistic development of children as one can notice in the life of Samuel and Jesus (1 Sam. 2:26; Lk. 2:51-52).[7]

This effort of the parents has implications for our parental responsibility of leading our children to Jesus if our children need to be blessed in life. The most suitable age for children to accept Jesus is between 4- 14, as Dan Brewster's theory of 4/14 Window shows.[8] Many children understand God's love for them and are receptive to the Gospel. Bringing children does not stop with teaching them but also enrolling them in the visible Body of Christ.

They need to be dedicated, baptized and trained to take part in the holy communion and ministries of the churches. Children need to be developed by families and pastors as disciples of Christ from their early childhood.

2.   Rebuking for Releasing

Secondly, the disciples rebuked the parents (v.13). The reason for objecting the parents bringing children to Jesus is not told. We can only assume that the disciples regarded the children so low in their society. Children were not given much importance in the Israelite society. They were regarded as small and a commodity like a property of the family. In their society, there existed a hierarchical structure in the family regarding husband as the man of high position and authority, wife secondary and children are the third category till they grow to the status of a father. Another reason could be that the disciples assumed themselves as the core group around Jesus and no one can come to Jesus as close they are, without their permission. We notice this kind of trend today in our Indian politics. Political leaders or ministers are surrounded by their own party men not allowing others to come closer to express their grievances to these public servants. The same trend can be noticed when religious gurus and babas come to a temple. The priests surrounding them allow only certain devotes to be blessed by these gurus. Or else they regarded children as nuisance and wanted Jesus not to be disturbed by children and their parents.

Whatever be the reason, thirdly, Jesus does not like their attitude and hindering children coming to him. The narrator records the reaction of Jesus. He was indignant to the disciples (v.14). He rebuked the disciples to allow the children to come to him. This is a challenge to release the children from the control of his disciples to enjoy the love and blessing of Jesus. Like Jesus, the leaders in the family, society, church and nation should either force or persuade those who are hindrances in allowing the children to come and enjoy their rights and privileges. The next move of Jesus is taking the children in his arms and putting his hands around and blessing them. This action of embracing is an evidence how much Jesus loved children and valued them.

3.   Teaching for transforming

Fourthly, Jesus goes one step further in teaching an important lesson to his disciples and parents around him and transforming their mind. He made it clear that children are part of the kingdom. The Kingdom of God belongs to children is a radical challenge and a big shock to the disciples because they were thinking that they are the first citizen of the kingdom and will have position and authority in Jesus' kingdom. They assumed that the rest of the people should be under the rule of their cabinet. Mark is aware that all the children are created by God but not all children belonging to different religious faith belong to the kingdom of God unless they accept Jesus as their personal Saviour (cf.Jn.3:16). So he is careful in phrasing his message, 'the kingdom of God belongs to such as these'. The Greek syntax is *'ton gar toiouton'* meaning 'not that the kingdom of God belongs to these children whom Jesus is touching now' but 'the kingdom of God belongs to such ones' emphasizing the nature and quality of children as loving, innocent, dependent, humble not seeking power and position and vulnerable (v. 15).[9] Children are examples for adults. As we become adults, we develop both good and bad nature in us. Our mind is corrupt and long for money, sex, power and authority. We do knowingly or unknowingly injustice in our administration, leadership and to children, families and communities. Relinquishing all bad nature and getting renewed by the power of the Holy Spirit is to be taught from the early childhood that we grow to be of transformed adults. That is why Jesus asked Nicodemus to born again like a child with a transformed mind and character (Jn.3.16).

i.   *Receiving the kingdom of God like a little child demands transformed life*

Jesus laid down the criteria to be in the kingdom of God (v.15). All the people including the disciples are required to receive the kingdom of God like a little child. We have to raise two questions to understand what Jesus meant. Why did Jesus use children as an example or illustration or a sign of the kingdom?[10] What he means by receiving the kingdom like a child? The main reason Jesus used children as an example because of the nature of children. In an another incident narrated in Matt.18:1-6, Jesus watched the arguments and quarrels among his disciples regarding being the greatest in

Jesus' kingdom. The disciples misunderstood the teachings about the Kingdom of God. They were expecting a political kingdom under the kingship of Jesus as fulfillment of the messianic prophecy. But Jesus was not talking about a political kingdom throwing away the Roman rule and becoming a king of Israel that the disciples plan for a position. In that context too, Jesus placed a child in the midst of them as an example or sign and asked them to become like a child to inherit the kingdom.[11] The one who inaugurated the kingdom of God on this earth by his incarnation is asking his audience to receive it. Jesus knew that his initiative of inaugurating the kingdom is not enough unless the people should receive it responding to his accomplishment . Otherwise it cannot benefit the most. It is interesting to note the way Mark and Matthew phrase this point. Mark writes, 'anyone who will not *receive* (GK. *dechetai*) the kingdom of God like a little child will never enter it' (v.15). Matthew says, '..unless you change and become like a little children, you will never enter the kingdom of heaven' (18: 3). Both are explicit and mean the same. To inherit or be a member of the kingdom of God, we need to become like little child who receives gladly without questioning or doubting but trusting the one who gives a sweet or chocolates. If so, then the action of receiving on the side of us includes, faith in the person of Jesus, trusting his power and love, manifesting humility, accepting him gladly and not sadly. These are such qualities one can notice in a little child. Corrupt persons in mind and life cannot be part of the kingdom of God because they are contradictory to the values and demands of Jesus. Justice and righteousness are expected from the people. Jesus used the opportunity either to place one child in the midst of his disciples or touching a group of children in front of them to teach the audience to be transformed like little children to be eligible for the kingdom of God.

ii. Welcoming Children demands the heart of God

In the context of objecting children coming to him, the disciples were asked to allow the children to be released from their control, touched, embraced and blessed by him. It is showing the way to the adults to accept children. It is not merely a symbolic action but a genuine action of Jesus demanding the disciples to follow him and welcome the children in a literal sense. The term 'welcoming' in the words of Jesus has a deep meaning. It has to reveal the heart of God for children. The adults are not only required to have a transformed life like a little child but to practice it by receiving, accepting, loving and blessing children. This kind of action towards children offers recognition, importance and dignity to them. This is lifting them from being 'last' in the family to be the 'first' to enjoy justice and rights. The action of welcoming children can influence the social structure of the family and community to treat children valuable and develop them holistically.

iii. Enabling little children to be part of the kingdom demands missional action

Mark records the teaching of Jesus to be servants of all and receive (Gk: *dechetai*) the little child. This Greek word used in 9:37 and 10:15 are the same but it is translated as 'receiving' or 'welcoming'. Receiving a little child is equivalent to welcoming Jesus and the God who has sent him. In other words, welcoming a child is receiving the kingdom of God. Mark reverses the saying from 'receiving the kingdom of God like a little child' (10:13-16) to 'receiving the little child' is receiving the kingdom of God (9:35-37). Does Mark equalize little children and kingdom of God one and the same? No. Children cannot be the kingdom of God except be part of it. They need to enjoy the goodness of the kingdom. If so, why he talks about welcoming little children? Welcoming a little child and thus welcoming Jesus demands a radical change in the attitude and actions of the adults. Welcoming a little child requires showing love, sharing, accepting, rendering justice and empowering children.

Welcoming could also mean working for the change in social structure particularly patriarchy and its influence in the families where children are regarded last. The disciples are asked not to stop the children coming to him but also to work for their justice by changing the oppressive social structure. This is understandable from the call of Jesus to the disciples to be 'servants of all'. The word 'all' includes children too. If the adults want to be servants of children, it demands them to relinquish their domination over the children. Furthermore, they need to extend charity to the needy children and struggle for the rights and justice of children. Socio-political actions are needed to enable them to enjoy the goodness of God's kingdom. This is one of the ways to make the kingdom of God belonging to children in each generation. That means serving children truly. Matthew and Mark say vehemently that the society should change and protect the children quoting the warning of Jesus. Those who lead or force children to sin or suffer rather than enjoy the good life should be brought to justice (Matt.18:6, Mark 9:42).

The insights one can draw from Matthew and Mark is that children are not merely examples or signs of the kingdom but also targets to enjoy the kingdom of God. How can the kingdom of God belong to these children (Mk.10:15)? In summary, children, on the one side, need to be instructed to believe Jesus and on the other side need to be supported by the action of adults to give them goodness of the kingdom of God here and now. Actions are demanded on children as they grow as well as on the adults. Let not adults deprive the rights of children to be part of the kingdom of God by suppressing them. Rather they work for them to be part of the kingdom.

III. NEED OF CHILD-FRIENDLY CHURCHES FOR HCD

Today, children are one-fourth (25%) of the world population. They are the future leaders in families and society. UNO is giving importance to children and their development through its programmes and financial support. Christian children are also members of the Body of Christ and they are served to develop their spirituality through Sunday Schools and Christian Education programmes. However, they are not getting importance in many churches.[12] Some churches do not have Sunday Schools or Vacation Bible School (VBS) to nurture them regularly. Some churches do not budget for the ministry to children. The teachers of Sunday Schools are left to raise the funds for their work among children. Many churches are not child friendly to develop children holistically - spiritually, socially, psychologically and educationally.[13]

Characteristics of Child-Friendly Churches

I can list many characteristics of a child friendly church but I emphasize only a few of them below looking into the context of South Asia.

i.   Giving importance to children as full member

Children do not get importance in families since our families are conditioned by Patriarchy system. Father is the head of the family and his wife and children are his property. Male preference to female child is still dominant in our families. The same social setting reflects in the structure of our churches in

India, Pakistan, Nepal and Bangladesh. Men are in the upper hierarchy, women below and children last in churches. Till they complete confirmation and cross the age of 21, children are lesser category in churches and they are not consulted or allowed to be part of the decision making body in churches. How many Pastorate Committees in churches have 'growing-children' as their members or invitees avoiding the requirement of getting elected. Their presence can challenge the elderly members to be role models in discussions and conducting themselves. They can also give valuable suggestions from their side and for their needs. Unless children are integrated in all the aspects of the life of the churches, they remain marginalized.

ii. Love, Care and Respect

Children need love, care and respect of the ministers and other members. In some societies, children are addressed with respect. The elders do not use abusive language and degrade children. They correct children not in front of others but privately counsel and guide them. Pastors and Sunday School teachers should understand each child fully particularly, their background, parents, relationship within the family and school, attitude, physical health condition, social and psychological needs. Since children are told about their caste by their parents and taught to maintain caste difference, careful attention is needed to shape each child to come out of this mind-set and see it as social evil and wrong to maintain it. The social, racial and material differences can cause ill-feelings among children if ministers or members express publically or practice it. Favouring children from upper caste and rich families and discriminating poor and lower caste cannot promote friendliness and equality among children. Love and care should unite children. Children of all background whether they are rich or poor, upper or lower caste should feel the churches as friendly and encouraging them to come up in life. Preferential option to lift up children of widows to study or get trained in technical school can help them to stand on their own feet later and take care of their widowed mothers, kith and kin.

iii. Prayer and social support for children

A child friendly church prays for children and goes one step further to help a child in *truma* or poverty or in financial need for his or her education. When they come to know that the members and leaders are praying for their studies, exams and needs, they are encouraged and gain more confidence in God and church. They feel one with the congregation and love the church. They are prepared to do anything for the church because they are attached with the church in their emotions and reasons. Small financial grants to needy children for their education, training and clothing help them to get educated and feel normal than coming to the church with inferiority complex and hopelessness. They start questioning God's care and love for them when they suffer but strengthen their faith in God when helped economically.

iv. Nurturing and Curriculum

Each child needs to be rooted in the Word of God. Preaching high sounding academic sermons cannot reach children. They need to be taught biblical truths in the way they can understand. When they raise questions in Sunday schools, the teachers or pastors need to be patient to listen and answer. Their doubts are genuine. They are seeking truths at their level. If the pastor and teachers are doubtful about the Scripture and do not believe certain texts in the Bible, children begin to doubt the bible. Child friendly church nurtures children in truth and train them to hold on God's word to lead their lives. The Christian Education curriculum should be designed to lead children to believe the Bible, divine values and broaden their perspectives about environment, gender equality, peace and harmony, handling crisis situation and to keep good relationship with all. They need to know the meaning of the rituals, symbols, imageries and traditions true to the Bible. Christian nurturing is not limited to imparting knowledge but enabling them to practice what they learnt. In doing so, leaders need to avoid threatening method or indoctrination approach or forcing the child to accept their views but to teach them the truth in love.

v. Developing the Skill and Talents of children

Many churches minister to children to learn the Scripture. But this is not enough. Many children need guidance and help to develop their skill in drawing, music and playing musical instruments. They cannot afford to buy their own instruments. Churches can provide tuition and instruments to such poor children to develop their talents. Some children in villages are finding it difficult to learn English and languages by paying fees for private tuition.

Spoken and written training in languages can be offered to such children. Church building or a hall can be left open with lights for the village children to come and study in the night time and do their home work. Youths can help them to do their home work as a voluntary service.

vi. Educating and training the congregation

Special effort should be taken to create programmes to educate the parents, elders and ministers in the churches about the rights of children and responsibility of parenting and caring them. Many pastors, elders and parents do not know the biblical laws and universal documents like Convention on the rights of Child (CRC) to protect the rights of children. My eyes were opened when I exercised re-reading the laws in the Old Testament about the protection of children particularly female child.[14] It is important that the churches take these laws in Ex. 20-24 seriously and teach them to the congregation. The CRC document can be studied by leaders, teachers and parents together. The newly emerging Child Theology is influencing churches to look critically into their age old doctrines about children written in colonial period and the structure of the Department of Children and make changes in the policies, doctrines, sacraments and budget to be friendly to children.[15]

More opportunities are coming up to train parents, pastors and teachers through Holistic Child Development educational programme in bible colleges in India and abroad.[16] Christian Forum for Child Development (CFCD-India), a common forum has developed the curriculum for HCD education and training faculty members of colleges offering MA and M.Th in HCD through Distance mode to be practitioners. HCD is a professional course for those parents and ministers to work among children. Churches can send their elders, Sunday School teachers and child care workers to get trained in HCD.

vii. Child Friendly Church campus

Usually churches provide facilities for adults. Many churches in rural areas conduct their Sunday School under trees on campus or roadside without facilities to show audio-visual presentations. In many towns and villages, mothers sit outside the church building keeping their kids and protecting them from running to the road. Since they do not have a room or kids corner to leave their children and participate in the worship, they miss a lot in singing and hearing sermons. They could not participate fully in the Sunday worship. Urban churches have parish hall for children to assemble and learn. Providing facilities of drinking water, proper toilets for children, play ground are lacking in many churches. Parents feel uneasy when their children cry during the worship service and afraid of pastors or a member sitting near could scold them. Some churches spend huge amount in decorations and printing and for committee meetings rather than providing needed facilities for children and mothers.

viii.   Celebrations friendly to children

Children love celebrations like birth day parties and fun. Moses instructed the Israelites to celebrate Passover, Feast of Tabernacle, harvest including children.[17] The main reason is to teach the meaning of these celebrations to children because they are to be connected with their history of liberation from Egyptian bondage, wilderness wandering and staying in tents as pilgrims and thanking God for granting a good harvest and food. Celebrations are not merely fun but to teach history and the religious traditions born out of their historical experience and became a belief. Usually Christmas, New Year and Easter are celebrated by adults and children to enjoy cakes, *briyani* and ice-cream. Our religious festivals and secular festivals such as Independence Day and Republic Day or Pongal are celebrated with children but not theologized to teach them to integrate history and faith. Harvest festivals in churches are celebrated for raising funds for constructing building or missions. Children get some food out of sale on that day. May Day (1st May of each year) as Labour Day never challenged us to stop child labour in our institutions. Children do hard jobs in many homes belonging to Christians. Can our celebrations bring more joy and meaning to children?

Churches which are giving importance to children and develop them are growing and producing men and women of God for the families and nations. When children are left uncared, they find their places in clubs, bars, cafes and hooked to the influence of mass media. Some of them may become violent and end up in prison. Others may cause a lot of problems to their families, schools and society. It is not for the sake of churches to boost the number of their members and sustainability but for the sake of that individual, families and society, we must evangelize children, nurture them in Christian faith and teachings and develop them as good leaders. Their relationship with the local churches and enabling the children to enjoy the goodness of the Kingdom of God here on earth depend on the attitude and action of leaders in Christian ministry and families and can contribute for the growth in quantity and quality.

Endnotes

[1] Refer to the articles in the book for issues and problems of children today: *Children at Risk:* Issues and Challenges (ed. J.B. Jeyaraj, Chris Gnanakan, T. Swaroop, P. Prasad), ISPCK-CFCD India joint publication), 2009.

[2] Roger Hedlund, *Roots of the Great Debate in Mission: Mission in Historical and Theological Perspective* (Bangalore: TBT, 1993) traces the debate on evangelism and mission in different consultations.

[3] See: J.B. Jeyaraj, *Christian Ministry: Models of Ministry and Training* (Bangalore: TBT, 2006), pp. 213-221 for discussion on Church and Kingdom of God.

[4] J. B. Jeyaraj, 'Liturgical Perspective of Family and Parenting' *Journal of Theological Education and Mission* (JOTEAM), vol. 3, Feb. 2012, pp. 61-80. Church of South India (CSI Synod) has revised the Order of Service in 2006 and elaborated the section on children.

[5] G.E. Ladd, A Theology of New Testament (Grand Rapids: W.B Eerdmans, 1979), pp.45-120.

[6] Ched Myers, *Binding the Strong Man: A Political Reading of Marks Story of Jesus* (Maryknoll, NY: Orbis Books, 1994), pp. 266-268.

[7] J.B. Jeyaraj, 'Theology of Development and Transformation of Children' in the book Holistic Child Development: Foundation, Theory and Practice (Vol.1, Delhi: ISPCK-CFCD, 2013) pp. 1-28.

[8] Dan Brewster, 'Themes and Implications of HCD Programming in Seminaries' in CAR book (ISPCK-CFCD, 2009), pp. 37-38.

[9] Tan Kim Huat, *The Gospel According to Mark*, Asia Bible Commentary (manila: ATA, 2011), p.231.

[10] Keith White sees children in these texts as sign of the kingdom. See his article: 'Children as Signs of the Kingdom of God-A challenge to us all' and critical responses in the book *Now and Next: A Compendium of papers presented at the NOW and NEXT Theological Conference on Children*, Nairobi, 2011 (ed. Keith White, Compassion International), pp. 35-80.

[11] J.B. Jeyaraj, 'Child in the midst: Incarnation and Child Theology' in the book *Children at Risk: Issues and Challenges* (Delhi: ISPCK/CFCD-India, 2009, pp. 49-72.

[12] Dan Brewster discusses this problem and several charateristics of Child -friendly churches in his book, *Child, Churhc and Mission* (Compassion International, 2005) chs. 5 and 8.

[13] See J.B. Jeyaraj, 'Theology of Development and Transformation of Children' which discuss the biblical text on holistic child development-

[14] J.B. Jeyaraj, 'Biblical Understanding of Children and their Protection' (Madurai: Jubilee Institute Publication, 2008), pp. 1-30 also reprinted in the book Children at Risk (Delhi: ISPCK-CFCD, 2009), pp. 1-31.

[15] Keith White and Haddon Wilmer, Introduction to Child Theology (UK: CTM, 2008) and J.B. Jeyaraj, 'Child in the Midst: Incarnation and Child Theology' in CAR book (Delhi: ISPCK-CFCD, 2009), pp.49-72.

[16] Degree progorammes such as MA and M.Th in HCD to be practitioners are offered in seminaries in Kerala, Bangalore, Jorhat, Nagaland. One core subject called CAR will be taught to students of B.Th., B.D. M.Div. in many seminaries related to Senate of Serampore and ATA.

[17] J.B. Jeyaraj, 'Festivals, Communication and Development' Journal of Dharma (Bangalore: Dharmaram Publication, 2003), vol. 28, 3.

CHAPTER - 4

Child in the Midst:
Incarnation and Child Theology

One may think that the Bible speaks of children here and there and does not give much importance to children. But a survey of the references on children in the Bible points to more than 1400[1]. Formulating a child theology has been neglected until recently[2]. A person who surveys the books written by scholars on Biblical Theology finds rarely a chapter on children. If some mentioning of children is found, it could be in connection with the doctrine of infant baptism or adult baptism or nurturing children in the knowledge of the Bible. Scholars writing commentaries on biblical books, either pay less attention to the texts where a child is mentioned or make a passing comment on the text without explaining about children in detail. Even books on Systematic Theology do not pay much attention to children except on the doctrine of baptism or the concept of 'children of God' and neglect to include a chapter on Child Theology. It may be disappointing to find that children have no place in the books written on history of Christianity. However, God did not leave the world without a voice for children in each generation. Some of their voices might not have been recorded in terms of books. But some theologians have written about children and the importance of knowing the thoughts of these theologians is being increasingly recognized. For example, what John Chrysostom, St. Augustine, Thomas Aquinas, Calvin, Luther, John Wesley, Jonathan Edwards, Friedrich Schleiermarcher, Karl Barth and Karl Rahner wrote on children is getting attention due to the emerging Child Theology and made known in some of the recent articles and books.[3] Yet, there is a tremendous need to write on children and relate them to theology and praxis.

I.   UNDERSTANDING TERMS AND PHRASES

The phrase 'Child Theology' is like any other phrase such as 'Liberation Theology', 'Creation Theology' or 'Eco-Theology'. But there are at least three kinds or strands viz. 'Theologies of Childhood', 'Theologies of Children' or 'Children's Theology' and 'Child Theology' with their own uniqueness and distinctions and relating to each other. Theologies of childhood focus in general on the various stages of the growth of a child, theories related to child development and nurturing the child. Marcia Bunge envisages that the 'Theologies of Childhood' will provide 'sophisticated understanding of children and childhood and our obligations to children'. But she believes that the 'Child Theologies' which 'reexamine not only the conceptions of children and obligations to them but also fundamental doctrines and practices of the Church' will develop more in different regions of the world.[4] She points out that 'Child Theologies will be able to offer new insights into central themes of the Christian faith, such as God, creation, Christology, theological anthropology, sin, salvation, faith, the Word, worship, sacraments, missiology and eschatology. Thus Child Theologies will build on strong theologies of childhood but have a broader scope'.[5] In my opinion, the third strand, 'Theology of a Child' or 'Theologies of a Group of Children' refers to the way children define God and explain their experience and could be linked to Child Theology. Some of these definitions coming from the Western scholars are useful but they are more academic and need to be analyzed. Nevertheless, the Asians, Africans and Latin Americans need to define their own 'Child Theologies' out of their biblical and cultural reflections.

Theologies are not new. But they emerge due to challenges of the context. During the early period, heretical interpretations about Jesus arose and the result was the articulation of creeds. Doctrinal theology followed out of the need for systematizing concepts and ideas. Contextual theologies such as Liberation Theology, Eco-theology, Theology of Pain, brahminical response of Indian Christian Theology, Dalit Theology, Tribal Theology and Theology of Religions emerged due to socio-economic changes, development of science and technology, identity and cultural conflicts and growth of pluralism. These insights are discovered from the Scripture, traditions and experience and articulated in the form of theologies. These contextual theologies are constantly shaped and experimented. As long as they grow, they can bring fresh insights and challenges. Child theology is also not new but recovered from the insights of the Biblical teachings on children. It is unique because it is based on biblical teachings and contributes to the holistic dimension of development of children. Other ideologies and philosophies also contribute to the development of children but they are based on a social or economic or psychological or cultural basis. They lack the spiritual dimension which is an important component of Child theologies. The Gospel is holistic and has universal applicability. The philosophy and schemes of a UNO or some NGOs or secular movements and charities need not necessarily have the basis of faith in God and the teachings of Scripture. But Child Theologies for Holistic Child Development (HCD) interpreted by the church and for the ministry of the church include spiritual, social, economic and other dimensions to meet the demand for the holistic development of children.

The Christian NGOs such as Compassion International, World Vision, KNH and Save the Children Fund that are based on the Bible and Christian conviction have contributed to the relief of the physical needs of children and are supporting millions of orphans all over the world, who are deserted and abused. These organizations and other similar organizations are doing a tremendous work in developing children physically, mentally and educationally. Christian Education ministries such as Sunday School, VBS and Bible Club Movement, and Scripture Union are working among children, nurturing them in Christian faith and biblical values and guiding them for proper ethical living. As far as I know, none of them brought out a child theology although they work on the biblical basis. Our Roman Catholic friends have given importance to infant Jesus. They called some of their churches and children homes as Infant Jesus Church or Homes and articulated their own *Infantalogy* of Jesus. I am not sure, whether or not their theologians or Protestant theologians belonging to other Christian traditions have used the phrase 'Child Theology' and promoted it as has been done by Child Theology Movement (CTM).[6] A thorough research on this issue in the history and development of 'Theologies of Childhood' and 'Child Theologies' is needed and should be taken up by some scholars and doctoral research students in seminaries.

In this new millennium, Haddon Willmer and Keith White, the key theologians in the CTM, have made a valuable contribution of highlighting 'child' as an important agenda in theological thinking. Both of them define Child Theology in their official document of CTM saying, 'Child Theology is an investigation that considers and evaluates central themes of theology – historical, biblical and systematic – in the light of the child standing beside Jesus in the midst of the disciples. This child is like a lens through which some aspects of God and his revelation can be seen more clearly. Or, if you like, the child is like a light that throws existing theology into new relief '[7]

Taking their cue from Mathew 18: 1-6 and Mark 9:33-37, they emphasize the phrase 'Child in the midst' and promote Child Theology through their conferences and consultations.[8] I will discuss Mt. 18 and my emphasis on Incarnation of Jesus as a child in the midst at a later stage in this paper. Another valuable contribution comes from Dan Brewster with his Holistic Child Development Movement (HCD). As the International Director for the Advocacy Programme of Compassion and General Secretary of Global Alliance for Advancing HCD, he emphasizes the praxis of developing children holistically. One of his main emphases is the 4/14 window focusing on reaching children for Christ and developing them spiritually in the age group between 4-14 since many children commit their lives to Christ during this period. According to him, Child Theology is one of the bases for HCD which is more inclusive of theological, contextual and other dimensions of children. He believes firmly that HCD is like an umbrella and accommodates various themes such as Child Theology, Children at risk, Theologies of Childhood, nurturing and raising future generation, etc.[9] The above survey points out the effort taken for the cause of children from various perspectives such as materialistic development, nurturing and spiritual formation, theological, historical and missiological.

II.   UNDERSTANDING TEXTS AND INTERPRETATION

It is not easy to explain all the texts related to children in one article. Volumes of books need to be written on these texts. I see three kinds of texts connected with children. One kind is *Problematic Texts* such as God asking Abraham to sacrifice Isaac (Gen.22:1-19), Jephtha sacrificing his own daughter to fulfill his vow for God (Jud. 11:32-40), the two women who planned to eat their own children due to a severe famine (2 Kings 6:24-31), hundreds of innocent children being killed by Herod for the sake of one child Jesus (Mt.2:13-18). These texts are hard narratives in the Bible and it is difficult to answer the various theological, historical and sociological questions raised by these texts. The second type of texts is the *Paradigm Texts* such as Mt.1:20-2:6, 18:1-6, Mk. 10:13-16, Lk.1:26-36, Jn. 1:1-16, 3:16 which focus on the child and provide a good basis for the formation of child theology. The third type is the *Progressive Texts*, which help us to progress in our understanding of and working for children. Fox example, passages which teach that both male and female children are made in the image of God (Gen.1:26-28), passages that assert that children are the gift of God (Ps.127:3), laws protecting children in the ancient Israelite society (Ex.21:7-11, 20-22, 22:16; 22:23, Lev. 18: 21,19:29, Dt. 22:13-19, Gal. 3:26-29) and instructions for disciplining and nurturing children to be responsible persons in the family, church and society (Dt. 6:1-9, 11:18-21, Prov. 1:8, 4:1-4, 5:1-6, Eph. 6:1-4, Titus 2:6-8). I will try to focus on one or two *paradigm texts* to contribute my insights for the progress of Child Theology.

A. GOD PLACED HIS CHILD IN THE MIDST OF PEOPLE – INCARNATION

Without the incarnation of Jesus there is no salvation for humanity in the world. Incarnation is the starting point or the central focus of many theologies. So it is important to study the event of the incarnation narrated in the texts of the Bible. There is a vast difference between *'incarnation'* and *'avatar'*. In Hindu mythologies, avatar of gods and goddesses are common phenomenon. The four main characteristics of *avatar* are viz. the appearance of gods and goddesses in human form need not be historical and proved with evidences, the appearance is temporary, can repeat and can be connected with sinless or sinful activities which are regarded as the *'play'* or *'leelai'* or *'holy game'* (*Thiruvilaiyadal*) of gods. Hinduism also speaks of gods placing or sending their sons in the midst of people. In the Vaishnavite tradition, Krishna appears as Bala Krishna steeling the butter in the home. He appears as Gobi Krishna in front of the girls, bathing and dancing with them. In Saivaite tradition, one of the sons of Shiva known as Bala Murugan asks questions and learns from his parents and other sages. He placed his abode on the six mountains in Tamilnadu and started dwelling among people as a symbol of wisdom. Ayyappan is another avatar of a god in Hinduism and has a number of devotees visiting his temple in Kerala during the months of November to January. In contrast to these characteristics of avatar, the incarnation of Jesus is historical, permanent in the sense that it happened once and does not repeat and not connected with sinful activities of 'play'. E. W. Thompson writes of the distinctiveness of the incarnation of Jesus by saying,

> When Christians speak of incarnation, they mean that God's very real self dwelt among men in a real human body, with a complete human nature, under the ordinary conditions of our humanity and subject to righteousness, for a moral purpose – the deliverance of men from the bondage of sin and the leading of them into a nobler life. This cannot be said of any avatar[10]

The incarnation of Jesus includes birth, growth, death and resurrection (cf. Philp. 2:6-8).[11] Theological discussions on incarnation focus on the question of virgin birth, historicity of Jesus, divinity and humanity of Jesus, substance of Jesus and the relationship of Jesus with the Father and Holy Spirit, place and status of Jesus in the Trinity, but do not relate the incarnation to Child Theologies. We need to bring together all the texts in the NT that speak on the incarnation of Jesus to develop Child Theologies. Nevertheless, it is not possible to explain all these texts in detail within the limited space of this article. I encourage other scholars to enter into this area of relating incarnation and other texts in epistles to child theology. I am making an attempt here with my limited knowledge based on the resources available to me to incorporate the insights of the texts on incarnation in the NT and to relate them to Child Theology.

Matthew and Luke narrate the story of the birth of Jesus and the glorification of the incarnated child by the angels, shepherds and wise men from the east.. St. John, the writer of the Gospel of John speaks of incarnation in philosophical term of 'logos' (word) being with God and sent to dwell among people. (Jn.1:1-16). But the same writer has brought out the concept of incarnation in simple words in Jn. 3:16 that every one of us can understand. This text is always looked at from the point of God, the Father and his initiative. The love of God, the Father for the lost world is emphasized by commentators. Nevertheless, we need to shift our focus on the child, the direct object of the action of God and explain the text from the perspective of child. We gain the following insights for Child Theologies.

1. 'The Word became flesh' *(Jn. 1:14)*

The Hebrew term *dabar* (word), signifying the word of God and its creative power in the Old Testament, is well known to Jews. Both the 'word' and 'God' cannot be separated in the understanding of the OT. The 'word' spoken by God is God's extended personality. 'The word of God is God himself in his creative action.'[12] John uses deliberately the Greek term *logos* (word) in the prologue of his Gospel. This Greek term, known to Greeks and Jews living in Hellenistic context, refers to the same and only God in John's Gospel. John emphasizes the eternity of God by saying, 'In the beginning was the Word, and the Word was with God and the Word was God' (1:1). Jesus is not a separate entity outside God, but Jesus is that 'word with God.' Being part of the Godhead, Jesus has a close relationship with the Father.

Commenting on John 1:1-2, Bruce Milne emphasizes three aspects of Jesus viz. 'Jesus shares God's eternity,' 'Jesus Christ was eternally with God' and 'Jesus Christ is one with God.'[13] He goes on to discuss the four implications of verses 1-2 viz. the finality, mystery, centrality and the supremacy of Jesus Christ.[14] The opening verses of the Gospel thus indicate the origin or source of the flesh, that is, Jesus. John using 'logos' to refer to God as well as to Jesus, goes on to say that 'the Word became flesh and made his dwelling among us' (1:14), meaning God has revealed himself in human form and that form is Jesus. Instead of using the Greek word for 'man' or 'body,' John uses deliberately 'flesh' (*sarx*) in order to emphasize the 'human existence in its frailty and vulnerability' and refers to the 'whole person' of Jesus.[15] In describing the incarnation of God in Jesus, Cornelis Bennema says, 'this is the greatest miracle in the history of humankind: the Creator entered his creation by becoming a creature.'[16] Bruce Milne's comments are worth quoting:

> The verb 'was made' (*egeneto*, from *ginomai*) expresses that a person or thing changes its property and enters into a new condition, becomes something that it was not before. The tense is aorist, implying a definite and completed action; there is no going back upon the incarnation. The act of self–humbling

on the part of God is irreversible, he is eternally 'Emmauel' God with us. God the Son, without ceasing for a moment to be divine, has united to himself, a full human nature and become an authentic human person, 'God with us.' In Jesus Christ, God 'was made man.'[17]

John makes it clear that Jesus is the beloved son whom God has sent to dwell among human beings because God loved the world so much (Jn. 3:16). He refers to Jesus as the 'son of God' and emphasizes the relationship between God, the Father and the Son (10: 30, 14:9). Luke describes Jesus through the words of angels to Mary—Jesus is the 'son of the Most High' (Lk. 1:26-33)—and to shepherds—Jesus is 'Christ the Lord' (Lk. 2:11). Paul brings out the significance of incarnation through the words of his beautifully styled song,

> Who being in very nature God,
> did not consider equality with God
> …but made himself nothing
> taking the very nature of a servant
> being made in human likeness,
> being found in appearance as a man,
> he humbled himself and became obedient to death
> —even death on a cross (Phil.2:6-8).

Paul not only describes the nature of incarnation but also connects it to his ministry of servanthood and death on the cross. God becoming flesh in human form and dwelling among people is a special revelation, an incarnation and an important event in history. Within the narratives of incarnation in the Gospels, Matthew, Luke and John affirm that Jesus is the only son of the only God and Christ, the Lord. They describe the important aspect of the person and work of Jesus. Through this special revelation, we come to know the nature, attributes and plan of God. John 1:14 says that we see the glory of God in Jesus, incarnation and God's grace and truth. By describing the incarnation of Jesus as a child rather than a grown up youth or adult and affirming that this child is Christ, the writers of the Gospel have laid the foundation of Christology for Child Theology. If so, we can say that Child Theology has a Christological basis and even claim that the Child Theology is Christological.

2. *'Made his dwelling among us'* (John 1:14)

The activities of incarnation are not happening in the celestial world as mysterious and mythological. Jesus is sent to dwell among human beings (cf. Jn. 3:16). The important questions we need to raise from the perspective of the child are viz. the nature of his dwelling, purpose of his dwelling and impact or result of his dwelling. First, Jesus was not born as a youth or adult but as a new born baby. He was like any child born of a woman (Gal. 4:4) and fed by his mother. He went through all the stages of growth a child would go through in this world. As a child, he depended on his parents for care and protection. He was weak, dependent and vulnerable. He played with other children and learnt like other children. He was trained by his parents on religious and moral instruction. He used his free will to do what is acceptable to God and required by Judaism. He was circumcised on the eighth day according to the prescribed religious ritual. All these activities prove that Jesus was fully human and was at risk like any child. 'Made his dwelling among us' refers not only to his human form but also that he was part of sociological background of his community. This includes his relationship with the members of the family and society.

Secondly, the purpose or significance of his dwelling among human beings is to provide the visible presence of God so that human beings can know God through his words and actions. His dwelling among people as Matthew describes it in his name 'Emmanuel' (God with us), quoting the prophecy of Isaiah (7:11-14), signifies his presence and identity with human beings. Jesus is not emanated from God as mythological stories describe gods and goddesses in some religions. He can live with people as one among them. 'Made his dwelling among us' signifies his solidarity with humankind. Luke looks at his dwelling among people 'as peace on earth' (Lk. 2:14). John describes his dwelling on earth as revealing God's glory, grace and truth (Jn. 1:14).

Thirdly, the impact of his dwelling among people is that the law of Moses is replaced by grace and truth which came through Jesus Christ (Jn. 1:17). People are no more under the law but under the grace of God. His dwelling among people is so helpful that we need not memorize different laws and feel guilty of failing the laws. We are free from the burden of paying penalty charges and performing sin offerings constantly (cf. Eph. 2:15). Human life is made not to become burdensome because of the death and resurrection of Jesus for our sins that we can live with the free offering of forgiveness from our guilt and shame. Our social life is under the grace and truth of God through the incarnation of Jesus and cannot be taken for granted. His incarnation among human beings is sociological in terms of his birth, growth, presence, relationship and consequences. 'Made his dwelling among us' and not in heaven or beyond the social context of earth underlines that the Child Theology has sociological basis in the incarnation of Jesus. Child Theology is not only theological but also sociological.

3.   'His kingdom will never end' (Lk. 1:31-33 cf. Mt. 2:6)

The birth narrative of Jesus links the child with the concept of the kingdom. The incarnation has a political dimension. In the story of Magi searching for the new born child, Matthew quotes the prophecy of Micah (5:2) that a ruler will come out of Bethlehem and will be the shepherd of the people of Israel. Kings in the OT are regarded as shepherds leading the people in the way of the Lord. First, the title "Christ' (Messiah-Anointed One) used in Matt. 2:4-6 referring to the child coming out of the Bethlehem signifies that the incarnated child is the expected Messiah and going to establish the kingdom. Luke also presents this message in narrating the incarnation of Jesus (Lk. 1:31-33). Unlike the usual royal tradition that the child born in the family of the king inherits the kingdom, it is God who is going to give the kingdom and kingship to Jesus. The coming of Jesus inaugurated God's kingdom on earth. The identity of the child in the narratives of the incarnation is Christ, the Messiah. In both the texts of Matthew and Luke, the expectation is for a political king in the line of David based on the prophecy of Nathan to David (2 Sam. 7:11-16).

Secondly, the disciples thought that the nature of his kingdom was ruling the people of Israel by throwing away the yoke of the Romans and securing the Jewish State as it was in the days of David and later in the days of Hasmonean Dynasty. Matthew and Luke look at infant Jesus as a future ruler with a political kingdom, but they understood the radical teaching of Jesus about the kingdom and write in their Gospels not merely about a kingdom in a political sense but also as a rule with spiritual dimension and divine values such as love, justice, equality, sharing of resources and welfare.[18] The kingdom of God is not limited to the people of Israel or confined to the land of Israel but transcends borders and communities.

Thirdly, Luke says that his kingdom will never end (Lk. 1:33), which could be based on 2 Sam. 7:11-14, Isaiah 9:7 and Ps.89:28-30. Although the thought in the OT is the continuing line of kings, Luke's statement means that the Messiah himself is to reign forever.[19] This implies that the political kingdom of Israel as well as its ruler will continue forever without losing the kingdom to foreign rulers hereafter. The Jewish state will continue forever. But there is a change in the thought that the rule of Jesus will be forever based on Messianic prophecy. Humanly speaking, Jesus also as a king will pass away one day, but the difference is that his resurrection continues the kingdom of God on the earth without the limitations of human leaders and time. Here the death and resurrection of the incarnated Jesus and the eternal continuity of the kingdom of God are integrated, providing a holistic dimension of the kingdom of God. Since the kingdom of God has political dimension and is linked to the incarnated Jesus as the Messiah, it can provide a political basis for Child Theologies and encourage socio-political struggles for the justice and rights of children.

4.   'He will save his people from their sins' (Mt. 1:20-21)
The missional dimension of the incarnation is stated by the writers of the Gospels. Matthew records the message of the angel to Joseph that the child should be named 'Jesus' (from the Hebrew root word 'yeshua' – to save) because he will save his people from their sins (1:20-21). Luke also records the same message given to Mary (Lk. 1:31). They reveal that the purpose of Jesus coming as a baby to this world is to save the sinners. John expresses the missional aspect of the incarnation by saying, 'For God *so loved* the world that he gave his one and only Son that whoever believes in him should not perish but have eternal life. For God did not send his son into the world to condemn the world, but to save the world through him' (Jn.3:16-17). The basis of sending Jesus is God's love and concern for the world. Bruce Milne writes, 'The *unfathomable depth* of the love of God is stressed: God so loved…. In his love, God went so far as to 'give (up)' his *one and only Son* (we should

probably see here a reference to incarnation as well as crucifixion).'[20] In describing the extent of God's love, the commentators say, 'This love knows no barriers of race, creed, religion, language, education, tribe or caste. It includes the wealthy, the proud, the clever, the capable and the socially acceptable. And it extends to the mean, the violent, the depressed, the hopeless, the victimized, the sick and the outcast. The limitless range of love's recipients are caught up in the one word *whoever*. It extends to everyone (15)...anyone, anywhere.'[21]

The purpose of giving the only child is to save the world. By declaring that Jesus is the 'Saviour of the World', the mission is not limited to Palestine or the Jewish community. It has a universal dimension. The mission of giving the child is for global redemption. Paul describes the mission as reconciliation between God,and humanity in Rom. 5:9-11. The child is the peace child, as Don Richardson describes in his redemptive analogy,[22] bringing peace to communities.

The main action of the child is to die on the cross to save the world. While God fulfills his purpose to redeem the fallen world by sending his child, people are expected to have faith in that child and his mission. Whoever believes in him shall not perish but have eternal life (Jn.3:16); this is the reward for those who believe Jesus.

The survey of 4/14 window shows that children in the age group of 4-14 are more receptive to accept Jesus as their Lord and Saviour.[23] The missional aspect of incarnation leads the believers to share this message with others. Proclamation, personal witness and sharing the love of God by deeds are necessary components of mission. If the incarnation has a purpose for the global mission, then Child Theology based on incarnation is missional and has universal validity.

5.   '... He gave the right to become children of God' (Jn.1:12-13)

The expectation of God in sending the child is that human beings receive and believe Jesus. The greatest result of fulfilling the expectation of God is inheriting the right to become children of God. Unlike the laws in the OT, the texts of NT do not describe the laws of protecting children. The idea of child in the NT moves on to the way a person can become a child of God. It focuses on the idea of 'Children of God' different from 'Children of Satan' (1 Jn.3:8-10) and emphasizes the faith and life of children of God. It is good to explore in the future the connection between the concept of 'children of God' and Child Theology.

Paul affirms the message of John in his letter saying, 'God sent his son, born of woman… that we might receive the full rights of sons' (Gal. 4:4) and that right enables us to call God 'Abba Father' and become automatically 'heirs of God' and 'co-heirs with Christ' (Rom. 8:16-17). The right of being heirs of God includes both 'suffering for Christ' and 'sharing in his glory.' First, the idea of inheriting the rights has implications for the Child Rights today. If God is granting the rights to children, then how much do we need to grant the rights of children in the midst of us.

Secondly, born of God and not of human beings is a spiritual birth into the family of God. As children inherit the right of membership in a family, all those who received and believed Jesus inherit membership in the family of God. The 'family of God' is not visible but it is an invisible relationship to an invisible family, experienced by that individual or community who believe and are born of God. This invisible family of God is spoken of as the 'Body of Christ' in the Epistles. The Body of Christ is visible in the form of local churches. This body has an important role in nurturing the children of God in Christ. Faith in the incarnated Jesus is an important component in Child Theology. Joining the visible church as an outward mark of the faith and being born of God adds *ecclesiastical dimension* to Child Theology. Child Theologies can be rooted in an ecclesiastical basis when we emphasize believing Jesus and joining the Church. The invisible membership in the family of God and the visible membership in the local church indicate that the Child Theology is relational. The implication for the children of God is that they must foster proper relationships with children of different classes, castes and races and empower the oppressed and marginalized.

In summary, by placing his own child in the midst of us, God taught humanity about his great love for people of all ages, castes and tribes; his redemption plan, eternal life and the need for his mission to be carried out by the church. As pointed out above, the incarnation is important for Child Theologies as God's paradigm since it provides *Christological, sociological, political, ecclesiastical and missional* bases.

B.   JESUS PLACED A CHILD IN THE MIDST OF DISCIPLES – AN ILLUSTRATION

Another key text on placing a child in the midst is in Matt. 18:1-6 (cf. Mk.9:33-37, Lk.9:46-48). Rarely commentaries explain the idea of child in the midst and relate it to the Child Theology. Let me explain these texts briefly and bring out a comparison between Incarnation and Illustration.

1.   Controversy among disciples (Mt. 18:1)

The context of the incident is the quarrel and argument about who would be the greatest in the kingdom of heaven. The version in Mark omits the last part of the phrase 'in the kingdom of heaven' to imply that the argument is about themselves becoming greatest when Jesus throws off Roman rule and establishes his political kingdom. The word 'greatest' in general refers to status, power, authority, fame and wealth. This kind of expectation in the minds of the disciples is a contradiction to the teaching of Jesus about Servant-Leadership (Mk.9:15).

2.   Action of placing a child and teaching (Mt. 18:2-6)

Jesus called a little child and asked him to stand among the disciples. The details of this child regarding age or family background are not stated by Matthew and Mark. This child could be a boy of very young age and was used as an illustration as well as to represent Jesus and his concept of kingdom of God. There is no indication in the texts that the child spoke or shared his views. Rather, this action of Jesus was followed by his teaching on the kingdom of God. Jesus tells them the truth of being greatest in the kingdom of God by the following five requirements.

The first requirement is *'change'*. Unless the disciples change their attitude and ambition from being powerful and famous to becoming a servant of God, they cannot be in the kingdom of God. Change of mind, thinking, ambitions and attitude at a later age is difficult. As human beings, we want to be the greatest in the world with all the wealth, power and authority, pomp and fame. The disciples have left their jobs and family and followed Jesus for nothing. They did not understand the teaching of Jesus in the right sense. They had an inner ambition of being powerful in his political kingdom. So Jesus wants them to change their understanding and expectations.

Secondly, Jesus asked them to '*become like a little child,*' using the boy as an illustration. The nature of little children is liked by all of us. They are innocent, weak, dependent, vulnerable, obedient, respectful of others and harmless. Jesus is asking the disciples to show these qualities of a child in their lives rather than being clever politicians among themselves by grabbing the top positions in the kingdom. Without having these good qualities of little children, disciples cannot enter into the kingdom of God because the values of the kingdom are divine values of love, sharing resources, helping each other, avoiding jealousy and envy, doing justice, relinquishing power and fame. An evil nature and wicked attitudes cannot have a place in the kingdom of God. That is why Jesus told Nicodemus that every one should be born again in the sense of becoming like a child in nature and qualities. It is worth noting that the Lukan version (9:46-48) does not speak of 'becoming like a child' to enter into the kingdom of God or the kingdom of God belonging to children, but only speaks of welcoming the child. Luke emphasizes that the 'least' will become 'great' among the disciples on this earth. The word 'least' means the way children are regarded as least and insignificant in society. Unless we interpret 'welcoming Jesus' to mean welcoming his kingdom and becoming a member of the kingdom of God, the Lukan version deals with the problem of leadership, recognition, power and being great in that group.

Thirdly, Jesus instructs them to '*humble*' themselves like a child. Humility is a virtue, but it is difficult for people who have money, wealth, education, position, man power and authority to humble themselves. Disciples should not take advantage of being with Jesus, who demonstrates power and authority in his mission, to be proud and seek positions. The nature of a good child is to be humble, friendly and relate with other children without being dominating and haughty.

Fourthly, the disciples should '*welcome*' children. 'Welcome,' in the literal sense, can mean receiving the child and accepting the qualities of children.

Children are taken for granted and not allowed to be in the decision making process. They are treated like property in the family and regarded as cheap labour and sexually abused in society. In discussing the Markan text, Ched Myers explains the way a child was marginalized in Jewish society of Jesus' time and at present in our societies.[24] Welcoming children in the name of God includes working for the welfare of children and empowering them. In a metaphorical sense, 'welcoming a child' could mean accepting the values of the kingdom of God. However, it is also understood in a figurative sense of a child representing Jesus and receiving salvation.

Matthew and Mark agree that anyone who welcomes a little child welcomes Jesus. Regarding this child as representing Jesus, Haddon Willmer says, 'Christ is received when he is represented by an Other. Christ is one who is ready to be represented, so ready and present in the representation that he may be really received in it.'[25] The Markan version adds '…and whoever welcomes me does not welcome me but the one who sent me' (Mk. 9:37). Welcoming a child means welcoming Jesus and welcoming Jesus means welcoming God, the Father who sent him.

It is not that the little child placed in the midst of them as an illustration is equal to Jesus. Jesus is relating the issue of being greatest in the kingdom with the radical interpretation of the kingdom using a child as an illustration. Jesus inaugurated the kingdom of God and children have a place in it because of their nature and qualities. If the disciples become like children, they can also have a place in the kingdom of God. In a sense, Jesus is telling them that he is represented by the child in the midst of them as Jesus was placed in the midst of them to represent God, the Father. The disciples need to accept and welcome him and his teaching. By doing so, they welcome God who has sent Jesus to be in the midst of them. The linking of the child standing in the midst of them with Jesus and God emphasizes the need for faith and action on the side of the disciples.

Finally, Jesus warns the disciples not to *cause the children to sin*. Two aspects need to be explained here. One is the phrase 'these little ones who believe in me' in Matt. 18:6. The Markan version omits this phrase. The identity of the little children here is those who have faith in Jesus. Does it mean only those children who believed Jesus or all the other children too? In the context of Matt. 18:1-6, it can refer to children who believed Jesus. Or it can refer to 'children' in the broader sense of all those who believed Jesus and became children of God as John and Paul describe them. If this is the meaning of the text, then 'children' can refer to anyone from a child to an adult who believe in Jesus. Since Mark omits the phrase, his text opens the gate to include all the children irrespective of caste and creed. No child on this earth should be caused to sin. However, I assume it has a wider implication of including all the children since his mission is beyond Jewish community and it is global. The other phrase that needs to be explained is 'causing to sin.' Adults can easily make children commit all sort of mistakes ranging from teaching or forcing them to tell lies, steal, yield to sexual abuse and become involve in crimes of violence leading to imprisonment. Leading children to commit sins damages their personality, spiritual life and leaves them to live in guilt, trauma and shame. Whoever does not build up the lives of children, but instead ruins them is accountable. These culprits deserve punishment to the extent of 'drowning them in the depths of the sea.' They deserve capital punishment so that these culprits do not live anymore on earth to spoil the lives of children. The message is to take care of children and develop them holistically.

The emphasis in Matthew 18:1-6 and Mark 9:33-37 is on the nature and requirements of the kingdom of God. This is identified with Jesus and illustrated by placing a child in the midst of people. The nature of the kingdom of God is indicated by the nature of a child. The requirement to be part of the kingdom of God is accepting Jesus and his values.

A comparison of Incarnation and Illustration

Comparing the incarnation of Jesus and the illustration of placing a child in the midst gives us some idea about the value of both the child Jesus and the child born of human beings.

INCARNATION OF JESUS

1. Jesus is the Son of God and has a close relationship with God.
2. Jesus is divine and human.
3. Jesus is the revelation of God.

4. Jesus answered the disciples.
5. Jesus is present among human beings as Emmanuel.
6. Jesus is weak, vulnerable and at risk.
7. Jesus represents God and is to be received.
8. Jesus and the Kingdom of God cannot be separated and they are integral part of the Gospel.
9. Jesus is the Saviour and Messiah of the world.

ILLUSTRATION OF A CHILD

1. The child is the son of human descent.
2. The child boy is a human being.
3. The child is an illustration for answering the disciples.
4. The child did not speak or shared his views.
5. A child's presence among us is temporary till the child lives.
6. The child is weak, vulnerable and at risk.
7. The child represents Jesus and is to be received.
8. The child belongs to the kingdom of God by faith.
9. The child is a human being and needs a Saviour.

How do these two categories of the child in the midst relate to each other? A few points can be listed below for further research.

1. The incarnation of Jesus is the important theological basis and cannot be ignored as the central focal point for Child Theology. It is God's paradigm for Child Theology.

2. As God placed his son in the midst of us, Jesus placed a child in the midst of disciples for the purpose of explaining the concept of the kingdom of God. God placing his child in the midst of us, in my opinion, is also the starting point for Child Theology.[26]

3. The teachings and ministry of Jesus sent by God is the basis to evaluate the views of the children placed in the midst of us and correct us while doing Child Theology.

4. God placing Jesus in the midst of us has a missional purpose and that is demanded by Jesus to welcome the child and not to lead them to sin but build them up holistically.

III. DEFINING AND DOING CHILD THEOLOGY

Whenever we mention the phrase 'Child Theology' in churches or seminars in India, the participants want to know the definition of Child Theology or at least some explanation of the concept. Exploration by Indian leaders in formulating theologies gained momentum during the British colonial period. The process of contextualizing theologies due to the challenges of socio-economic and religious pluralistic context of India and the influence of Liberation Theology from Latin America demands theological basis for any action programmes. Indian theologians expect theology and praxis to go together transforming society.

A. WHAT IS CHILD THEOLOGY?

It is important that children define God and create their own theology. In fact, Child Theology should be formulated and articulated by children from their perspective and context. A rich child may define God as a 'God of Blessing and Prosperity'. A poor child may see God as poor and powerless to overrule injustice and provide food and shelter and may reject God, the Creator. Every child born of Indian parents is a caste child. He or she inherits a caste by birth and the caste cannot be changed. A dalit child may define God as a dalit God or God is discriminative. A black child may define God as black or a biased God. Another child could define God as an angry God or always punishing people. For an orphan, God could be a parent or father or mother. A disabled child may curse God for being created blind or lame. Leaving children to define God could bring out the positive and negative elements of their theology. This kind of 'Theology of a Child or Children's Theologies' could be pluralistic and sometimes contradictory. In my opinion, adults can formulate a 'Child Theology' on behalf of children based on hearing the views of children, the theological dimension of children in the Bible and leave room for adding a contextual dimension if it is not contradictory to the biblical teachings on children. CTM defines Child Theology differently with the emphasis on Jesus placing a child in the midst of his disciples as pointed out above.[27] Although it has left out the significant step of God placing the child Jesus in the midst of us as a lens through whom we can know more about God, we cannot ignore the significance of incarnation as an important basis for Child Theology. Let me summarize and define 'Child Theology' out of the theological dimension discussed in my booklet[28] and on the above explanation of incarnation. Whether one agrees with it or not, it can help to motivate further exploration:

> Child Theology is the theological reflection on the nature, status, role and reality of children, placing the children to be at the focus, not replacing God to shed light on theological and practical issues and leading us to receive and work for children particularly children at risk. For, all children irrespective of their race, caste, religion and class are created and loved by that one God. Both male and female children are created in God's image. There is no discrimination in the sight of God against the male or female sex. Children make fatherhood and motherhood more meaningful and help us realize the parenthood of God. Jesus, the incarnated child was at risk at the time of his birth and sought by the political authorities. The incarnation of Jesus in the midst of people reminds us of the weak, dependent and powerless nature of children and becomes the hope of salvation. The dimension of Jesus' incarnation, childhood, vulnerability, his ministry in the temple of Jerusalem in front of the religious leaders at a young age and relating the kingdom of God to children, his death and resurrection forms the Christological, sociological, political, ecclesiastical and missional bases of Child Theology.

Child Theology is not an exclusive theology for one group of children but an inclusive theology embracing all children irrespective of their caste, colour and creed, listening to them and working for them. Although the perceptions, attitudes and approaches of children of the rich, middle class and poor; and of different castes and races and religious traditions can differ, the truth that all children are created by God in God's image challenges the differences between children. The Child Theology has a universal applicability since the Christological basis is universal and the children in the universe are God's own creation. However, child theologies need to be contextualized to the local context taking into account of the biblical teachings on children, giving preferential option to children at risk and marginalized, addressing their problems and initiating programmes and actions for their liberation, protection, welfare and empowerment. Child Theology is not for polarizing and dividing the children but being an inclusive theology and universally applicable. It has all the ingredients and potentials for uniting children of all communities and the parents for their holistic development.'[29] Holistic Child Development is the over-arching umbrella or goal for which Child Theology provides a theological basis for actions. Since Child Theology is biblical and the Holistic Child Development is the ultimate goal of this theology, they are integrated as theology and praxis and should not be separated.

A.   HOW TO DO CHILD THEOLOGY?

Child Theology is not a theoretical exercise and limited to the boundaries of academic institutions. It is deeply rooted in the Bible and related to the Body of Christ with a mission dimension. Various movements and NGOs are doing Child Theology. One of the ways used by CTM as reported in their document is to call and place a child in the midst of a group of people sitting in a circle and learn from that child.[30] If a child is not available, the group can 'imagine a child' in the midst of them and have their conversation. Haddon Willmer uses the term *logos* in Jn. 1:1 in the sense of 'conversation' about a child placed in the midst of the disciples.[31] The outcome of this interaction depends upon the class, caste and racial background of that child standing in the midst of the group or imagined by each member of the group. The child can teach a lot to us about God from his or her perspective and the situation of the society in terms of the problems and prospects. In this approach, the theology of rich, poor, dalit, tribal, black, orphan or disabled children, as stated above, can show positive or negative understandings of God and create tensions in society and controversies about God. The members of the group may not arrive at a common consensus or may formulate a Child Theology based on the conversation about the child in the midst.

Another way of doing Child Cheology, in my opinion, is to go to children in a particular area like slums, juvenile homes, industries employing child labour, HIV/AIDS homes and orphanages and listen to their theological understanding of God and society. This method of doing Child Theology is the other way of 'placing ourselves in the midst of children' as Jesus placed himself in the midst of children by welcoming them around him (Mk. 10: 13-16) and listening to them. 'Imagining a child' can give us theological reflection but not the skill and action plans unless we go and place ourselves in the midst of the children where they live and know the real situation of their context.   Both ways of doing theology can challenge our understanding of children, traditions of the churches as well as children's attitude to God and the world.

While the first step of *placing* a child or ourselves in the midst and the second step of *listening* to children are important in doing Child Theology, we should go further in our praxis. Keith White says, 'Child Theology is tenacious in the angle of its approach and the specification of outcome. As noted already this approach respects the experience and voice of the subject by letting the child speak, rather than attempting to do something to or for the child; and the result is intended to be somehow theological. The outcome will be fresh and more accurate readings of the Scripture, a reformation of Systematic theology with a child in the midst, new readings of the history of church and theology... and new understandings of church and mission, and new operative theology....'[32] Experimentation on Child Theology should not stop with placing a child in the midst of a group of people and listening to the 'theology of a child or children'. Doing Child Theology in a third world context, in my opinion, needs further steps to go beyond being theological and academic. The third step in the approach is the *critical analysis* of their background and context which can help us to know why the children have such a theology. The fourth step is to raise our *theological response* to their questions as well as correct our own theology. A healthy inter-action in theological exercise demands checking the interpretation of biblical texts, accepting their valuable subjective experience and correcting the wrong notions in accordance with the biblical teaching and bringing freshness into the mission of God. Such an interaction can contribute to the development of Child Theology and be made relevant contextually. The fifth step in doing theology is to be involved in *action* for the holistic development of children. Doing Child Theology having the basis of God's paradigm of placing his only child in the midst of us, following Jesus' example and using the above five steps can transform children, our thinking and lives and create a child-friendly society.

Endnotes

[1] Roy Zuck, *Precious in His sight: Childhood and Children in the Bible* (Grand Rapids: Bakar Books, 1996).

[2] Child Theology Movement in UK, Global Alliance for Advancing HCD, Malaysian Baptist Theological Seminary, Fuller Theological Seminary and Christian Forum for Child Development-India, are involved in developing Child Theologies.

[3] Marcia Bunge (ed.), The Child in Christian Thought (Grand Rapids: Eerdmans, 2001).

[4] Marcia J. Bunge, 'Theologies of Childhood and Child Theologies: International initiatives to deepen reflections on Children and Childhood in the Academy and Religious communities' *Dharma Deepika*, Chennai: DET, July-Dec. 2008, p. 35.

[5] Marcia Bunge, 'Theologies of Childhood and Child Theologies', pp. 42-43.

[6] CTM Limited is registered in UK.

[7] Keith J. White and Haddon Willmer, An Introduction to Child Theology (London: CTM, 2008), p.4.

[8] Refer to CTM Reports of the Consultations held in various countries (London:CTM)

[9] Dan Brewster, 'Themes and Implications o HCD Progrmmes in Seminaries' (A paper presented in GA-HCD South Asia Consultation on Curriculum and Resource Development (SAC-CARD) held in Bangalore from 11-14th Feb 09.

[10] Quoted in the Asia Bible Commentary, *Gospel of John*, written by J.J. Kanagaraj and Ian S. Kemp,(Bangalore: ATA, 2000), p. 123.

[11] Bruce Milne, *The Message of John* (BST Series, Leicester: IVP, 1993), p.77.

[12] Bruce Milne, *The Message of John*, p. 31.

[13] Bruce Milne, pp. 32-34.

[14] Bruce Milne, pp. 35-36.

[15] Bruce Milne, p. 46.

[16] Cornelis Bennema, *Excavating John's Gospel: A Commentary for Today* (Delhi: ISPCK, 2005) p. 25.

[17] Bruce Milne, p. 46.

[18] J.B.Jeyaraj, *Christian Ministry: Models of Ministry and Training* (Bangalore: TBT, 2007), pp. 159-162, 217-227.

[19] Howard Marshall, *Commentary on Luke* (NIGTC, Grand Rapids: Eerdmans, 1989), p. 68.

[20] Bruce Milne, p. 77.

[21] J.J. Kanagaraj and Ian S. Kemp, *Gospel of John* (Asia Bible Commentary, Bangalore: TBT, 2000), p.156.

[22] Refer to Don Richardson' book: *Peace Child,*

[23] Dan Brewster, *Child, Church and Mission* (Colorado Springs: Compassion International, 2005).

[24] Ched Myers, Binding the Strong Man: A Political reading of Marks's Story of Jesus (Maryknoll: Orbis Books, 1994), pp. 266-270.

[25] Haddon Willmer, 'Child Theology and Christology in Matthew 18:1-5' in Dharma Deepika, July-December 2008, p. 72.

[26] Keith White, however, expresses a different opinion that Mt. 18:1-6 is the starting point of Child Theology in his article, 'Insights into Child Theology through the Life and Work of Pandita Ramabai' in Dharma Deepika, July-Dec. 2008, p. 80.

[27] Keith White and Haddon Willmer, *An Introduction to Child Theology*, p. 4. The danger of over emphasizing Mt. 18:1-6 as the only text for Child Theology can lead us to read too much into that text and over stretch it deliberately to relate to other texts in the NT. We need to consider other texts also in their own merits to build Child Theology. In future, we can expect different Child Theologies such as Dalit Child Theology, Tribal Child Theology and Feminist Child Theology emerging from our Indian context if these communities reexamine the concept of children in the Bible, tradition of the churches and context.

[28] J.B. Jeyaraj, *Biblical Perspectives on Children and their Protection: Towards a Child Theology*, Madurai: JIP, 2007, pp. 20-22.

[29] J.B. Jeyaraj, Biblical Perspective on Children and Their Protection: Towards a Child Theology, pp.20-22.

[30] Haddon Willmer, Experimenting Together: One Way of Doing Child Theology (London: CTM,2007), p.6.

[31] Haddon Willmer, Experimenting Together: One Way of Doing Child Theology (London: CTM,2007), p.6.

[32] Keith White, 'Insights into Child Theology' p. 79.

SOCIOLOGICAL PERSPECTIVE

CHAPTER - 5

Invisible Children:
Infanticide, Foeticide and Abortion

Invisible children are of many categories. Children are conceived and grew for a few months in the mother's womb and disappear due to natural abortion or using medical treatment for various reasons. Some children are born but become invisible on the next day due to infanticide. They do not see the second day of their birth. Some of them are kidnapped for money, kidney, sex-work or for bonded labour, from their families and vanish to an unknown place from where they cannot return. They are alive but uprooted, suppressed and kept underground, not to be visible. Some other children are controlled by rebel armies and trained to be suicide bombers and thus vanish in their young life. Many children exist in front of our eyes but we do not see them. For many of us, disabled children are not important and we do recognize them. Some children sit in a lonely place and shed tears without making their cry audible because they are abused or accused unnecessarily or need some food or financial aid or counselling. Our eyes may notice them but our minds do not perceive them as children in crisis. Some children come to school with sadness and hopelessness because of their alcoholic father scolding them or refusing to pay their fees. So they may not be able to concentrate on learning in the class room. Some teachers do not see their difficulties and shout at them. These children need sympathy and encouragement. Some children come from divorced or single-parent family longing for the love of teachers and friends but they are unaccounted in their sight. Blind, deaf and lame children try to cross the road waiting on the platform for a long time but we drive our scooters, autos and cars without letting them to cross the road safely. Moving fast on roads whether there is a signal or not, has blinded our eyes to these children in need. Their plight is not visible to us to recognize and help them. The age limit to be regarded as children varies in different cultures. But UN has regarded those who are below 18 years of age are children.

The Prophet Isaiah of 8th century BC spoke of the invisibility of the Israelites in seeing the injustice and violation of human rights in their society. He brought out this lack and arrogance on the part of the people of Israel by saying,

> Keep listening, but do not comprehend
> Keep looking, but do not understand.
> Make the mind of this people dull,
> and stop their ears,
> and shut their eyes,
> so that they may not look with their eyes,
> and listen with their ears,
> and comprehend with their minds,
> and turn and be healed - (Isaiah 6: 9b-10).

God called Isaiah to go and proclaim his message to the people in southern kingdom. When Isaiah obeyed God's call to be a prophet, God gave him this message to tell the Israelites. The above text is to point out the sad situation of the people not having the willingness to see the injustice in their society, apostasy in religious life and correct their lives.[1] During the 8th century BC, the people of Israel had economic prosperity. The rich people accumulated wealth while the poor became poorer. Lands were alienated from the rural people to the rich money-lenders and court officials. The ruling class became wealthy whereas the poor lived in debt, poverty and hard labour. The exploitation and sufferings of the poor were ignored by the rich people. Their difficulties and misery were not taken seriously by the rulers and business community. The court was corrupt and perverted justice due to the victims. Many Israelites sought to worship Baal and Astharoth, the god and goddess of the fertility cult forsaking their God who brought them out of Egypt into freedom and gave them the promised land for ethical living. God wanted them to be sensitive to the needs of others but they were selfish. God expected them to practice justice and righteousness but they perverted justice. They were required to share their resources with widows, orphans, aliens and all the poor and powerless but the rich and ruling class added land to land and house to house and accumulated wealth and assets. A section of their society turned a blind eye to the problems of the poor, deliberately ignored them and refused to help the needy by hardening their hearts. So God had to point out this callousness and arrogance on the part of some people in the society sarcastically by telling Isaiah to make their minds dull and stop their eyes and shut their ears. This was the situation of the people and therefore they need to be made accountable. Their invisibility in terms of lack of sensitivity, showing sympathy and empathy, willingness to help and empower the needy who are in their midst pained the heart of God. In spite of sending several prophets and messages, they did not change but continued their practices and ruined the lives of many. The punishment for such an attitude of the people has been spelled out in verses 11-13.

Other prophets in Israel point out this fact in their messages. Jeremiah who came on the scene in 6th century BC felt the same attitude in the people of his times. They were described as 'senseless people' who had eyes but do not see and had ears but do not hear (Jer. 5:21) indicating their unwillingness to listen to God and obey his commandments. Ezekiel too noticed this attitude in the people of his time and had to proclaim God's message whether they hear or refuse to hear implying their indifference to God (Ezek. 3:11). The Psalmist points out the arrogant nature of the oppressors as people with the heart of fat and gross (Ps. 119:70).

People with an indifferent attitude to God, divine values and problems of society are present in every generation. Selfish people can found in each society. Jesus noticed this trend in his time when ministering in Palestine. He used the prophecy of Isaiah discussed above in his message to point out this kind of attitude in people to his message and ministry. In the context of explaining the nature, role and value of the Kingdom of God through parables, Jesus mentioned about the people who do not want to perceive or understand (Mt. 13:13-18; Mk. 4:10-12; Lk. 8:9-10).[2] Again in the context of speaking about his death and resurrection, Jesus pointed out the unwillingness of people to believe him by referring to Isaiah's prophecy of people having blinded their eyes and hardened their hearts failing to understand Jesus (Jn. 12:40). Paul in his letter mentioned the hardening of the heart on the side of Israelites to the Gospel of Jesus Christ (Rom. 11:8). Like the early Israelites, Christians and their churches are quite often turning a blind eye to a social problems particularly to children since they are small and taken for granted. However, there are a few people who have eyes to see the plight of the children, ears to hear their cries and heart to understand their problems and willingness to help them. As Jesus said about those who have more, more will be given (Mt. 13:13), the people with vision for children grow in their concern, develop their service and abound in achievements. The reports of various churches, organizations and NGOs and the Commissions of the governments in different parts of the world prove the progress in their service to children. Yet, find this task needs the entire humanity to have the 'visibility' to understand children. The purpose of this booklet is threefold viz. to point out briefly the history, reasons and consequences of infanticide and feticide, to raise Christian response from the biblical view on abortion, murder and euthanasia and to draw challenges for Christian service.

According to the Oxford Illustrated Dictionary, the term *infanticide* means 'murder of infant immediately after birth' or 'custom of killing newborn infants'[3] The Orient Longman Word Master – Learner's Dictionary of Modern English defines 'fetus' as 'an unborn baby that is almost fully developed'[4] 'Feticide' means killing the embryo by using medicines or surgery or cruel methods of removing the embryo from the uterus by hand, an illegal practice which still goes on secretly in villages, towns and cities at the risk of the life of the mother. This is a horrible practice of harassment meted out to women and an insult to the newly formed child who did not commit any mistake.

I.   MALE INFANTICIDE IN ANCIENT HISTORY

Killing of male children happened in different periods of history but we do not have sufficient details about this practice. In some ancient religious traditions, male children particularly the first born in the family were preferred as a special sacrifice to gods and goddesses. It was observed as ritualistic for various reasons such as to propitiate the anger of the deities or to please them to have mercy on the population by not sending epidemics, to save the village from chaos and calamities or to achieve desired result.[5] The practices of child sacrifice was found in the ancient Near Eastern culture. The king of Moab gave his first born son and heir as a whole burnt offering upon the wall to save his country from the attack of enemy (2 Kings 3:27). The Ammonites sacrificed children to their god Molech. The ancient Israelites who lived among these nations and followed this practice of offering their children as burnt offering in the valleys was condemned by Jeremiah (7:31). Pre-Columbian cultures too show evidences of child sacrifice. Greek mythologies speak of kings sacrificing children to gain favourable weather for invading other territories. In the rural cultures of India, children were sacrificed to get rain if the monsoon failed and famine prevailed for two or three years.

Some Magicians prefer the eldest boy child in the family and so they kidnap and take them to forest or cremation yards and perform the sacrifice and use the blood or ashes for their tricks or to spread over the doorposts of the newly built houses and other buildings or bridges. Some of them believe that the skull of the boy could be a medium for receiving messages from the spirit world and foretelling the fortunes to people. This happens even today is reported in the newspapers or TV. Such magicians or priests are arrested and kept under police custody. New born babies are thrown into the rivers as a special offering to gods and goddesses due to the superstitions among some families in India.

The Bible narrates a few incidents of killing male children. The Pharaoh of Egypt ordered the killing of the male children in his kingdom to reduce the male population of the Israelites to avoid any insurrection or political coup. He allowed the female babies to live in order to have women as cheap labour force who would not fight for freedom or rebel against the government. An attitude of racial discrimination and the control of immigrant population to be in minority always were the policies of Pharaoh (Ex.1:7-2:22). Although the midwives saved the male babies disobeying the order of Pharaoh, we do not know how many Israelite families were forced by the Egyptian neighbours and commanders to throw their male child into the river Nile (2:22). Moses as a baby was saved from infanticide because his mother was unwilling to kill her baby and the daughter of Pharaoh showed concern for this baby floating in the river. The daughter of the Pharaoh could have ignored this baby and allowed to drown in the river. She knew the rule passed against the male children in Israelite families and not against Egyptian families to throw the child in the Nile river. She could have understood the child belongs to a Hebrew family. Moses could have been an invisible child and faced death but the compassion of the daughter of Pharaoh saved this child and a great leader arose. We attribute the miraculous saving of the child to God's providence. But we should not forget the contribution of human beings like the daughter of Pharaoh in saving the child disobeying the order of her own government. Mere rescuing would not save the child. She had to devise a strategy to save the life of the child from the law of male infanticide. She had no other option except adopting the child as her own and nurturing the baby (2:5-10).

Another similar incident of infanticide by political order is recorded in the Gospel of Matthew (2:16-18) during the birth of Jesus. Herod, the king of Judea ordered the killing of all babies below the age of two in and around Bethlehem. Male child could be a rival for his position and political authority. We can assume, therefore, his target was mainly the male child who could rise up as king of Jews in the future. Joseph had to escape with Mary and the child to Egypt to save Jesus. But the rest of the children below two years were massacred for political gain. The pain of this cruel act in society is expressed by the prophecy of Jeremiah (31:15) where Rachel, representing the entire women folk of the nation, is crying for her children. Mothers feel a deeper pain when they lose their children since they conceive, carry in their womb for nine months and deliver the children after hard labour. Mothers and children are attached biologically and psychologically. Ruthless leaders do not have eyes to see and heart to feel the pain of killing children. They want to strengthen their position and power at any cost even if it means suffering of innocent children.

Children, particularly boys, dying due to wrong political reasons happen all the time. Hitler killed millions of Jews including the children during the World War. Wars created by the leaders of tribal communities in Africa, politicians of the North America and religious leaders of Middle East Islamic countries have killed millions of innocent children in the past. It seems, more children may die or become orphans because of the policies of some leaders who need to open their eyes to see, ears to hear the cry of people and mind and heart to understand the value of life.

II.   FEMALE INFANTICIDE IN INDIA

Killing female children at their birth goes on in different countries for various religious, social, economic and political reasons. Female children are more at risk today in our modern society from the day they are born. Female infanticide and feticide are important issues in medical ethics, gender studies and Child Theology. Female infanticide is also known as 'gendercide'. The sex ratio of females per 1000 males, according to statistics, shows an alarming decrease in female population. At the beginning of the 20th century, the female population in India was 972 per 1000 males in 1901 and by the end of the century, it declined to 933 in 2001. The risk of female children dying between the ages of one to five is 43 per cent. It is difficult to trace the origin and the spread of the practice of female infanticide in the world. But female infanticide was practiced from ancient times in many civilizations.[6]

1.   Historical Survey and Reasons of Infanticide in India

When the practice of female infanticide began among some communities in India, is not known clearly. But the existence of this practice among some caste groups in North, West and South regions of India, controlled by the British rulers, was discovered in 1789 and brought to extensive discussion, to stop female infanticide.

Northern and Western Regions

In his article, L.S. Vishwanath narrates in detail with evidences, the attempts made by the Bristish to put an end to female infanticide in India.[7] The documentary evidences used by Vishwanath proves the practice of female infanticide among the castes of Rajkumar Rajputs, Jedeja Rajputs, Suryavamsha Rajputs, Bedi Khutris, Jats, Gujars, Ahirs and Moyal Brahmins in the North and Lewa Patidars, Lewa Kambis in the western India. The empirical study of the British rulers and Christian missionaries brought to light the declining sex ratio of females in these communities. They had difficulties in collecting the data about the exact number of children killed, and at what day or weeks after they were born, because these communities were not willing to reveal the details to others. However, the information collected by interviewing some of the members of these communities, appointing informants and the Census Report, affirm the fact of female infanticide.

Rajputs

Among the Rajputs, L.S. Vishwanath lists a census of 37 girls to 332 boys in Deogam of Azangash District in 1856 and 805 girls per 1000 boys in 1931. Suryavamsha Rajputs had only 72 girls to 729 males in Amroha region in 1856. In the region of Kutch and Kathiaward, it is estimated that 20,000 female children belonging to Jedeja Rajputs were killed in 1808, 15 girl children were left out in 1816 and only one girl child left out in 1817. Through the interviews with local people, the British rulers found out that the practice of female infanticide among the Rajputs is their custom.

i.   One of the reasons could be regarded as political for their customary practice of their warrior-ideology of conquering neighbouring regions and increasing their territory and income through spoils of war was threatened by the firm control of the British. This control on their war restricted the Rajputs communities from accumulating wealth for dowry and spending huge amounts on the marriages of their daughters. These restrictions led them to resort to killing female children.

ii.   The sociological reason is their practice of *hypergamous* marriage. The high caste Rajputs accepted brides from the middle caste Rajputs for the sake of the huge amount of dowry but refused to give their daughters to the grooms in lower caste Rajputs. This led the middle and lower caste Rajputs within the stratification of the Rajput community to reduce the number of female children by practicing female infanticide.

iii. Another sociological reason is that maintaining the high status of their caste limited them to seek marriage alliance for their daughters from other castes and practice inter-caste marriage. When finding suitable boys for their daughters within the same caste or upper caste in the hierarchy of Rajputs became difficult, these caste groups tried to reduce their female population.

iv. The economic reason is that the Rajputs were asked to pay heavy revenue to the British which resulted in falling of their economic capacity to maintain their high status and pay for the marriage of their daughters. The British colonial rule identified political, social and economic reasons for female infanticide among the communities of Rajputs but did not find any religious reason or sanction from the Shastras and Puranas of Rajputs to justify the custom of female infanticide.[8] On the other hand, they found out that the Shastras and Puranas are against female infanticide.

Lewa Patidars and Kambis

In the Western region of India, the Census record points to the fact, that the Lewa Patidars who were of higher status than the Lewa Kambis, practiced female infanticide. The Lewa Patidars living in Kaira Village had only 39-59 girls to 100 boys in 1872, Baroda region had 707 girls per 1000 males in 1901 and 717 girls to 1000 males in 1911. Lewa Kambis in Kaira village had 73 girls to 100 boys in 1872. Unlike the Rajputs, the Lewa Patidars and Kambis practiced female infanticide secretly for socio-economic reasons. The main reasons identified for the practice of female infanticide among the Lewas are the practice of *hypergamous* marriage, decline in their landholding, demand of high revenue by the British and paying huge dowry to marry off their girls to higher caste grooms.

Jats, Gujars, Ahirs, Rewari, Khurtis

Due to the decline of the Mogul power in North India, many Jats, Ahirs and Rewaris emerged as new and regional kingdoms and claimed royal status. But choosing grooms for their daughters, maintaining status and spending for dowry and marriage expenses forced these castes to resort for female infanticide. Jats had 789 female children per 1000 males in 1921 and 805 in 1931. Gujars had 778 females to 1000 males in 1921.

Another caste, Bedi Khurtis belonging to the Sikh community in Punjab also practiced female infanticide like the Rajputs for sociological and economic reasons. This is clear from the low female ratio in 1981. It seems, Moyal Brahmins too practiced infanticide but detailed information is not available.

Southern India

The assumption that female infanticide is not found in the South India was shattered when the sociologists studied the population statistics and infant mortality rate (IMR) in the census. They noticed that the female infant mortality rate is high in some villages in Tamilnadu particularly among caste groups such as Gounders, Khonds, Kallars, Vanniyars and Todas, a tribe of Nilgris hills. The practice of female infanticide may have originated in 1800 but went on secretly in the south for the past 200 years. This was brought to the notice of the public through newspapers and cinemas in the1980s and publication of research articles and books.

Gounders

The report of the study of 12 villages in the North Arcot-Ambedkhar District between 1987-89 shows that the Gounder community is a majority to the tune of 56 per cent in the villages and practiced female infanticide.[9] Out of the 33 female babies born, 19 female babies died which amounts to 72 per cent of female infanticide in the villages. The mortality rate of female babies born in the community of Gounders is documented as 100 females per 1000 males in 1999 in Salem District and 130.8 in Dharmapuri District. However, it declined to 103 in Salem by 2000, 65 in 2001 and 42 in 2002.

Kallars

Kallars are one of the sub-groups of the Thevar caste in Madurai District. They are regarded as the most backward caste (MBC). Practicing female infanticide due to economic and social reasons is common among the Kallar community in the region of Usilampatti and this has been documented in various books.[10] A survey of the sex ratio shows 939.8 females to 1000 males in villages where female infanticide is practiced in contrast to 1018.6 females in other villages in that region where female infanticide is not practiced.[11] Out of 570 female babies born in Usilampatti region, 450 die due to the practice of female infanticide. This accounts to 80 per cent of female infanticide among the Kallar caste of this region.[12]

2.   Methods and Consequences of Female Infanticide

The study of female infanticide in the North, West and South India has discovered the following methods used to kill the female infants.[13]

i.   by giving the child some opium or poisonous sap of plants mixed with mother's milk.

ii.   By inserting paddy (rice with its husk) into their throats to swallow and bleed to death.

iii. by pouring hot chicken soup in the mouth of the child.

iv.   Feeding the baby with a combination of solution of soap, salt and water.

v.   Covering the child's face with a wet cloth to struggle for breathing.

vi.   Exposing the child to heat or cold

vii. Refusing to feed the baby so that the baby is left to embrace natural death.

The persons involved in the infanticide are the child's family members particularly mother-in-law, father of the child, the village nurse, relatives of the family and the mother of the child.

Female infanticide has severe consequences on the mother, family and community. Mothers go through guilt feeling, depression, grief, shame and psychological trauma for killing the baby. Some women have gone through hypochondria and others experience a sense of losing control over their wish and ambition of having children in the family. A few others hesitate to have a proper sexual life with their husbands due to the fear of conceiving another girl baby. The family practicing female infanticide is looked down upon by other castes living in that village or region. The male children born in that family have no sisters to relate to and their social bonds are limited to the boys. When they grow up, they question the action of their mothers and fathers killing of the female children born in the family. The impact has far reaching consequences in the sex ratio of that community. Among the Bhati community of Rajasthan, according to a Report in 1988, population of women was a record low - 550 to 750 for 1000 men.[14]

III.   FETICIDE IN INDIA

The decline in the practice of female infanticide and the increase in the sex ratio of female child shown in some districts indicate some improvement in eradicating female infanticide due to the effort of the British administrators, Government, NGOs and other religious institutions. For example, female infanticide deaths (FID) decreased from 1048 in 1997 to 657 in 1999 in Dharamapuri, 125 to 79 in Madurai, 281 to 231 in Theni.[15] However, it is not a hopeful sign because people resort to technological methods to abort the female fetuses. Gabriele Dietrich, in her paper, discusses the way the female feticide replaced the female infanticide.[16] According to statistics more than 78000 to 1,00,000 female fetuses have been aborted by couples who had volunteered for tests in the state of Maharastra between 1979-1985.[17] The Bombay Metropolitan city witnessed the highest abortion of female fetuses - an estimate of 45,000 in 1985.[18] The UN estimates appx. 2000 female fetuses are aborted illegally every day and more than 10 million female infanticides were committed over the past 20 years in India. These alarming numbers of children killed indicate clearly that the move is towards the abortion of female fetuses is from the age old practice of female infanticide.

The practice of female feticide is seen not only among the families in India but also found among the Indian born families living in UK. One of the studies undertaken in the recent years at the Oxford University about the Indian women in UK, estimates more than 1500 girl children missing in England and Wales from 1999-2005.[19] The study revealed the alarming truth that Indian women come to India, undergo Sex Determination Tests and abort their girl babies.

Reasons and People involved in feticide

Unlike female infanticide practiced by the few communities identified above, female feticide is found in many families irrespective of caste and class. The following are some of the main reasons for families accepting the practice of female infanticide. The reasons are applicable to feticide too.

    i.   The Indian society is patriarchal in nature and functioning. Naturally, therefore, parents prefer boys to girls. A daughter has to go to her husband's home after marriage. But the sons remain with the parents and involve in the profession of the family and take care of the parents in their old age. Son-preference in the patriarchal system has led families to control the birth of girl child.

ii.   With the availability of sophisticated medical tests, equipments and technology of Utra-sound scanning, amniocentesis and other Sex Determination Tests (SDT), parents are able to get information about the sex of the child in uterus and go in for abortion. Doctors, Nurses and Brokers and Agents are promoting scanning centres and SDT for a commission.

iii. Families are of the opinion that a scientific way of abortion is safer and more acceptable than the cruel way of practicing female infanticide and being caught by the police or neighbours. Fear of being informed about their practicing of female infanticide to the local officials and being punished, has led them to use medical science and technology, which are respected and sanctioned legally, to get rid of the female fetus.

iv.   The Mothers' attitude towards the girl child is also an important reason for feticide. The Indian society does not give equal value to women to enjoy all the rights. They are looked down upon as second or third class citizens, a financial burden on families and have no economic value for families. Since women have gone through the experience of discrimination and sufferings, they fear that their daughters too would go through similar sufferings. Therefore they hesitate to have girl children.

v.   Economic reason such as expenses for the education, dowry, marriage of daughters contribute to female feticide as have contributed to infanticide. However, the changes in land-holding and tenure in villages and cities have forced many families to reduce the number of female children.

Madhu Kishwar writes: The most important and far reaching of the changes introduced by the British involved imposing changes in land ownership patterns. Cultivators now ended up as tenants of a much more interventionist and rapacious State. While creating these new tenancy rights, women's rights in the land were disregarded and bypassed. Even among communities where women were the primary workers on the land, in the process of converting communal property rights of the clan into individual property rights, women were almost completely excluded. Labour power is more valued in societies with surplus land and scarce labour. As land become scarce and population pressure increases, a woman's labour power loses its value and possession of land becomes the all important asset. If ownership of land is vested mostly or exclusively in the hands of men, women begin to be treated like mere dependents and considered as liabilities rather than assets.[20]

A similar view is expressed by Gabriele Dietrich when she says:

It is evident that women in areas like Usilampatti have been more and more marginalized in agriculture and lost control over traditional agricultural methods while green revolution methods took over and bride price was substituted by dowry. A lot of feminist research has shown that women's access to land, water and decision making in agriculture is a very crucial factor not only for their well-being but for their very survival.[21]

Selling of agricultural land due to debts or industrial developments or for real estate reduced the value of women who were once employed in agriculture. This has led to their being regarded as useless and unwanted in families.

vi.   The rapid urbanization of rural areas has led couples to opt for female feticide. Villages after villages vanish in many regions of India particularly in the surrounding vicinity of cities like Delhi, Kolkata, Bangalore, Pune, Chennai because of the construction of computer, automobile and garment industries and multi-storied housing apartments. Rural people have not only lost their land and sustenance but are being influenced by city culture to have small family and resort to abortions.

vii. The influence of mass media particularly cinemas and TV serials focus their attention on male child in families and promote patriarchal system. Advertisements promote small families to enjoy high standard of living owning double bed room houses, small cars and educating their one or two children in international and English medium schools. The driving force set by the media is to limit the number of children, particularly with male children.

viii. The process of globalization of bringing MNCs to various countries with their latest scientific techniques and technological equipments like scan for SDTs, people are encouraged to use them to their advantage. International travel becoming common among the middle class. People travel to India for medical treatment which is not costly when compared to the West and make use of SDTs and resort to abortion.

IV. ABORTION

Abortion is part of feticide. The history of abortion dating back to ancient times shows evidences of pregnancies being terminated through a number of methods viz. using *abortifacient* herbs, sharp needles and knifes, application of abdominal pressure, injecting poison directly into the uterus and other techniques.[22]

Since the population of India is growing fast and has crossed the mark of one billion the Government of India has appealed to people and families to control the birth of children. Various Family Planning projects and programmes are promoted by using the media. Many parents now want to limit the number of children to one or two preferably male. Some families accept the idea of having one daughter rather than the second or third female child. The Sex Determination Tests (SDT) and the Medical Termination of Pregnancy Act of 1971 (MTPA) allow parents to go on for abortion of a second female child. The MTPA allows abortion for particular reasons.[23] First, the abortion of fetus can be carried out for *therapeutic* reason if the life of the pregnant woman is in danger or would affect her mental health rendering her useless care for the baby or because the life of her child was at risk. The second reason is *eugenic* in the case of the conceived child who would born with serious physical and mental handicap due to the effect of German measles, chicken pox or small pox, viral hepatitis, toxoplasmonia or radio-activity or invisible – ray treatment on the pregnant woman. The third reason is based on *humanitarian* ground, that is, abortion of the fetus if conceived due to sexual assault and rape. The fourth reason is of *social* concern of pregnancy occurring on account of the failure of contraceptive device. This issue of abortion will be discussed from the biblical perspective later as a Christian response to infanticide and feticide. Roy Zuck has dealt with these issues in the Bible in his book which is recommended for further reading.[24]

Many '**Pro-Choice**' advocates justify all the above reasons for abortions. According to the 'Actuality Principle' of *Functionalism*, a fetus is not a person. Only when a person begins to act as a moral, spiritual and intellectual, being, then he or she is human.[25] Human organisms have a right to life if only they can act with self-consciousness and personal thought. On this basis, abortion or euthanasia of a defective child is valid.

i.   These advocate of pro-choice see abortions are the only way to control the increase in population.

ii.   They also argue that abortion is necessary in the interest of the health of women and saving the life of the mother.

iii. Sexual assault resulting in pregnancy can cause many problems in the family and so abortion is the remedy to get rid of the fetus and to maintain relationship within the family.

iv.   To help the female child escape discrimination and misery in her life, abortion is resorted to.

v.   Women have a right over their reproductive system and can decide when and what gender of child they want. At this juncture, it is important to note the key reasons for the Western Feminists demanding women's right to abortion. Young people in the west like to refrain from child bearing to enjoy freedom and a good standard of life, for fear of ecological decline and nuclear and toxic effect on health and life of children and over emphasis on the rights of women.[26] Increasing divorce rate, separation and single parenting are another reason for abortion.

Some '**Pro-Life**' promoters take either the stand of 'Potentiality principle' in Functionalism which emphasizes the right to life if that fetus can develop with self consciousness and personal life.[27] Other Pro-Life promoters follow the principle of *Essentialism* which emphasizes that a human organism is a human person and has a right to life because it is member of human species and as such a fetus is a developing person.[28] Modern medical science points out that the tiny heart of the baby begins to beat by third week of pregnancy.

The head and body are distinguishable by the fifth week and the brain starts functioning by the seventh week. Therefore, abortion cannot be allowed. Many of the Pro-Life advocates criticize the loopholes in the MTPA that allow couples to have abortions done easily at the cost of Rs.150 (USD 4) to Rs.500 (USD 13) in private clinics. This group points out various consequences of using modern techniques for sex determination and abortion of fetus.

i.   It is risky for the fetus, as some believe, to draw amnetic fluid through uterus for aminocentasis test to determine the sex of the fetus. The child can have some defect or physical deformity.

ii.   The method of Chorionic Villi Sampling (CVS) by vaginal extraction in 8 to 16 weeks of pregnancy can cause infection and result in fatality to the pregnant woman or have the side-effect of spontaneous abortion.

iii. The Ultra-sound scanning method in sex determination is unreliable and can lead to the abortion of the fetus of a male child by mistake.

To promote pro-life emphasis, Gabriele Dietrich points out, the Indian society needs to be educated on the value of life. Children and Women cannot be separated. To address the problem of children, the focus has to be on women also. Instead of punishing the mother who allowed infanticide or feticide, it is important to heal her self-value of being a woman. In our patriarchal society, women as custodians of life should be emphasized to promote the welfare of women and female children. Not only women but the entire society should realize the shame and guilt of infanticide and feticide.[29]

V.   EFFORTS OF THE BRITISH, INDIAN GOVERNMENT AND NGOs

Efforts were taken by various groups to stop infanticide and feticide. Some of these efforts are briefly listed below.

1.   British Administration

The British administrators particularly Jonathan Duncan, Warren Hastings, Alexander Walker and Elphinstone had taken various efforts to stop female infanticide. Some of their attempts discussed by L.S. Vishwanath are listed below.[30]

i.   The British administrators during their rule did not find any evidence for female infanticide in the Hindu puranas and shastras. They, however, noticed that the *Bretemo Bywurt Pooran* (Brahma Vaivarta Puran) speaks of punishment for taking a life of even a fetus. The killer shall suffer in hell or be born again as a leper and afflicted for sin. So the British administrator used this purana to educate the Rajputs to stop female infanticide.

ii.   They made the Rajputs and Jedeja community to sign an agreement, which included the punishment as stated by the shastra, to persuade these castes to relinquish the practice of female infanticide. Although the practice was stopped for a short period, it continued and the agreement became a 'dead letter', as noticed by the British officials.

iii.   The communities were persuaded to expel those who practiced infanticide and not have any relationship with such families.

iv.   The British administrators created Caste Council to educate communities not to go in for *hypergamous* marriages to avoid dowry demands and to overcome social and economic factors forcing them to practice female infanticide.

v.   Some of the British officials insisted on a 'coercive' approach. Informants were appointed to bring to the notice of the Government these families practicing female infanticide. But others opposed this coercive system as an intrusion into the domestic privacy of the communities and warned the informants with threats of the danger of their being alienated from their local communities. As an alternative approach, police surveillance encouraged some villages to control female infanticide to a certain extent.

vi.   The British administrators insisted on compulsory registration of births and deaths in areas suspected of female infanticide and encouraged the panchayats to co-operate in the registration process.

The attempts of the British administration in the North and West of India brought about awareness on female infanticide and yielded some significant results in the control of female infanticide, although it could not eradicate the practice completely.

2.   Government of India

Both the Central and State governments are aware of the problem of female infanticide and feticide and have taken various steps to control and eradicate these practices. Their approach was two fold viz. one, to deal with the issue of infanticide and feticide by enacting laws and implementing them and the other, for promoting welfare schemes for children, particularly girl children, and awareness programmes for women. It is not possible to discuss the achievements and failures of these schemes in detail here except for listing briefly that the government is concerned about children.

i.   Since the problem of female infanticide is connected with various sociologically complex issues such as the marriage system and dowry, prostitution and abortion, divorce, preference for sons over daughters and the patriarchal structure of society. The government passed laws against dowry system and sati which caused misery to women and forced families to reduce the birth of girl children, involve in prostitutions and illegal abortions. But the Indian government is unable to challenge the patriarchal structure of society by laws and bring equal status to women. The practice of caste system, dowry demands, prostitutions and abortion are still going on unreported but can be controlled by the intensive implementation of laws.

ii.   Son-preference and female feticide are challenged by laws controlling pre-natal diagnostic tests. No woman can be forced to go in for SDT. The Pre-conception and Pre-Natal Diagnostic Techniques (Prohibition of Sex Selection) Act and Rules 1994 as amended up to 2002 state clearly the rights of women to refuse SDT. The scan centres and the clinics involved in Sex-Determination Tests and carry out abortion are controlled by the same law enforcing powers the Enforcement Authorities of Central and State Supervisory Board. Yet, feticide goes on, failing to bring the medical centres and the doctors to accountability.

iii.   Laws in Indian society can bring some results but cannot solve the problem fully unless the public and officials co-operate and are willing to stop the practices. Combined with the rules and regulations, the government has launched several literacy programmes and projects to educate women about family, marriage, children, health and hygiene and child development programmes like Danish International Development Assistance (DANDA), ICDS, Tamilnadu Area Health Care Project (TNAHCP), Cradle Baby Scheme, Girl Child Protection Scheme, etc.

3.   Non-Governmental Organizations

Many Non-Governmental Organizations are involved in dealing with the problems of children. Some of them have contributed to the welfare of orphans, the mentally affected and the physically challenged, by establishing or supporting financially the orphanages, homes, health clinics and schools for these children. Others are fighting against child labour and for the rights of children. A few others are involved in helping children who have been sexually abused. Two of the NGOs I know viz. Society for Integrated Social Upliftment (SISU) and Society for Integrated Rural Development (SIRD) based in Madurai, are concerned about female infanticide and feticide and initiated programs to educate the families of the Kallar community against female infanticide. These NGOs organize seminars and give training against feticide and have launched non-violent struggles against Pre-natal Diagnostic Techniques and abortions. Similarly other NGOs are working among the Gounder and Vanniyar communities in north Tamilnadu. The welfare schemes such as loans for purchasing cows, improving agriculture and small businesses and grants for educating girl children either instituted by the NGOs with their funds or recommended to the government, to improve the economic and social status of these communities and thus stop the practice of infanticide and feticide, brought about some results initially but it did not last.[31] Some NGOs work closely with leaders of local communities and the state government. The Street Theatre programme of 'Kalaipayana Kuzhukkal' supported by TNAHCP brought about an awareness of infanticide and mobilized village panchayat officials, community leaders and health officials to educate their local communities.[32] Their preventive and controlling approaches rather than the developmental schemes, achieved good results in reducing the practice of infanticide and feticide. However, a detailed evaluation of the achievements of NGOs is needed and the process could take a long time.

VI. CHRISTIAN RESPONSE TO INFANTICIDE AND ABORTION

Christians, as individuals and local churches, have responded to social problems ever since the time of the Apostles. The Gospel values have compelled them to involve in social transformation. Christian response is in the form of theological basis as well as practical action.

Missionaries and Churches

i.   Missionaries living in North India during the colonial rule wrote extensively about the way the female infanticide was practiced and its consequences. They published their findings to bring about awareness on this practice and mobilize the British administrators to pay serious attention to this problem and pass necessary laws to eradicate it.

ii. A research conducted in Tamilnadu to know the involvement of the churches and Western Mission societies (CMS, LMS, ALC) in addressing the problem of infanticide shows that these missionaries focused their attention more on the care of orphans and providing primary health care and schools for the education of the children rather than on eradicating the practice of infanticide.[33] Churches also followed the same social service of health care, education and establishing orphanages and children's homes for the needy. Whether churches in various regions of India were hesitant to address the problem of infanticide, or attempted and failed or simply ignored it, needs detailed research.

iii. In addition to continuing the social service to children in various capacities, churches need to discuss the issue of abortion from theological and sociological perspectives. For, Christians are divided on this issue of abortion and euthanasia. Roman Catholic Christians, following either the Potentiality Principal of Functionalism or

Essentialism reject abortion. Other Protestant churches have varied opinions because of the way they interpret the biblical texts. In fact, the Bible does not state clearly on abortion but some texts have been used for the case of Pro-Life and Pro-Choice.

Theological Response

Pro-life advocates quote Ps. 139:13-16, Jer.1:5 and Lk.1:41-44 to support their views but the following examination shows that they are not speaking of the right to life or against abortion. The emphasis of Ps. 139 is on the omniscience of God. The Psalmist acknowledges that God knows man from the time he is conceived in his mother's womb because God has created man wonderfully. He cannot hide himself from God. The message of Ps. 139:13-16 is about God's creation of human beings and his constant watch over them rather than against abortion. John Stott believes that this psalm is speaking about the value of life and explains it to prove his pro-life position.[34] Similarly Jer.1:5 speaks of creating Jeremiah to set him apart for prophetic ministry and not about right to life. Mary's greetings to Elizabeth in Lk 1:41-44 made her rejoice. She could feel the baby leaping in her womb. These texts appreciate the mystery of God creating human beings in the womb of women that they can realize the wonderful work of God and serve him.

Another text which is against killing of human lives is in Ex. 20:13, 'You shall not murder'. Both pre-mediated murder and incidental murder are wrong and the punishment varied according to the case, in ancient Israel. The message of this text is applicable to a person born and growing day by day. This includes the case of infanticide or euthanasia of terminally ill children but this becomes controversial in the case of feticide due to the question of when the zygote becomes a person.

The controversial text is Ex. 21:22-24 used by both groups to support their pro-life and pro-choice stand.

> If men who are fighting hit a pregnant woman and she gives birth prematurely but there is no serious injury, the offender much be fined whatever the woman's husband demands and the court allows. (v.22).

> But if there is serious injury, you are to take life for life (v. 23)

Scholars differ in their translation and interpretation of this text. According to Gershon Brin, this text is not double laws but one single law with two principal parts namely, 'miscarriage and yet no harm' (v.22) and 'if any harm' (v.23) and with two different degrees of damage caused to the pregnant woman and varying punishments.[35] The damages caused to a pregnant woman are the miscarriage and assault on her life. If the second part (v. 23) is understood as injury to the mother's life and death penalty is imposed, then this issue is not directly related to the question of abortion. However, the problem lies in the first part of the text (v. 22). Is it right, first of all, to translate the phrase 'gives birth (a child) prematurely' or 'miscarriage'? The second problem is to understand the Hebrew word *ason* – 'harm' or 'injury' in v.22. The third problem is to find out the main focus or thrust of this text. Is it on the life of the pregnant woman or the losing of the child or fetus?. According to Alan Cole, this text is not about the issue of abortion. Its focus is on the injury caused to the mother when she interferes during the fight between her husband and another man. He points out that the miscarriage should be compensated because it is an injury to the mother without discussing the meaning of miscarriage as fully formed fetus or unformed fetus.[36] Cornelis Houtman quotes the view of Fensham that the word *ason* refers to a permanent damage done to the woman who can no longer be able to bear children as a result of injury. But he disagrees with Fensham because the issue is not whether the woman is still fertile or not.[37] Susanne Scholz focused her attention on the literary aspect of the text speaking of her husband deciding the amount of penalty to be paid to him for the injury caused to his wife and criticizes the male dominated language and the patriarchal values of the society rather than discussing the issue of miscarriage.[38] Joseph Blenkinsopp emphasizes the economic value of children as a resource for families and the need for compensation to the husband without discussing the issue of miscarriage as referring to premature birth of fully formed child or unformed fetus.[39] John Durham sees 'miscarriage' in two possible ways viz. premature birth of a child and no harm to the life of the mother and the baby or the loss of fetus which is *ason* (harm) and such an injury demands penalty. He is not discussing the issue of abortion except emphasizing the effect, harm and compensation.[40]

Jack Cottrell taking the Pro-life position argues that the translation 'miscarriage' is not appropriate in v. 22 which can mean only the loss of fetus. He points out another Hebrew word *shachol* used in Ex. 23:26 and Hosea 9:14 to refer to miscarriage (cf. Gen. 31:38, Job 21:10 referring to animals, 2 Kings 2:19, 21, Malachi 3:11 referring to the land and plants not producing mature fruit).[41] On the basis of the words *yeled* (child) and the verb *yatza* (to go out, to come forth) used in v. 22, Cottrell interprets this text as meaning the premature birth of a child and not the destruction of a fetus. Furthermore, he says that the text does not make any distinction between harm done to the child or to the mother. The fine or the penalty is not based on this point of view but from the very fact that the mother and child are exposed to danger and distress. V. 23 introduced with 'if' clause can have effect if the mother dies of injury. For him, this text cannot be used as a justification for liberalizing the law of abortion.

Extensive discussion is taken by Stanley Isser in his article on Ex. 21:22-23.[42] He compares this OT law with the laws in Ancient Near Eastern Countries and Greco-Roman period. Out of his study he points out two possible understandings of the word *ason* in v. 22. It can mean not fully formed fetus and so compensation according to the months of the fetus levied as penalty. Or else it could also refer to a fully formed fetus equal to a human person. If so, then death penalty is demanded for taking a life. The growth of the fetus aborted naturally due to the injury during the fight between a woman's husband and the other man can be judged only by the elders of the village with the help of the nurses in their society. It is possible that the judgment was awarded according to the details collected and verified in ancient Israel about which we have no further information in the OT. The harm could be against the unformed fetus or fully formed fetus. The focus of the text, however, is on the unexpected and incidentally happened abortion in the context of fight between men and not pre-planned and deliberately induced abortion. Both Pro-life and Pro-choice promoters can claim this text but have to solve the problem of interpreting it and seek medical advice about the growth of the fetus as unformed, semi-formed or fully formed into a baby and the rules of the nation.

Instead of searching for a proof of text in the Bible to prove either of the positions, it is important to emphasize the creation theology of the Bible. God who created both male and female in his own image, values human life.[43] The Bible does not say that murder or infanticide or abortion will never happen. It criticizes the inhuman practices of sacrificing children to gods and goddesses, dedicating female children to be cult-prostitutes in temples as is seen in the *devadhasi* system in India or using them as medium for sorcery. These superstitions and rituals may have contributed to the practice of infanticide and feticide. The world-view of the people and the cultural practices based on the world views need to be challenged by the creation and redemption theology of the Bible combined with the ideology of humanism. The Gospel of Christ for new humanity should be proclaimed and promoted to emphasize the value of life for the present and future generations.

It is easy to leave the discussion of abortion open for further discussion without stating any conclusion. We can leave it to the views of Christians to take their own stand on abortion. But there are certain situations like rape, mental illness of the mother or child, forced pregnancy by the husband, illegal pregnancy in prostitution and failure of contraceptives and surgery demand a stand on abortion and the congregations are looking for a clear guidance from their authorities. Should one's mother, sister or daughter be made to bear the brunt of having the child, conceived when raped? Should one be made to have a child when mentally ill? Who will be the father of the child in the case of gang rape? Will that child born be acceptable to the husband and family members? Who will marry a girl if she is raped and has given birth to a child? Should the deformed and mentally retarded child be borne by the mother? Should both of them with their family members suffer life long? On the other hand, when abortion is done, the woman and the family may feel guilty of killing a child. The most affected person is, undoubtedly, the mother who has to live with the guilt of having lost her child. She undergoes trauma for life.

In my opinion, Christians should take into account, three factors viz. i). the way they understand the biblical teaching, ii). the law of the Government and medical ethics, and iii). the humanitarian aspect which includes sociological relationship. Proper guidance and counseling are necessary to the woman and family members, before and after abortion, if it is done for valid reasons at an early stage of pregnancy. However, one particular view cannot be imposed on everybody. Both male and female child as well as the mentally retarded and physically challenged children should have the right to life. Families all over the world should be trained to care for them. Societies should be educated to accept them not as a burden but as a challenge to their spirituality and an opportunity to develop them. The Governments are also responsible to legislate appropriate laws, modify the existing rules and implement them effectively. Churches, Seminaries, Missions and Christian colleges and schools need to include the concern of children and build up the future generation in their programmes, projects and curriculum

Endnotes

[1] John D.W. Watts, *Isaiah 1-33* (WBC No. 24, Waco: Word Books, 1985), p. 75.

[2] Donald A. Hagner, *Matthew 1-13* (WBC No. 33, Texas: Word Books, 1993), pp. 373-376.

[3] *The Oxford Illustrated Dictionary* (ed. J. Coulson, Oxford:OUP, 1981),   p.430.

[4] *Orient-Longman Word Master-Learner's Dictionary of Modern English* (ed. Usha Aroor, Chennai:OL P Ltd, 2004) p.207.

[5] 'Child Sacrifice' in *www.answers.com*, accessed on 7th Dec. 2007, pp. 1-7.

[6] R. Muthulakshmi, *Female Infanticide: Its Causes and Solution* (New Delhi: Discovery Publishing House, 2003), p. 7., Pari Titus, 'Female Infanticide in Salem, Dharamapuri and Madurai Districts of Tamilnadu and Its implications for Christian Mission' unpublished Thesis submitted to CIME, Bangalore, 2007.

[7] L.S. Vishwanath, 'Efforts of Colonial State to suppress Female Infanticide: Use of Sacred Texts, Generation of Knowledge' *Economic and Political Weekly* (EPW, Mumbai, vol. 33, No. 19, May 9-15, 1998), pp. 1104-1112.

[8] L.S. Vishwanath, pp.1106f.

[9] Sabu George, Rajaratnam Abel and B.D. Miller, 'Female Infanticide in Rural South India', *EPW*, vol. 27. No. 22, May 30, 1992, pp. 1153-1156.

[10] Raj Kumar (ed.), *Violence against women* (New Delhi: Anmol Publication P. Ltd, 2000), ch.13, pp. 139-140., R. Muthurlakshmi, pp. 20-23.

[11] S. George, et.al, p. 1115.

[12] S. George, et al. p. 1154.

[13] Pari Titus, unpublished thesis ch. IV, Vishwanath, p 1108, 'Born to Die' *India Today*, June, 28, 1986, pp.28-33.

[14] Raj Kumar, pp. 141-142.

[15] V. Athreya and S.R. Chunkath, 'Tackling the Female Infanticide: Social Mobilisation in Dharamapuri, 1997-1999' in *EPW*. Dec. 2, 2000, pp. 4345 to 4348. These authors point out in the same statistical Table No. 1 on p.4346 that FID has increased in other districts of Krishnagiri and Salem between 1997-99.

[16] Gabriele Dietrich, 'Sex-Selective Abortions Replacing Female Infanticide: A Feminist Perspective' in *Female Feticide in Tamilnadu: Report of the State Level Consultation-Dec.23, 1998, Chennai* (eds. Sabu M. George and P. Phavalam, Madurai: SIRD, 2000), pp. 25-34.

[17] Raj Kumar, pp. 134f.

[18] Raj Kumar, p. 134.

[19] 'UK Indian Women aborting girls' in *www.news.bbc.co.uk* accessed on 7th Dec. 2007, pp.1-4.

[20] Madhu Kishwar, 'When Daughters are Unwanted: Sex Determination Tests in India' in *Manushi*, No 86, Jan-Feb. 1995, p. 20 discusses how the changing land-tenure system contribute to devalue women and causing feticide.

[21] Gabriele Dietrich, p.27.

[22] 'History of Abortion' in www. Answers.com. assessed on 7th Dec. 2007, pp. 1-20.

[23] K. Kumar and Punam Rani, *Offences against women: Socio-Legal Perspectives*, (New Delhi: Regency Publication, 1996), p. 37.

[24] Roy B. Zuck, *Precious in His Sight: Childhood and Children in the Bible* (Grand Rapids: Baker Books, 1996), pp. 71-89.

[25] Robert N. Wennberg, 'The Right to Life: Three Theories' in *Readings in Christian Ethics: Issues and Application* (Eds. D.K. Clark and R.V. Rakeshtraw, Grand Rapids: Baker Books, 2000), vol. 2, pp. 36-46. Virginia Ramey Mollenkott, 'Reproductive Choice: Basic to Justice for women', *Readings in Christian Ethics*, pp. 26-31.

[26] Gabriele Dietrich, pp. 29-31.

[27] R.N.Wennberg, pp. 38-39.

[28] Robert E. Joyce, 'When does a Person Begin?' pp. 46-51, R.N Wennberg, pp. 42-44. Also the introductory comments on 'Abortion' in page. 24 by the editors D.K. Clark and R.L. Rakestraw. Op.cit.

[29] Gabriele Dietrich, pp. 31-34.

[30] Vishwanath, pp. 1106-1111.

[31] Pari Titus, ch. VIII.

[32] V. Athreya and S. R. Chunkath, p. 4346.

[33] Pari Titus, ch. X.

[34] John R W. Stott, *Issues Facing Christians Today* (Basingstoke: Marshalls, 1984), pp. 280-288.

[35] Gershon Brin, *Studies in Biblical Law: From the Hebrew Bible to the Dead Sea Scrolls* (S.No. 176, Sheffield: JSOT Press, 1994), p. 20.

[36] R. Alan Cole, *Exodus* (TOTC, Leicester: IVP, 1973), p. 169.

[37] Cornelis Houtman, *Exodus* (HCOT, Leuven: Peeters, 2000), vol. 7, p. 170.

[38] Susanne Scholz, 'The Complexities of 'His' Liberation Talk: A Literary Feminist Reading of the Book f Exodus' in *Exodus to Deuteronomy: A Feminist Companion to the Bible* (ed. Athalya Brenner, Sheffield: SAP, 2000), p. 34.

[39] Joseph Blenkinsopp, 'The Family in First Temple Israel' in *Families in Israel* (eds. Leo G. Perdue and others, Louisvelle: Westminster John Knox Press, 1997), pp. 69f.

[40] John I Durham, *Exodus* (WBC, No. 3, Waco: Word Books, 1987), pp. 323f.

[41] Jack W. Cottrell, 'Abortion and the Mosaic Law' in *Readings in Christian Ethics*, vol. 2, pp.32-35.

[42] Stanley Isser, 'Two Traditions: The Law of Exodus 21:22-23 Revisited' CBQ, 52, 1990, pp. 30-45.

[43] Refer to J.B. Jeyaraj, *Biblical Perspectives on Children and their Protection: Towards a Child Theology* (Madurai: JIP, 2007).

CHAPTER - 6

Children Rights to Education: Holistic Child Development Training for Parents and Trainers

Dr. A.P.J. Abdul Kalam, the former President of India spent most of his time in meeting children and youths in schools, colleges and professional institutes, teaching them values of education, science and technology and the need to build the nation of India with peace and harmony. He has a high hope on educational institutions to transform the lives of younger generation and said, 'I would even go to the extent of saying that if parents and teachers show the required dedication to shape the lives of the young, India would get a new life'. Knowing very well the burden of colonial rule and the great need to develop India, Mahatma Gandhi emphasized the elementary education of all children combined with manual labour and development of skill. He believed that mere academic knowledge is not enough for the holistic development of children and so wrote:[1]

> I am a firm believer in the principle of free and compulsory Primary Education for India. I also hold that we shall realize this only by teaching the children a useful vocation and utilizing it as a means for cultivating their mental, physical and spiritual faculties. It will check the progressive decay of our villages and lay the foundation of a juster social order in which there is no unnatural division between the 'haves' and the 'have-nots' and everybody is assured of a living wage and the rights to freedom. - (Harijan, 11.9.1937).

History of the development of education is a long story[2]. Each country has its own history of the development of education in its soil. The *gurukula* model of education in the early period was focused more on learning religious Vedas. Pandits taught languages, basic mathematics and administration to the members of the royal families in palaces. Learning under the feet of a guru or a pandit was the right of the rich and upper caste people. The caste system prevented the lower caste people to have the right of education or perform rituals in the temples[3]. The colonial period of the West also encouraged the people of upper caste to learn English in schools and colleges to work for their administration in India.

But Christian missionaries from the West realized the need of establishing schools for all irrespective of caste, class and religion to educate children and liberate the society from superstitions and oppressive customs and practices[4]. They believed that India can progress in all respects through their educational service. Many leaders and parents acknowledge the valuable contribution of western missionaries through their educational and medical service to all people irrespective of their class, caste and religion. Today, one can notice three kinds of Christian schools viz. i. Schools established and managed by churches for the poor and middle class. ii. schools established and managed by Christian business men or families mainly for the employment of members belonging to their families or caste and as commercial endeavour for profit. Most of these schools are English medium with better facilities but cater for the rich and upper middle class. iii. The third category is the schools established by national missionary organizations in the post-independent period in their mission fields and educating the poor tribals and their generations. In addition to these schools, both the state and central government have thousands of schools all over India. It is estimated that India had 43,000 elementary schools in 1950-51 but this has increased to 7,75,100 in 1996-97. The state of Tamilnadu is a pioneer in establishing schools at least elementary level to middle level in each panchayat providing free mid-day meal to all children to enable children in rural area to have basic education. Many more schools are mushrooming in the recent years due to the policy of privatization of education by the government. A survey conducted by my own students some years ago in the city of Madurai reveals that the schools are class oriented. Children belonging to rich and upper middle class families are afford to pay the high fees and study in high class private schools. Children of middle class families go to ordinary schools managed by some churches. Children of poor families go to schools of the local panchayat or municipalities or corporations where facilities are not good enough. The economic divide of the society is reflected in the schools. Unfortunately, the interactions and sharing between the children in these schools are lacking that generations are growing in schools without understanding each other. It is sad that the management of many schools is not serious about the widening gap between the children of rich and poor families in schools.

Many temples, mosques and guruduvas have their own schools combining secular and religious education. Rich families of other faiths have established private schools and collecting high fees. The parents and others who are against commercialization of education are asking the government to take some actions on these schools to reduce the fees and provide better facilities. The Government of Tamilnadu is bringing some rules and regulations on this issue and the owners of these schools are opposing the regulations of the government through legal actions. During the struggle for independence, Mahatma Gandhi emphasized the importance of education of all and created an alternative model of *Ashram* without rejecting formal education in schools for imparting ethical values and his three key ideologies of Sarvodaya, Swaraj and Swadeshi[5]. He was critical of the traditional model of education of the west emphasizing only the academic excellence. But the policy of privatization of education has led to ignore the ideals of Gandhism and to establish schools only for academic purpose calling their schools with western names such as 'Cambridge School', 'Oxford School' or 'Harvard College'. The gap between education and ethics is widening can be noticed by the way the educated children, youths and adults are behaving in families, offices and society. So, many questions are raised today on education. What sort of education we need? What is the purpose of education? Should we continue the traditional model of education of academic emphasis or overall development of children? Will the parents and government accept the alternative model of education of the holistic development of children?

I am not going to answer these questions. This essay is not a detailed research paper but I am sharing some of my views and ideas on the rights of children to get educated, role of parents, teachers and the emerging Holistic Child Development education to train parents, teachers, social workers, pastors and trainers of trainers in the following pages.

I.   CHILDREN RIGHTS TO EDUCATION

Even though many questions are raised on the present state of education, there is always a need for formal education of children in schools. The elementary education is the right of every child because it enables the child to develop the following[6]:

1. To develop and realize child's full potential as a human being
2. To develop the ability to think, question and judge independently
3. To develop a sense of self-respect, dignity and self confidence
4. To develop and internalize a sense of moral values and critical judgment
5. To learn to love and respect fellow human beings and nature
6. To develop civic sense, citizenship and values of participatory democracy
7. To enable decision making.

However, millions of children are not getting even the elementary education. According to one statistics, 73 million children between 5-14 years of age are engaged in child labour. But this estimate is questioned because of the difference of opinion regarding defining 'child labour' and 'child work'[7]. A girl working as domestic maid or a boy working in a cattle farm to earn a small amount for their families is regarded as 'child work' and not included in the statistics of child labour. Another report points out that the children out of schools in India alone are 100 million. Although statistics vary, it is clear from the news in media coming out constantly that millions of children are in child labour or on the streets unable to have basic education.

Various reasons can be stated briefly for children not getting elementary education.

1. *Poverty:* More than 40% of the population lives below poverty line. Poor parents are unable to send their children to schools because they cannot pay fees, transport expenses, buy books and uniforms.

2. *Attitude of Parents:* Many parents who are illiterate and poor want to keep their children for work in agricultural fields, gardens, plantations and industries to earn income for the families.

3. *Broken Homes:* Children suffer a lot if their parents are separated or divorced. The first problem they face is their struggle for food and shelter or losing their right to continue education in schools and look for a job.

4. *Lack of Schools:* Many villages and hills do not have elementary schools. It is a serious problem in many states of North and North West India. While the Constitution of India promotes the right to have education, the state governments do not establish schools in interior villages and tribal areas of forests. Children who want to get educated cannot reach schools afar. So parents ask their children to work with them in villages and forests and estates.

5. *Poor facilities in schools:* Many schools of the local panchayats or municipalities or corporations in rural and urban area do not have basic infrastructure of class rooms, black boards and toilet facilities. These schools do not have enough teachers to teach and they go on leave quite often.

6. *Subjects and Teaching Methods:* The curriculum used in elementary and middle schools is designed to memorize many lessons. Children find mathematics, history and English so difficult. The evaluation method is based on passing the exams. If they fail in subjects, they have to repeat the course remaining in the same class. The teaching method is also not developing the skill of learning and encouraging the struggling students in studies. The teaching-learning methods are exam oriented rather than oriented to build the student holistically. They are not conducive to continue their education. Some children, although began to enjoy their right to learn, drop out of schools before completing the elementary education to the level of 5th standard.

God has created each child in his own image, loves them and wants their rights to be protected. Jesus showed remarkable knowledge of his learning from parents and religious centers and answered those who questioned him. He taught as an effective teacher to his disciples and transformed the lives of his listeners. Jesus spent time with children and warned those who would do injustice to children. I have discussed the value of children, their rights and laws protecting them from biblical perspectives in my article and so do not want to repeat it here.[8]

The rights of children for food, shelter, health, education and welfare got more attention that UNO has created Convention on the Rights of the Child (CRC) and mobilized countries to sign and implement the Convention. While the Universal Declaration of Human Rights addresses the rights of all people, CRC focuses its attention on the rights of children[9]. Since other scholars have discussed CRC and Indian Constitution in detail, I make a reference to these documents briefly below.

Convention on the Rights of the Child (CRC)

The Convention on the Rights of the Child adopted by the UN General Assembly on 20th November 1989 is a significant land mark for the welfare of children all over the world[10]. The rights of children can be categorized under three "P's" viz. Provision, Protection and Participation. Thus, the children have the right to be provided with basic needs such as food, shelter, clothes and services of health care and education. Children have the right to be protected from exploitation, oppression, abuse and torture. They have the right to participate in decision making process which affects their rights. These essential features are further expanded in 54 Articles in CRC dealing with each aspect of the life of a child. More specifically Article 28 and 29 of CRC deal with the right of all children without discrimination to have free education.

Indian Constitution

The Constitution of India upholds the right of children particularly to get educated. The Articles 45 and 46 guarantee their right of education[11].

Article 45 - Provision for free and compulsory education for children:

> The State shall endeavour to provide, within a period of ten years from the commencement of this Constitution, for free and compulsory education for all children until they complete the age of fourteen years.

Article 46 - Promotion of educational and economic interests of Scheduled Castes, Scheduled Tribes and other weaker sections:

> The State shall promote with special care the educational and economic interests of the weaker sections of the people, and, in particular, of the Scheduled Castes and the Scheduled Tribes, and shall protect them from social injustice and all forms of exploitation.

Furthermore, Article 28 provides freedom to attend religious instruction and protects the child from any information of religious instruction through educational institutions. The recent Amendment Act on education (Article 51-A) compels the parents to send their children to schools as a fundamental duty. Thanks to the effort of the Central and State Governments in promoting the elementary education as free but compulsory that the literacy rate is increased. The survey of literacy rate in India says[12]:

> The results of 2001 census reveal that there has been an increase in literacy in the country. The literacy rate in the country is 64.84 per cent, 75.26 for males and 53.67 for females. Kerala retained its position by being on top with a 90.86 per cent literacy rate, closely followed by Mizoram (88.80 per cent) and Lakshadweep (86.66 per cent).

> Bihar with a literacy rate of 47.00 per cent ranks last in the country preceded by Jharkhand (53.56 per cent) and Jammu and Kashmir (55.52 per cent). Kerala also occupies the top spot in the country both in male literacy with 94.24 per cent and female literacy with 87.72 per cent. On the contrary, Bihar has recorded the lowest literacy rates both in case of males (59.68 per cent) and females (33.12 per cent)

II.   PARENTS: NEED TO GET EDUCATED

Parents play a key role in educating their children. We can classify parents on the basis of their educational level into three broad categories viz. i. Parents who are uneducated and illiterate, ii. Parents who are educated to a certain level and iii. Parents who are highly educated and earned degrees. The education of their children depends on their attitude, values and expectations. Most of them want their children to read, write and get qualified for a job. Others want their children to be highly qualified professionally to take up their business or work abroad. Most of the parents have a different understanding of labour, work and service and value jobs related to manual labour or agriculture or farming or serving for community development as low and therefore they want their children to go for white-color jobs in offices or teaching in institutions or engineers in IT companies. However, they are not paying attention to the holistic development of their children. They expect them to speak fluent English and earn thousands of Rupees and lead a high standard of life. But most of the parents give less importance to spiritual, physical and skill development and emphasize more on getting high marks in the exams to enter professional colleges and become Doctors and Engineers. They compel the children to go for private tuition offered by the teachers at their homes or private tutorial institutes.

Problems of children in schools

1. Because of the pressure of parents, some students gain academic excellence but lose health or social relationship with others.

2. Those children who cannot make up academically become frustrated in life and go through trauma.

3. Other children become violent and problematic to their families and schools.

4. Orphan children are looked down and they struggle for their identity and recognition.

5. Children belonging to Dalit and Tribal communities are humiliated by other students and staff and discriminated in lifting them up in their studies.

6. Some girls and boys go through crisis in their mind due to problems in families and they go through loneliness and seclusion. Some go for alcohol or drugs or run away from their homes.[13]

7. Some children are rough and bully other children and terrorize them to do whatever they say to these weaker children.

8.   Some use abusive language against other students, teachers and parents

9.   Rich children with lots of money misuse their money without accountability.

10. Boys as they grow learn from their peer groups to have gender bias and look down girls as secondary citizens to be suppressed or sex objects. Some of them misbehave with girls in the schools.

Parents and Need of HCD Training

The problems of children are so many that the parents and teachers need to have training to address these problems and develop children. Many parents assume that the schools will teach everything to their children and their responsibility is to find a good school, pay the fees and arrange transportation. Their role is over with feeding and sending them to schools regularly. If their children are problematic at home or society, they blame the schools for not shaping their children. They should know that the schools have their own limitations. Many parents do not understand their children fully as they grow and to guide or discipline them properly. They also need some education for the holistic development of children. Usually the Parents-Teachers Association (PTA) in schools discuss about the fees collected or exams conducted or raising funds for constructing buildings. But PTA can take effort in co-operation with the Management Board of the schools for the constructive training of parents

This education is not formal education to read and write but an awareness education developing their ability and skill to shape the children spiritually, critically, physically, psychologically, sociologically and with values, spirit of patriotism and commitment to society and nation. The schools can arrange one hour session per week for the parents and offer a Certificate course on HCD inviting some specialists in the local area to teach the parents. This course can be a short term course for 10-20 weeks in the evening on the campus of the schools. The following important subjects can be taught to the parents to gain some basic awareness about the children and some skills to deal with them at home.

1.   Developing the spirituality of children

2.   Nutrition and health fitness

3. Environmental awareness
4. Gender equality and rights of girl child
5. Non-violence and Peace
6. Media, Information Technology and Sex
7. Understanding problems and skill of counseling children
8. Relationship between Children-Parents-Teachers
9. Stewardship and Accountability
10. Marriage, Family and Parenting children

Schools can add some more subjects according to their context. These subjects when offered to parents not only will enlighten them but also will change them first to be role models to their children. This kind of certificate level training will lay the foundation for many parents to understand their children, give due recognition to enjoy their rights and enable to discipline them as responsible kids at home, schools and in neighbourhood. The quality of parenting their children will certainly improve.

III. TRAINERS: NEED TO GET TRAINED

The term 'Trainers' includes teachers who train the students, pastors training their congregations and sociologists training the staff of NGOs. Although they are trained in their own field of teaching history or language or science or commerce, preaching and pastoral care and social work respectively, they need special training for HCD.

Teachers and HCD education

The Government has rules and regulations regarding the appointment of teachers in schools. Teachers should have proper qualification and trained in the approved Teacher Training colleges. The curriculum of teacher training programmes include subjects on the history of education, philosophy of education, teaching methods, psychology of students, practical work, etc. The main emphasis of these subjects is centered on academic achievement. Some private schools employ teachers without proper qualification to teach and pay them less. Even if they are trained in institutes or colleges of education for teaching, they should know more about children and not merely their syllabus. The students in schools are not mere customers to consume our teaching but valuable personalities to be built as responsible leader to lead his or her family and the nation in future. The other side of the children particularly the personality development at every age, influence of peer groups and media, socio-economic need, background of their parents and situation in family, feelings of being abused, loneliness, discrimination on the basis of caste, colour and class, need of identity and recognition, etc.

Schools are responsible to send their teachers in batches for HCD training or organize HCD Refresher Course and programmes in their schools to educate their staff to develop the children holistically. They need to learn not only the content of the following subjects but also the way to use the insights to shape the children in their schools. Mere theoretical knowledge is not enough. The subjects of HCD should include the development of critical analysis, creating skills, approaches and techniques and a heart for the children.

1. Understanding Children's background – their family, socio-economic status, culture and locality where they live and helping the poor children.

2. Children at Risk (CAR – Reasons, Consequences and Remedies)

3. Child Rights – UNO document (CRC), Human Rights, Indian Constitution and Policies

4. Critical understanding of the influence of Media and Information Technology on children

5. Skill of handling and guiding peer groups in classes

6. Creating the spirit of peace, harmony and patriotism

7. Counseling methods for children in crisis (CIC)- Abused, Discriminated, HIV infected, Separation of Parents and siblings, Alienated from Parental love and care.

8. Creation and Caring the Environment

9. Marriage, Family and Parenting children

10. Gender Equality and Rights of Girl children

11. Role of religion and liberating children from oppressive customs and practices.

Some schools do address on these aspects to children in the general assembly conducted in the morning or evening. But the training of teachers for HCD gives them more confidence to handle children. Children spent most of their time in schools learning subjects and look at their teachers as role models. A Certificate level training on HCD to all the teachers will be useful in developing themselves as well as children under their care.

Pastors and Christian NGOs

Church is not mere institution with buildings and rituals to perform but a community of believers. Families join and make up the churches. Church is people oriented. The pastors have played a key role in educating the parents and their children through the ministries of preaching, teaching, Christian Education programmes and counseling. The ultimate goal of ministering to children is stated as follows.[14]

> As ministers to the child, we seek to meet fully his present and unfolding needs, to the end that we bring him to self-fulfillment and maturity in Christian faith characterized by (a) personal acceptance of Jesus Christ as Saviour and Lord; (b) mature decision-making and behavior reflecting the internalized Christian values; and (c) righteousness, true holiness, and the fullness of the stature of Jesus Christ.

This ultimate goal is expected to be achieved with specific tasks and programmes based on certain intermediate goals. For example, most of the churches have their own Sunday Schools to teach scripture to children and build their spiritual life. The main focus in serving the children so far in many churches is to root them up in Christian faith, nurture and catechism and not necessarily developing them holistically addressing their problems in families or schools or neighbourhood. Nor helping the needy poor children with financial grants to get educated or dealing with their psychological trauma of discrimination, being abused or lacking recognition and encouragement. A critical analysis of the Christian Education programme in India and the need of a holistic curriculum for holistic development of children has been discussed in a recent article.[15] The need for change in curriculum is felt but the same old doctrine oriented methods of teaching continues in Sunday Schools because the churches are not getting the help of experts of Christian Education. Effective net working between them is lacking. A systematic HCD programme to teach the way Christians should develop their parenting of children is not offered in many churches. Biblical teachings on parenting as a sacred and required duty should be taught periodically to parents as they pass through different stages of their married life.

The curriculum used in some theological colleges is western and outdated. Even in the academic programme of colleges, the dimension of children did not get enough attention. One or two subjects on children are included in the syllabi of Christian Education Department to teach students to conduct Sunday Schools and youth meetings. Some important subjects focusing on children in different discipline such as 'Understanding of Children from Biblical Perspectives', 'Children at Risk and their Rights', 'Marriage, Family and Parenting Children', 'Child Theology', 'Child, Church and Mission' and 'Counseling Children in Crisis' are missing in our theological education. Although there is a difference of opinion about defining and doing Child Theology, the exploration from biblical, theological, contextual perspectives taken up by individuals and institutions in different parts of the world is challenging us for new hermeneutic and developing biblical, theological and missional foundations for HCD.[16] Many issues identified from the context are demanding a paradigm shift in our understanding of children, curriculum of teaching and learning process and mission to them.[17]

Various dimensions such as biblical, theological, historical, contextual, pastoral and missional are combined to make the curriculum. It demands the integration of theory and practice in their training. The Curriculum of HCD with more than 30 subjects is published in India and distributed to various institutions in Ethiopia, Kenya, South Africa, Philippines, Singapore, Nepal and Sri Lanka offering HCD courses. Although this curriculum provides a frame work for offering the courses, the seminaries can modify the syllabus of the subjects to suit to their cultural context. The well-being of the families and societies and having able leadership in various sectors of our nation are in the hands of present and future generation. The urgent need is to bring a vision for children, develop a heart for them and mobilize the co-operation of institutions such as family, schools and colleges, religious centers of worship and government to raise up a new generation to transform the world.

Endnotes

[1] M.K. Gandhi, *India of My Dreams*, Ahmedabad: Navajivan Publishing House, 1995, p.187.

[2] J.C. Aggarwal, *Modern Indian Education: History, Development and Problems*, Delhi: SHIPRA Publications, 2003 (spl. Chapters 1-4 Pages 1-31). J.B. Jeyaraj, 'Higher Education: Models and Value Orientation: An Indian Perspective', *TBT Journal*, 7, 1. 2005, pp. 54-67.

[3] Louis Dumont, *Homo Hierarchicus: The Caste System and Its implications*, Delhi: Oxford University Press, 2008, 33-64. Anita Diehl, *Periyar E.V. Ramaswami*, Madras: B.I. Publications, 1978, pp. 50-52. Bipan Chandra, Mirdula Mukherjee and Adotya Mukherjee, *India After Independence 1947-2000*, New Delhi: Penguin Books, 2000. p. 449.

[4] J.C. Ingleby, *Missionaries, Education and India: Issues in Protestant Missionary Education in the Long Nineteenth Century*, Delhi: ISPCK, 2000,   (chs. 6, and 10).

[5] M.K. Gandhi, *India of My Dreams*, Ahmedabad: Navajivan Publishing House, 1995, pp. 184-189, *Hind Swaraj Or Indian Home Rule*, NPH, 1994, pp. 77-82 and *Constructive Programme: Its Meaning and Place*, NPH, 1994. P. 14.

[6] Asha Bajpai, *Child Rights in India: Law, Policy and Practice*, Delhi: OUP, 2006, pp. 326-329.

[7] Manu N. Kulkarni, 'Child Survival Programmes Revisited' *Economic and Political Weekly*, New Delhi, 7th Jan 2006, pp. 28-30.

[8] J.B. Jeyaraj, 'Biblical Perspectives on Children and Their Protection' in Children at Risk: Issues and Challenges (CAR), Delhi: ISPCK/CFCD-India, 2009, pp. 1-31.

[9] S.K. Kapoor, *Human Rights Under International Law and Indian Law*, Allahabad: Central Law Agency, 2001, ch.3, pp. 23-27.

[10] www. Convention on the Rights of the Child, See: Thomas Paul, 'Child Rights Approach and Child Participation' in *Children at Risk: Issues and Challenges* (eds. J.B. Jeyaraj, C. Gnanakan, T. Swaroop and P. Phillips), Delhi: ISPCK/CFCD, 2009. Pp. 93-103.

[11] www. Indian Constitution, Section 'Right to Education'.

[12] www. Literacy-Profile-Know India: National Portal of India, pp.1-2.

[13] Each year thousands of children aged between 6-14 run away from their homes and found in the streets of towns and cities. One of the Christian NGOs called Bosco Mane rescues hundreds of children coming to Bangalore .Ref. G. Kollashany (ed.), *Street Presence: Bosco's Innovative Approach to Reaching Children on Streets*, Bangalore: NRDC, 2006.

[14] Roy B Zuck and Robert E Clark (eds.), *Childhood Education in the Church*, Chicago: Moody Press, 1978, pp. 23f.

[15] Varghese Thomas, 'Beyond Sunday School: The Indirect-Curriculum for Children in the Church' in HER Journal, Chennai: Hindustan Bible Institute, 3, 2008-2009, pp. 45-64.

[16] Keith J White and Haddon Willmer, *An Introduction to Child Theology*, London: CTM, 2006. Roy Zuck, *Precious in His Sight: Childhood and hildren in the Bible*, Grand Rapids: Baker Books, 1996, Marcia J Bunge (ed.t), *The Child in Christian Thought*, Grand Rapids: Eerdmans, 2001 and her article 'The Child, Religion,and the Academy: Developing Robust Theological and Religious Understanding of Children and Childhood' in Journal of Religion, 86, 4, 2006, p.549ff., Douglas McConnell, Jennifer Oroa and Paul Stockley (eds.), *Understanding God's Heart for Children: Toward a Biblical Framework*, Hyderabad: Authentic Books, 2007, J.B. Jeyaraj, 'Child in the Midst: Incarnation and Child Theology' in *CAR: Issues and Challenges*, Delhi: ISPCK/CFCD, 2009, pp. 49-73. Dan Brewster, *Child Church and Mission*, Colorado: Compassion International, 2008.

[17] More than 30 contextual problems and issues of children are discussed in various articles in the book *CAR*, Delhi: ISPCK/CFCD, 2009. Also see: Glenn Miles and Josephine-Joy Wright (eds.), *Celebrating Children: Equipping People working with Children and Young People Living in Difficult Circumstances around the world*, Cumbria: Paternoster, 2003.

CHAPTER - 7

Mission Agenda
of Holistic Child Development

The word 'Mission' picked up from Christianity, is now widely used by various religious communities to refer to their organizations, schools and projects. It is not appearing in the Bible to be called as biblical term but it is used as a theological term introduced in the later period of history of Christianity. My concern is about recognizing the contemporary movements working for the welfare of children. Often the study of mission or focus on missionary legacy is about the history or theology of the traditional and colonial missions and missionaries. I agree, that there is so much to explore on colonial missions. But the study of mission is not giving that much importance to the work done among children. Some of the Indians who did missionary work among children in villages, tribal areas and slums are not yet studied and documented. The biblical teachings that motivated them to work for children throughout their life is not explored. Their understanding of mission to and with children are not formulated as their legacy.[1] Children are the future leaders of the family, church and nation. My concern in this paper is to emphasize the mission agenda of reaching with the Gospel, liberating and rooting in faith and ethical life and empowering children holistically and to make it important in our ministries. Let me explain first the concept of HCD with some biblical illustrations and move on to discuss the basis of the agenda. Finally I point out briefly the names of modern movements with HCD agenda.

I.   BASIS FOR THE AGENDA

An 'agenda' is described generally as a matter of business to be discussed and implemented. Mission of God (*missio Dei*) cannot go on without agenda. In studying and doing the mission, the Great Commission in Matt.28:19-20 is regarded as an important agenda.   The evangelical agenda emphasizes evangelism and church planting and charitable service as important mission. The Lausanne Covenant is a comprehensive and well balanced agenda for mission including the Great Commission and the Great Commandment of loving God and people (Mt. 22:38; Jn. 15:17; Rom. 13:10). The ecumenical missiology emphasizes humanization, liberation and inter-faith dialogue as important mission. Who sets the agenda for mission? What is the basis to draw the agenda? In my opinion, we can recognize three important sources for drawing agenda namely, Biblical demand, contextual challenge and ecclesiastical responsibility.

1.   Biblical Mandate

We can know God's mandate for mission from the Scripture. Since we are selective in our reading and emphasizing what we like, we fail to see the agenda for the various sections of society particularly for the children who are regarded as the last and least in the society. Missiologists look for a statement or command to do mission as in Matt. 28:19-20. I call this kind of statement or command in the Bible for mission as *'explicit mandate'*. The statement is self- explanatory and any reader can easily understand it. The literal meaning of such commands is enough for action. But we cannot limit the mission agenda to explicit mandate alone. We need to use a different hermeneutical approach in discovering the mission agenda from other texts narrating events or stories. They need exposition and articulation of the meaning of the text into a form of mandate. I call such a formation of mandate through exposition as *'expositional mandate'*. For example Isa. 61:1-4 and Lk. 4:18-21 need explanation to make it a mandate for liberation. Similarly references and stories about children need to be articulated in the form of mandate for the mission to/ with children. In the mission of holistic child development, we find a few explicit mandates in the Bible and we need to bring out expositional mandate. I have highlighted below some texts for both kinds of mandate.

It is surprising in this process of studying the texts related to children to note that the mandate tells us that the mission of holistic child development has two sides – on the one side, it is a mission to children by the adults regarding children as objects of our mission and on the other hand, children are also agents of mission together with adults serving God and the community.

Mission to Children

More than 1400 references are about children in the Bible[2]. A detailed study of these texts reveal the theological significance of children that they are gift of God, created in the image of God, teach us parenthood and challenge our ministry[3]. Dt.6:6, one of the explicit mandates for mission to children regarded as *Shema*, speaks of developing faith and spirituality in children. The families of ancient Israelites were told to teach the law of God to their children and their generations and practice the divine values. Another explicit mandate is to 'train up a child in the way he should go' (Prov. 22:6). The word 'way' is used in many places in the Book of Psalms to refer to the way of the Lord, that is, the divine law and will. The imperative verb 'to train' (*hanak*) means to dedicate or consecrate. In the ancient Israel, each child is to be dedicated to walk in the ways of the Lord . The Israelites did not separate life into spiritual and secular. For them it is integrated. Walking in the ways of the Lord means living to the expectation of God in their spiritual and secular life. Their entire life is based on the commandments of God. The book of Deuteronomy emphasizes this integration that they can enjoy life in the promised land (Dt.8:1).

The law of God demanded them to take care of the orphans, widows and the family of the sojourners in the midst of them (Dt.10:14-19James 1:26-27). Orphans need food, clothes and shelter. Similarly the children of the sojourners needed physical and economic growth. The community of Israel cannot ignore the physical and economic development of the marginalized children in the midst of them. They need to provide for their growth and development. In relating to such needy children, they are asked to maintain their sociological relationship and not to discriminate them. The children who are orphans and belonging to the families of sojourners who are dependent on the society need not feel bad for being at the receiving end.

God, as the parent for orphans and guardian of the families of sojourners has taken care of them by instructing a mission mandate (Ex. 22:22, 23:9, Dt.14:28-29; Prov. 14:31, 21:17) to the rest of the community to develop these children in the midst of them. God is not asking for a charitable service to them but an obligatory mission of development to help them till they can stand on their own feet. That is why taking care of orphanages is not a sort of business but a missionary work to empower the needy children.

Mission with the children

Holistic child development can be fostered more when adults work with the children. HCD is not like one way traffic to make children at the receiving end and adults treating them as consumers of their help. HCD is an inclusive mission to develop the receiver and the giver. Both parties can learn from each other. Children gain more experience from the expertise of adults and develop their thinking and skill. Adults learn simplicity, humility and can identify the needed area of the development of children. That is why Jesus used a child as an example to his disciples (Mt.18:1-6). Nicodemus was asked to be born again in the sense of being transformed like a child (Jn. 3:1-10). Eli, the priest of the temple at Shiloh worked closely with Samuel. In spite of his failure to train his own sons to fear and obey God, he encouraged Samuel to respond to the call of God and receive God's word (1.Sam.3:1-18). Eli was not jealous of Samuel and did not suppress him. Rather, he guided him to receive the word of God. He trained Samuel not to hide anything from him even if it is against him. His encouragement gave Samuel courage to stand for truth, honesty and openness and led Samuel to tell everything to Eli. He did not curse Samuel but acknowledged what he said. His response to Samuel was theological (v.18). He taught Samuel even at that situation that Yahweh is the Lord and the righteous judge. Eli would have learnt that God can use a child to receive and proclaim his word and he should support Samuel in God's ministry. The immediate formula following the response of Eli in the story points out that Samuel grew up (v.19) and not marginalized. He enjoyed the favour of God. The Lord did not fail him in proving the words Samuel proclaimed. Thus he got the support of God, Eli and the rest of the people from Dan to Beersheba. The mandate we can formulate out of the exposition of the story of Samuel from the perspective of HCD is that the leaders need to recognize the gift, and ministry of children and co-operate with them for mutual learning and development.

Another case of the mission of a child for the nation can be seen in the life and achievement of David. He was not well recognized in his family. His brothers were unable to defeat Goliath. Saul, the king did not know how to deal with the danger of attack on Israel by the Philistine kings. David came forward to kill Goliath. The king and his warriors allowed him to go and defeat Goliath. They could not discourage David and stop him from going against Goliath with his sling and stones (1.Sam.17:29-55). Their support to David came after seeing the victory. They went for war with David after defeating Goliath and completed the task. A child did the mission of liberating the Israelites from the constant attack and suppression of the Philistines[4]. The mission of David was political. The event would have developed David more to work for God and his people. It gave him immeasurable experience to develop his faith, reason and personality to contribute for the political and social development of the nation. The people also developed their faith in God and thinking by joining the mission of David. He grew in the favour of the King and people till Saul turned against David later. The mandate out of this event is to allow and support children who can do liberative mission and develop the nation.

Children can be part of God's mission as we notice in the service of the servant girl of Naaman (2 Kings 5:3, 15-16). Again we notice in the case of a child coming forward to give his five loaves and two fishes to Jesus during his mission of preaching and teaching the five thousand people (Jn.6:1-14). The child could have kept the food for himself but willing to share what he has, reveals his concern for others. The child is socially developed to have concern for others and share the resources for feeding the people. Jesus accepted the boy as a partner in his mission. He did not ignore his small resource offered for others. Many could be the children among the five thousand who received the food. They did not return to their homes in hunger and thirst. The boy would not have imagined that Jesus would do a miracle of multiplying the resource he gave to Jesus. In fact, Jesus worked with the boy using his resources to be multiplied to feed the five thousand. The rest of the disciples took part in the mission of distribution admiring the willingness of the boy and the power of Jesus multiplying the resources. This mission, as an example, is an aspect of social development albeit a single incident. The mandate we draw from this incident is that if each one can share their resources to deal with hunger and poverty as the small boy did, greater development of the society can happen. Many children can be benefited. The mandate is to share the resources, as an example set by the child, is a challenge to the rich and the well developed nations of the world.

2.   Contextual Challenge

Not only the Bible sets the agenda but also the local context. I have discussed the problems and prospects of children in other articles[5]. I need not elaborate it here because my essay gives some statistics. The websites of UNO and other NGOs are providing alarming statistics on child abuse[6]. My concern to include the contextual challenge is to take the context serious for the mission of HCD. Many children are facing so many problems that demands for holistic development of children. Millions of children need food, shelter and clothing. They need physical development to be healthy and strong. Many other children are in child labour to support their families with the meagre income they earn. They are deprived of their childhood and education. They need social, economic and educational development. Many young girls of 10-15 years from rural and tribal areas are forced to be sex workers. Some boys are kidnapped for the sake of taking their kidneys or forced to sell drugs and steal. Millions of children are celebrating their mothers' day without their mothers since they died of AIDS/HIV. Siblings get separated because of divorce and separation of husband and wife. The various sociological, economic, political and psychological reasons indicate the urgent need of developing the children in these areas. Christian mission cannot be limited to charitable service alone as I pointed out earlier. The agenda must be wider and inclusive of overall development of a child.

3.   Ecclesiastical Responsibility

Another important basis for the holistic child development is the responsibility of the Church. God has given his mission to the church to serve humanity[7]. The Church that received the mission and interprets God's word exists not only for worship and fellowship but also to do the ministry to the community within and outside the church. The Church is the sole agent of God on the earth to serve the entire creation. Children are one of the key stakeholders of the church and members of the Kingdom (Matt.18:1-6, Mk.10:14-15, Lk. 18:17) and local community.[8] They are part and parcel of the church either through infant baptism or dedication, born to Christian parents or in a non-Christian families but joined the church because they heard the Gospel and started coming to the church and attend Sunday School with the plan of getting the baptism. However, they are regarded as the least because they are still dependent on their parents and marginalized in the process of participation and decision making.[9] Without children in the local church, there is no guarantee for the existence of the local church in the future. The churches without the present generation of children can be closed down without members in the future. Many churches in the Western countries were closed down because they ignored the development of children, their key stakeholders. The survival of the local church itself depends on the development of the present generation of children. The leadership of the church and the growth of human and financial resources of a local church depend on the effort spent in developing the children. Bambang regards children as the partners in mission and writes, 'Children and youths are in the best position to relate positively to people of all ages, races, and social status...Sadly the church has not seriously considered children as partners for mission and has not adequately equipped them for the work. In the context of mission and transformation, children and young people have been either invisible or sidelined.'[10] Should we develop children for the sake of maintaining a local church? Can a local church, a visible body of Christ on earth neglect children, one of the members of its own body?

Dr. Dan Brewster sees the cry and demand of Rachel asking Jacob, 'Give me children or I shall die' (Gen.30: 1) as a prophetic voice for today's church. Unless the churches take this prophetic cry as a mandate for them and develop children, they have no future. I notice a socio-political aspect in the cry of the same Rachel when described by Jeremiah (31:15) and Matthew (2:17-18) as the mother representing all Israel weeping for her children who were victims of war and political injustice. Although the mothers of the children need consolation, Rachel's cry is relevant even today indicating the need of development of the social, psychological and peaceful life of children in society. The church has a mandate to develop children and that is why many churches and organizations have mission to children and engaged in various activities to develop the children. Nevertheless, many churches do not see the importance of ministry to children inside and outside their walls and do not have proper budget or staff trained in HCD to work in the Sunday School, VBS, CBS and orphanages or Community Development Project.

MODERN MOVEMENTS WITH 'HCD' AGENDA

Many mission movements have emerged with distinctive emphasis in different decades because of realizing the contextual challenge and in effect re-reading the Bible. The traditional mission of proclamation, witness and social service is continuing. Nevertheless, missionary organizations with specific focus and action such as eco-movements, feminist movements and human rights movements emerged and are contributing for justice and peace and development. I am not denying the contribution of churches, NGOs and missions for the welfare of children over the centuries. Ministry to children goes on from the time of founding the ancient Israelite society.[11] However, each institution gives priority to meet the need of spiritual or physical development except some missions in tribal or rural situation meet the holistic need of spiritual, physical, social, psychological and educational development

Some movements such as ViVa-International, 4/14 Window, Child Theology Movement, Global Alliance for HCD and Jubilee Institute of India have taken the agenda of HCD as their primary mission.[12] They may continue as a catalyst movements promoting the vision of holistic development of children, developing missiological basis for HCD and training parents, pastors, seminarians, activists and teachers for the cause of children or gradually become established missionary organization in the sense of sending missionaries to work with children.

Ministries either done by churches or missions or pare-church organizations need to include the agenda of holistic child development in their programmes, budget and activities. Children and youths are one third of the population in India. This large segment cannot be ignored in our ministries.[13] I firmly believe that the HCD education in the seminaries, training institutes of missions and NGOs can sustain the vision and the mission for children for years to come.

Endnotes

[1] The limited information I have is that books are written about the life, theology and ministry of Amy Carmichael and Pandita Ramabai for children. But not much is explored about the life, theology and ministry of Serampore Trio, P. Samuel of Bethel, Danishpet, School of Bangarapet with the team of Hamiltons contributing for Christian Education, Ms. Huldah Buntain of Calcutta, the influence of 'Paliar Nesan' of CSI Thirunelveli Diocese, national missionaries in North India, North West and North East India. Reports, biographies and souvnirs are published. Yet, their theological understanding of children are not analysed and articulated. Seminaries should encourage students to write their thesis on these leaders from the perspective of mission to and with children that they can provide resources for further research and writing.

[2] Roy Zuck, *Precious in His Sight*, Grand Rapids: Baker, 1996. See: Index and References at the end of the book.

[3] J.B. Jeyaraj, 'Biblical Perspectives on Children and Their Protection' *Children at Risk: Issues and Challenges (ISPCK/CFCD, Delhi, 2009)*, 1-31.

[4] Gustavo Crocker and Karissa Glanville, 'Children and God's Mission' in *Understanding God's Heart for Children* (eds. Douglas McConnel, Jennifer Orona and Paul Stockley), Hyderabad: OM-Authentic Books, 2007, p.268f.

[5] Refer to various articles in CAR book, 2009.

[6] A brief list of websites are given in the *HCD Education: Curriculum Book for MA, M.Th and Ph.D*, (CFCD-India, Bangalore, 2010), pp. 251-265.

[7] Different models of ministry given to the Church are discussed in my book, *Christian Ministry: Models of Ministry and Training* (TBT, Bangalore, 2002) and reprinted 2006. I discussed the issue of relationship between the Church and the Kingdom also in the same book.

[8] Bambang Budijanto, 'The Ecclesia of Jesus Christ' – unplublished paper and quoted by Dan Brewster in his book, *Child, Church and Mission* (Compassion International, USA, 2011), Revised Edition, p.87.

[9] I discussed the missisological aspect of liturgy and worship related to children in my article, 'Liturgical Perspective of Family and Parenting' in *Journal of Theological Education and Mission* (JOTEAM, (New India Bible Seminary, Tiruvalla, Kerala), 3, Feb. 2012,pp. 61-80.

[10] Bambang Budijanto, 'Children: New Energy for the 21st Century Mission' *Emerging Missions Movements: Voices of Asia* (ed. Bambang Budijanto), (Compassion International, 2010), p. 48f.

[11] I discussed the different laws protecting children in ancient society in my article, 'Biblical Perspectives on Children and their Protection' *CAR* Book, 2009, pp. 1-32.

[12] Refer to their publications and website to know more about the history, theology and contribution of these movements. I had already written briefly about these movements in my article, 'Holistic Child Development: Initiatives and Impact in South Asia' in the book *Repairer of Broken Walls: Essays on Holisitic Child Development* (eds. J.B. Jeyaraj, Rosalind Tan, Shiferaw Michael, Enrique Pindedo, ISPCK/CFCD/GA-HCD, 2014) pp. 289-302.

[12] Enlarged version of this essay is published in ACTS Theological Journal (Vol. 16, 2011), Korea, pp. 273-292.

CHAPTER - 8

Raising up a New Generation: Vision and Mission

Human generation continues on this earth ever since God created human beings. The planet earth faced many threatening forces which could have destroyed the planet completely and wiped off all human beings and leaving the earth empty. The covenant with Noah reminds us God's concern and commitment not to destroy the world (Gen. 9:11-12). The Lord God who created the heaven and earth and male and female in his own image pronounced the blessing to multiply and fill the earth (Gen. 1:26-28). This blessing of procreation is a precious gift of God to humanity. God did not withhold the power to procreate but given it to human beings that they will have children of their own. Their biological connection would develop naturally love, affection, care, joy and responsibility towards their offspring. It is an inseparable bond which will continue throughout their life with their children may be increasing steadily or in varying degree whether their children live closely or at a distance. The bond of the parents with their children and grandchildren continue till death. It is a privilege to see the children of their children and enjoy the presence of their descendants. We long to see not only our sons and daughters but also the future generation living in good health enjoying wealth and status. This blessing cannot happen automatically. It demands a great responsibility of raising up our own children and their descendants. The age limit of a generation cannot be fixed. One generation may live for 70-80 years if they are healthy (cf. Ps. 90:10). The OT points out a cycle for one generation is 40 years. However, I focus on developing children from birth to 18 years of age for the purpose of this essay. This essay is not written out of research but out of my concern for having good generation at present and in the future. I am listing briefly the six requirements of actions if we want to raise a new generation.

I.   NEED FOR RAISING UP A NEW GENERATION

1.   Contemporary situation of Children

We notice a rapid change in our civilization. The socio-economic and political factors influence the society at large and families, the basic unit of the society. Children are at risk in every society. Many children are unable to overcome the problems they face and become victims of the conditions in which they live. Many statistics and issues of children discussed in journals and books are not repeated here.[1] However, these problems can be classified as spiritual, social, economic, psychological and cultural. Lack of effort to orient children in spirituality, religious and moral instruction and providing opportunities to develop their spiritual life through prayer or bible studies or youth fellowship affected them to have a deep root in their religious beliefs and tradition. Liberal theologies of local churches or too much emphasis on secular way of life have led many children and youths to avoid church and hate their own religion. Neither these children have a religious base nor proper ethical life and became a prey to lead a loose living. When facing crisis in their lives, they do not have strength to overcome the pressure by their spirituality. They may like to use drugs or alchocol or commit suicide. Social problems such as pressure from peer groups, lack of identity, losing parents and being orphans or living with single parent due to divorce and separation of parents affect children so much that they either run away from home or drop their studies and accept labour for cheap wages or trafficked to sexual abuse. Some of them become a problem to their families, communities and nation. Parents and teachers do not know how to handle and help them to overcome their problems.

2.   A Definition of 'New Generation'

How do we define the phrase 'new generation'? Many of us understand it in a simple sense of having grand children, the next descendants for our sons and daughters. But it is not limited to having next generation. The word 'new' here means something different and of good quality. It is of value and worth having in this world. It refers to generation with good health, values, principles, broader outlook for peace and harmony, sense of stewardship and high ethical life. The Bible places importance on loving, fearing and obeying God. The Israelites were asked to pass on the teachings of God to their next generation.

> 'These are the commands, decrees and laws the Lord your God directed me to teach you to observe…so that you, your children and their children after them may fear the Lord your God as long as you live... Love the Lord your God with all your heart and with all your soul and with all your strength. These commandments that I give you today are to be upon your hearts. Impress them on your children…" - (Dt.6:1-9).

All the commandments in the Old Testament have both vertical and horizontal dimension. Obeying the law of God includes relating to others. One's vertical relationship with God should result in relating horizontally to the people in society. Jesus brought out this importance explicitly in his teaching to love God and our neighbor (Mark 12:28-31). He challenged his disciples and audience to prove it by being light and salt to the people that God may be glorified by seeing and benefitting out of their good work (Mt. 5:13-16).

Paul, having studied the Law and practiced the Law came to know the Lord Jesus Christ. His experience with Christ brought a radical change in his thinking and life and gave a powerful definition for 'new generation' as 'new creation'. If anyone is 'in Christ' (*en Christo*), every aspect of his or her life becomes new (2 Cor. 5:17). Such a person is re-generated as new in Jesus Christ. The bad old nature is cleansed by the blood of Jesus shed on the Cross and passes away. That person inherits the new nature by accepting Jesus as his or her personal Saviour and the authority of the Bible as normative for life. The teachings of the Scripture are valid for generation to generation that we practice them and train our future generation to accept and practice them in their lives. Paul makes it clear that there will be always a struggle between the old nature and new nature but re-generated person can overcome bad nature with the power of the Holy Spirit given to the person (Rom. 8:12-16).

II.   MISSION FOR RAISING UP NEW GENERATION

Raising up a new generation cannot happen without some actions taken by the present generation. A traditional African proverb says, 'It takes the whole village to raise a child'. These actions have to continue in each generation to raise up a new generation.

1.   *Recapturing the vision for children*

Children do not get importance often in our society because of either patriarchal structure or taken for granted till they become youths. When some voice is raised suddenly about children in the newspapers or Television, we remember children and pay attention to their problems narrated in the media. If those children are not our own or living far away, we sympathize with them for few moments or a day and then we forget them. The media can only touch our emotions but we need an enduring vision for children. Having vision for children need not necessarily be limited to understanding the problems and prospects of children but more in terms of concern for building the children as a new creation.

Although the Bible has hundreds of references to children, we fail to notice and capture the vision for children. Some writers of the narratives mentioned the problem of children (e.g. Hagar leaving the child to die in her desperate situation – Gen.16:7-16, death of a child of a sex worker and a quarrel to claim the living baby – 1 Kings 3:16-28; agreed to boil the child and eat during the severe famine – 2 Kings 6:24-30).[2] But the prophets of different periods challenged the generation to recapture the vision for children through prophecies. Their prophecies having everlasting validity, challenge us today to gain the vision for children as we read the Scripture.

Joel who lived in the Southern kingdom possible between 8th-4th century BC, mentions many things in his prophecy but did not fail to have vision for children and youths.[3] He prophesied that sons and daughters will receive and use the gift of prophecy (2:28-29). The Israelites understood that the gift of prophecy is given to adults particularly to the prophets. Joel challenged his audience to have a new vision of children as valuable instrument in the hands of God. They should not ignore the role of children in God's ministry. When the Priests, Pharisees, Sadducees and Scribes dominated the ministry and showing themselves as authority over the Law and Prophets, children were not even thought of as instrument of God that they can receive the gift of prophecy as the prophets of the OT period. In that situation, this prophecy was quoted again by the Apostle Peter to awaken his audience not to ignore children. They were asked to recapture the emphasis of Joel that children will be used by God (Acts 2:17-18).

In the pre-exilic period around 8th century, Isaiah of Jerusalem did not forget to mention about children. His prophecy about Immanuel – God with us- is always remembered in connection with the birth of Jesus. Nevertheless, he challenged his people that children are important in the sight of God and the society cannot ignore them. He pointed out that children and ferocious animals such as lion, wolf and leopard can sit together without harming each other. A little child will lead them (Isa. 11:6). Again, he mentions an infant will play near the hole of the cobra and the young child put his hand into the viper's nest (v.7-8).[4] It is unbelievable and not practical. Using this metaphor, he is calling us to understand that a child, first of all, can have safety only when powerful people do not abuse them. Secondly, a child can lead in the sense of being an instrument in God's ministry or society only when the powerful relinquish their authority and control over them and pave the way for their leadership. This vision of Isaiah requiring changes in our structures and approaches needs to be captured by us today to raise up a new generation to do ministry to them as well as with them.

The Prophet Zachariah who prophesized during the post-exilic period of restoring the country had a vision for children.[5] He rejoiced that the streets of the city of Jerusalem will be filled with boys and girls and they will be playing without anyone to harm them (8:4-5). The vision for children includes creating cordial and safe environment. We always emphasize the development of moral when we think of raising up a new generation. But raising up a new generation requires providing good environment that children can learn and develop themselves in right direction.

Malachi too had a vision that the hearts of the fathers will be turned to their children and the hearts of children to their fathers (4:5).[6] He concludes this prophecy with the warning from the Lord that the land will be cursed if the turning of the hearts failed to happen (v.6). The action of 'turning the hearts' here is an important requirement. First, this text is linking fathers and children in the action of turning to each other. Usually, the text of Proverbs demands children to turn their hearts and mind to God and parents (4.1-6; 6:20-21; 13:1; cf.Ps. 119:9). Fathers represent the adult or older generation and children represent the present generation. The older generation is asked to turn the heart to the present younger generation and vice versa for a purpose. Second, the word 'turning' (Heb. *Shub*) is not simply listening (Heb. *Shamea* – to hear) but more than listening.[7] The Prophet used deliberately the word 'heart' than 'ears'. Heart is regarded as the seat of emotions and desires. One can open the heart for listening or developing desires or showing mercy and grace or harden it as Pharaoh did. Turning the heart means, paying attention, giving importance and fulfilling responsibility. This is demanded of both fathers and children. Fathers turn their attention to children, understand their situation, need and develop them. They are expected to develop the generation according to the principles of the Word of God. On the other hand, children are asked to pay attention to their fathers who impart values and develop them in godly manner. They need to co-operate with their fathers if they want to rise up as a renewed generation. Third, failing to raise up a new generation can result in having sinful generation in Israel. Such a result is a curse is told to the Israelites (Dt.28-29). The nation will lose God's blessing because of the failure of raising up a renewed generation. The land shall face a lot of social problems in the family and society.

Jesus gave importance to children in his ministry. He challenged his disciples to welcome children and to keep them in front of their eyes as a role model to become like children manifesting the nature of children in their lives to enter the kingdom of God.[8] Jesus gave a radical declaration that the kingdom of God belongs to children. He asked his disciples to make it possible to each child in each generation (Mt. 18:1-6; Mk. 9:33-37, 10:10-16).

2.   *Re-reading the Bible and formulating Theologies related to children*
Why should we re-read the Bible and formulate Child Theology to raise up a new generation? Many Christians read again and again the Bible as a routine exercise for their devotion and draw spiritual message to strengthen their faith. Re-reading is a technical term meaning reading the text with a particular

perspective or approach or methodology. One can read the text with a perspective of leadership or environment or counseling or children. This exercise is needed to study what the text says on that particular focus or issue.

In doing re-reading, some basic hermeneutical principles should be applied. First, the text should have mentioned that issue or topic. If the text is not speaking about it, then we cannot insert our own idea into the text and interpret it. Second, the meaning of the text should be seen in its historical context before applying to present day context. Third, the reader should see the purpose of the author for writing this text and the way the writer has connected the text with preceding and following passages. Fourth, keeping the text in focus, exposition can be developed out of the verses in that text. The articulation or interpretation should be centered on the text. Using these guidelines of hermeneutics, feminists have brought out new insights on texts speaking on women. Reading the texts from the perspective of environment brought out Eco-theology. Management experts have extracted insights on leadership and administration from those texts speaking on resources, conflicts and stewardship. Counselors have re-interpreted many psalms to console the persons in suffering. In a similar direction, many started re-reading the texts on children and developing theologies such as theology of childhood and child theology.

Scholars may have difference of opinion on these theologies related to children and raise their critical comments. Nevertheless, theological basis is to be developed through re-reading and re-interpreting texts for various reasons. Secular books say different theories of child development. But, first, we must know what the Bible says about children if we want to raise a new generation. Secondly, developing children holistically includes their spirituality. Secular ideologies or theories of psychology or sociology may speak of developing children physically, cognitively, emotionally, educationally, economically and socially. They often omit the aspect of spiritual development because it is connected to religious teachings. Each religious community has its own scripture and theology for their spiritual development. For Christians, it is the biblical teaching about God, parents and children contribute for the development of spirituality. Third, theologies developed out of re-reading texts on children, help us to evaluate the doctrines and teachings on children. Many denominations have created doctrines, liturgies and rituals during the colonial period and using them till today without evaluating and revising them. The status, rights and role of children are not given much importance in such kind of doctrines and liturgies. The result is that churches neglected preaching and teaching on children and training parents with new insights to develop their children as new creation and as a witness in today's context. Many children and youths do not cherish to be part of the ministry of the churches. Fourth, developing child theology or theology of childhood out of biblical insights and contextual challenges gives us a theological basis and moral support to continue the ministry to children. This can give some guiding principles to churches and families and guard children against the influence of liberal ethics or universalism or to be part of gender discrimination or terrorism when setting new directions in serving children in this post-modern age.

One important caution is to be mentioned here as I mentioned elsewhere in formulating theologies relating to children.[9] The child could be 'in the midst' as a focus or sign of the kingdom of God or an illustration but not to be glorified. The starting point and the center of theology are God and what God says about children instead of what children say about God. It is good to listen what children say about God, their problems, need and see their theological understanding of their Creator and society. But such explanations about God could vary from children to children who are conditioned by their socio-economic situation, personality, geographical condition and culture.

3. Revising the Curriculum and Approaches

Written theologies can remain in books and journals and be used in academic circles for discussions. Unless they are used in training the pastors, evangelists and missionaries and caregivers in NGOs, development of children may not be so enriching. Most of the seminaries have only one or two subjects on children for their students focused on Christian nurture through Sunday Schools, VBS or Christian counseling for youths. Students in seminaries are not given training to develop children holistically except their spiritual life. NGOs give training to their staff to meet the physical need of children. Teachers in schools are trained to develop the academic knowledge of children. Although seminaries, NGOs and schools give importance to one aspect of the development of a child in their ministry, holistic dimension can be included if they are willing to revise their curriculum. The task of raising up a new generation challenges us to raise them up holistically in all the areas of their life. Therefore, we need to focus our attention on revising the existing curriculum or create a new curriculum to train pastors, parents and teachers.

The survey shows that children spent average 10-12 hours at home, 7-8 hours in schools, 2 -3 hours in games or with their friends each day and 2-3 hours in the church on Sundays. If so, then parents need to be trained more that they can help their children to grow spiritually, physically, socially and academically. Many parents do not know how to handle their children. They expect the pastors and school teachers to develop their children and are disappointed when their children are becoming problematic at home or in the church or school or society. Churches should call the parents in batches and teach parenting in different sessions. A simple but practical curriculum can be written by the pastor to train the parents to raise up their children with strong faith in Christ, values, discipline, stewardship of money and resources, honoring others, good in social relationship and be a better citizen of the country. This kind of training need to be based on content as well as developing the skill of parents to use some positive approaches rather than negative approach of scolding with abusive words, canning, corporal punishment, sending them out of homes or placing them in juvenile correction centers. Parents need updated knowledge on nutrition, health and hygiene, using medicines, emotions of children, their peer groups, demand on academic performance and counseling methods if they want to develop children to be good and achieving in this competitive world.

Teachers in schools are well trained in the field of education to contribute for the cognitive development of students. But most of them are not concerned about the rest of the aspects of the life of children. If anyone evaluates the curriculum of education used in the Teacher Training Colleges or Institutes of Education, he or she can notice the lack of emphasis for the holistic development of children. Some of their brilliant students ranking high in academic performance, fail in relating to others properly, showing good manners, love and sharing. Raising up a renewed generation is also the responsibility of the schools. In addition to their training in education, teachers need to be trained in understanding the children to be developed holistically through periodic refresher courses.[10] They need to be aware of the CRC and Child Protection Policy of the institution. The Parent and Teachers Association (PTA) can meet periodically to discuss about each child and enhance the co-operation between parents and teachers.

4.   *Resource development and net-work cooperation*

Training progrommes can be effective only resource materials are developed on the various issues of children. Two kinds of resources are needed. One for the trainers like pastors, parents and teachers in schools. The trainers learn what the Bible says about children, the patriarchal structure of the society and the status of children in families and communities, different psychological theories of child development, the nature, case studies of children in local region, causes and consequences of the problems children face today and the various approaches to help them. The content of these courses can provide theoretical, theological knowledge and practical skills to understand and develop children in their vicinity. It need not necessarily be highly academic or scholarly. These courses should combine knowledge and skills to practice their training.

The other set of resource material is to train children of different age groups providing self-study material and work-book. The standard of each course should vary according to the age group. The content of these material provide knowledge about God, Scriptural values, stories of children in the Bible, caring body, food and nutrition, health, bad habits, manners, controlling emotions, cultivating social relationship, patriotism, care of nature and environment, sex and marriage, parenthood and value of education. These topics can be spread out in different work-book according to the level of age group. Some of these issues can be done at a primary level and sensitive issues can be taught when they come to the age between 13-18 years. The lessons can be studied with the help of pastor or mother or father or teacher who deal with the children. Children use the material under such tutors and get the clarification and answer from them to have proper knowledge.

In order to train pastors, parents and teachers, co-operation of churches, families and schools is needed. The leaders of these institutions in a city or town or village can come together and work out programmes to teach children. To prepare course material for the above mentioned two groups of Trainers and Children, a higher level networking of Denominations of churches, NGOs, seminaries, Christian Education Organizations, social workers, Managers of schools, Missions and representatives of families is necessary. Net-working can help in various ways to avoid duplication of material, improve the quality of content of the courses, organize training programmes for the trainers and share financial resources.

5. Reforming the programmes of churches and missions

Many churches are satisfied with their ministry of worship, prayer meetings, Sunday Schools, bible studies within their four walls and outreach programmes of evangelism and charity. Some churches conduct annual retreats or convention or gospel meetings. Celebrating Harvest Festival, Mission Day, Children Day, Women or Youth fest goes on with elaborate preparation to raise funds for particular need. These activities are good and needed. But periodic evaluation of these ministries inside and outside the church to know whether they are contributing for the welfare and development of children in churches and neighbourhood or not is not done in many churches. A reform is needed in the ministries of churches if churches to be powerful agents of transformation of children. Christian mission of transformational development can reform all aspects of their lives. I have listed a few principles of action to bring transformational development for children.[11]

One of the important areas of reform needed is in modifying the organizational structure of the church to give priority for the ministry of children by creating a special department for children and appointing a fulltime pastor for children, enhancing the budget to develop the spiritual and social needs of children and promoting advocacy conferences and consultations besides annual retreat and conventions. Dr. Dan Brewster has analyzed the functioning of many churches and suggested reform in the areas of worship, songs, prayers, liturgies, sermons, teachings and infra-structure to make churches to be child-friendly.[12] If churches want to contribute for raising up a new generation, they should take bold step to reform their theological understanding of children, doctrines, organizational structure and programmes of ministry. Furthermore, the attitude of churches and seminaries towards children as consumers of the programmes and service needs changes. They should see children and youths as potential partners in mission. The new dimension is to speak of ministry not only to children but also for and with children.

6. Reaching the children of other faiths

Christian children are living in the midst of children belonging to communities of other faiths. They are constantly influenced by their friends in schools or in their neighbourhood and attracted to some of their superstitions, customs and festivals. Not that all the children of other faiths lack good values or principles. Most of them have good values and principles and lead a practicing life. Nevertheless, their world views are based on their religious traditions and culture. Some of them can be contradictory to the teachings of the Bible. The resurgence of religious fundamentalism in many regions of the world has led them to be resistant for any reform in their philosophies and world views. Rather, it is making them to be more fundamentalist. The socio-religious culture of these communities can be a hindrance for children of Christian faith. Raising up a new Christian generation is connected to the task of raising up a new generation of children of other faiths. Doing evangelism and teaching the Bible to them in some places is difficult to change the mind set of children of other faiths. At the same time, it is important to raise them from their views and practices based on superstitions, worship of creation, fertility culture and attitudes of fatalism holy war and terrorism. One of the ways to transform their views and practices is to give value education to the children of other faiths in schools. Value education can change their mind set and look at their views and customs critically to bring some reform in their religion.

Churches can add many more actions to the list mentioned above. Vision for children and a heart to care for them do not emerge easily in the lives of many people. They learn it by their own experience with children in their families and neighbourhood. We need to pray for a revival in the hearts of people and children. Prayer for the work of the Holy Spirit to turn the hearts of the fathers to their children and the hearts of children to their fathers can raise up a new generation and bring blessing to the families, communities and nations. All God's people say with the prophet Zachariah 'Amen'.

Endnotes

[1] See: CAR book.

[2] J.B.Jeyaraj, 'Biblical Perspectives on Children and their Protection', Children at Risk: Issues and Challenges (Delhi: ISPCK-CFCD, 2009), pp.1-30.

[3] See: Commentary on Joel for his period.

[4] J.B.Jeyaraj, 'Biblical Perspectives on children' in CAR Book, pp. 1-31.

[5] See: Commentary on Zachariah for his period.

[6] See: Commentary on Malachi.

[7] BDB Lexicon.

[8] See: J.B. Jeyaraj's artices – 'Churches and Kingdom of God: Relationship and Development of Children' in the booklet titled Churches, Kingdom of God and Children (GA-HCD Study Document Series, 2013) pp, 25-42 also repeated in this book: chapter 3 and 'Child in the Midst: Illustration and Child Theology' in CAR Book, 2009, pp. 49-72.

[9] J.B. Jeyaraj, 'Child in the Midst: Illustration and Child Theology' in CAR book pp. Also refer to Keith White and Hadden Willmer, *Introduction to Child Theology* (UK: CTM) 2009.

[10] J.B. Jeyaraj, 'Children Rights to Education...' Guukul – discusses in detail the need and the list of courses for training teachers.

[11] JBJ Theology of Development.

[12] Dan Brewster, CCM, ch.8.

MINISTERIAL PERSPECTIVE

CHAPTER - 9

Holistic Child Development: Innovation in Theological Education

This essay deals first with the scenario of theological education and the need for innovation and quality enhancement and then proceeds to discuss the emerging Holistic Child Development programme that could be one of the innovative and professional courses in theological education in different parts of the world as this millennium focuses on the cause of children to build the future generations.[1]

Theological education in India is a big enterprise with the mushrooming of bible colleges in some cities training pastors, evangelists and missionaries. One can notice six major streams of theological education in India viz. seminaries affiliated to the Senate of Serampore College (SSC), institutions accredited by the Asia Theological Association (ATA), independent bible colleges not part of SSC or ATA, Christian Studies Department in the secular Universities in Madras, Mysore and Madurai, private Christian Universities such as Allahabad Agricultural University, Martin Luther University and William Carey University in Meghalaya and Distance Education by TAFTEE, AIT, and IIM-RC. A number of students are studying in these streams to work as fulltime or part-time ministers and secular witnesses.

Indian theological education is also unique since we have promoted indigenization of theological education as soon as we got independence from the British colonial rule and created Indian Christian theologies. Indigenization in the early period (appx. 1947-1975) was in terms of developing Indian forms of worship, liturgy, using bhakti traditions, national leadership for churches, missions and seminaries, teaching courses in seminaries in regional languages and producing literature and text books focusing on Indian context. Indian theological education moved from indigenization to contextualization after 1970s by formulating theologies such as liberation, humanization, dalit, tribal, environment and feminist emerging from our own context. While the process of indigenization and contextualization goes on and significant achievements can be reported, Indian theological education still depends on the West for new ideas and funds. Theological discussions going on in the West (e.g ordination of women as priests or consecrating women as bishops and arch-bishops, homo-sexuality, combating racism, inter-faith dialogue, church growth, power evangelism and prosperity theology) set the theological discussions in India in similar fashion. Of course, it is not possible to come out of the global net work and influence. Nevertheless, it is important to discuss common issues, concerns and trends in the light of Indian context. Innovative programmes and approaches can be encouraged to make theological education relevant for the changing scenario in churches and communities.

I.   INNOVATIONS AND QUALITY ENHANCEMENT IN THEOLOGICAL EDUCATION

Theological education in many parts of Asia is still traditional following the western pattern of Departments, subjects, class room teaching methods, assignments and evaluations lacking inter-disciplinary approach, practical involvement in society and learning through experience. Some churches have not yet revised their curriculum and training method for their seminaries for more than 30-50 years. Some seminaries have emphasized evangelism and not the holistic dimension of training. Some are donor-driven to offer only those subjects and programmes dictated by their donors. Either due to these constraints or out of ignorance, innovations are not happening in the educational process of most of the seminaries. Let me mention briefly three major areas for innovations.

New Programmes

There are some seminaries particularly regional medium seminaries established decades ago with the B.Th programme, have not introduced any new programme. Upgrading their existing B.Th programmes as well as introducing new programmes such as BD or M.Div and M.Th is not happening as expected. Even if the leadership proposes to upgrade and introduce new programmes of higher level, the proposal is not accepted either by the faculty members or the Board. Most of the ATA colleges are still having B. Th. as their main programmes. B.Th programmes of colleges in SSC still go on but a development has been made to face out B.Th gradually by integrating it with B.D. Since B.Th and BD/M.Div are regarded as basic training for ministry with a number of courses drawn from different departments and practical work, many seminaries are not interested in introducing new progrmmes like MA, M.Min. or M.Th or D.Min particularly HCD. Other constraints of having qualified faculty to teach at Post-graduate level, constantly building resources in the library, infra-structure facilities of class rooms, raising funds and getting accreditation or approval for the new programmes from the ATA or SSC restrict the institutions not to introduce new programmes either at certificate or diploma or degree or doctoral level. In addition to these constraints, there is some sort of restriction on those colleges affiliated to SSC that they cannot offer new programmes (e.g. MA or M.Th in HCD or Worship, Liturgy and Music or Urban Transformation or Organizational Administration or Handling Natural Calamities, Conflicts and Resolution) which are not available in SSC, in co-operation with ATA or NGOs. This affects the freedom of the colleges to offer new programmes and serve the churches or NGOs who demand such specialization for their pastors, evangelists or social workers. Similarly, ATA should not restrict itself with accrediting only traditional programmes like B.Th, M.Div. and M.Th, in line with SSC but should come forward to support innovative programmes created and proposed by some colleges to offer more specialization and train the candidates with upto-date skill for the demand in society. Nevertheless the quality of the programmes, which will be discussed later in this paper, should not be compromised.

New Courses

The package of the subjects in the curriculum of B.Th, B.D/M.Div. include key courses from different departments. The students may learn 2 or 3 subjects only from each discipline within the 3 or 4 years of their programme. Specialization of biblical studies or theology or religion or counseling or communication or social analysis is difficult in BD or M.Div programme. Unless Choice Based Credit System (CBCS) is introduced at BD/M.Div. level helping students to select courses on the area of their interest along with certain number of core subjects, specialization in a particular area is not possible. Graduates of B.Th and B.D/M.Div come out of the seminaries studying 26-32 subjects but without having a skill for special task in churches and society. In the case of women students on some men students who want to minister among children in churches or communities, they are also expected to learn like majority of the men students prepared for pastoral ministry or missionary work. Why can't they specialize in a particular field of ministry to women, children or musicology? Many women students want to learn courses on Holistic Child Development for their future ministry with families or NGOs or mission societies. But at present such HCD programmes are not available for them to specialize during their basic degree programme or even at M.Th and Doctoral level. However, specialization built within Under-graduate progrmmes and at Post-graduate programmes are developing gradually in India and abroad. More than 20-30 subjects on HCD and 60 research topics are listed to offer fullfledged M.Min, MA, M.Th and Ph.D in HCD.[2]

New kind of Institutions

Innovations are not only in terms of new programmes and courses but also in terms of creating new kind of institutions and different models of training with or without big infra-structure but with suitable pedagogy to offer some of these programmes. For example, separate institutes offering MA or M.Th and Ph.D for Reformation or Ecumenical Studies or Counselling or Managaement or Leadership or Urban Studies can create more subjects on that particular field, work out different mode of learning either fully residential or fully distance mode or partly residential and partly distance mode. Special institutes focusing on one particular area of study can provide in-depth study of subjects, practical work, placement opportunities, take up focused research and attempt for more publications. Already a few institutes such as IIM-RC is offering Missiology. Christian Institute of Management is offering leadership and management. Similar institutes with distance model of education may increase in India focusing on certain area of study like HCD. This cuts down the cost of education and enables the students to continue in their job and get qualified. Demand for such special institutes offering special progrmme is gradually increasing in India. Many involved in ministry may not prefer to go to the traditional seminaries which require 2-3 years of residential stay and collect high fees. Yet, the students may not get what they want in their field of specialization. On the other hand special institutes may use professionals from other institutions, universities, NGOs on contract basis and On-line library and internet to make the students more professional in that field of study. Their net-working with businesses, missionary organizations, churches and NGOs provide fertile ground for carrying out the field research, thesis project and employment opportunities. In addition to offering courses on HCD in existing seminaries, special institutes are needed to offer fullfledged HCD programme of MA, M.Th and Ph.D in South Asia. Many NGOs are looking for such training institutes for their staff members get trained. Graduates of BD/M.Div. are looking for more professional training at Post-graduate level. It is important to note that the traditional programmes of B.Th, B.D or M.Div. will survive in the long run because they are the basic degree to enter into ministry. However, these programmes should be made more innovative periodically by the seminaries with CBCS for specialization. Otherwise such seminaries will be regarded outdated.

Some seminaries, as we are aware, have been closed down. We notice the signs of few others are at the verge of closing down due to lack of vision, innovation and effective training progrmme, students and qualified staff members, able leadership, and politics of the members of the Board, financial difficulties and severe competition. These struggling-seminaries can be turned into special institutes for special programmes focusing on one or two areas of training like Urban/Rural Ministry or Communication or Bible Translation or HCD or Gender Studies or Counselling, Peace Studies, etc.

Will the traditional seminaries draw more students for their M.Th and Ph.D or Special institutes meet the demand of the market? Whose training will be more professional and effective in the field? – are yet to be seen in the future. My observation is that the post-graduate theological degree programmes will be taken up more by specialized institutes emerging in the future in South Asia. Many traditional seminaries may have a set back in offering quality programme combined with professionalism and drawing students for their PG programmes since they have to do justice to basic ministerial programmes of BD/M.Div. These traditional seminaries will have a constant struggle to do justice to all their UG, PG and Doctoral programmes demanding too much from their faculty members, building a mega infra-structure to provide facilities and resources for all their programmes and raising funds to run their programmes. As small is beautiful and effective, decentralizing some of their programmes to special institutes or limiting themselves either with basic or advanced training is the way to reduce their burden and to do justice and enhance the quality.

Quality Enhancement

'Quality' is the word today in the market economy. Parents are looking for quality education and willing to pay any amount of fees to educate their children. Educational institutions from the level of schools to colleges and professional programmes like engineering, medical and business administration are facing cut-throat competition to woo students to them by building modern buildings with all sorts of facilities, creating new courses and training programmes, net-work with overseas universities and companies for placement, appointing well qualified staff members and hiring professionals from companies and NGOs. For them, quality in all the areas is the criteria for their survival and becoming excellent institutions in the ranking of the government, companies, media and public. Unfortunately many churches and seminaries are far behind in quality in terms of their programmes, qualification of staff members, infra structure and producing graduates who would prove themselves honest and effective in ministry. Some of the problems for enhancing the quality of theological education in India can be listed below.

1. Continuing the Western pattern of compartmentalized education than using inter-disciplinary and integrative approaches.

2. Not revising and updating periodically their traditional programmes like B.Th, BD, M.Th. and keeping the curriculum outdated.

3. Suspicion on the part of the Founder, Trustees, Governing Board or Faculty members for any innovative courses and programmes.

4. Lack of funds to develop infra-structure to offer new programmes

5. Complacent attitude of colleges that they got their affiliation or accreditation.

6. Lack of demands on teachers to upgrade themselves, publish papers and books, involve with local communities and take up research projects.

7. Lack of proper evaluation of the performance of teachers and providing Refresher courses by accrediting and affiliating agencies.

8. Lack of effort on the part of the SSC or ATA or University to demand its member colleges for innovation and monitor quality enhancement of programmes, staff members, infra structure and holistic development of students.

9. Lack of Quality Control Mechanism in each institution to evaluate their programmes, curriculum and the performance of each office, departments, staff and student. ISO helps each institution to develop their standard and quality. Seminaries can seek the help of ISO or some other Consultancy Service to evaluate them each year.

10. Lack of accountable relationship with churches and thrust on holistic dimension of ministry.

Innovations without setting standard and monitoring the quality will certainly lead to poor performance of the programmes whether they are existing old or the newly introduced programmes.

II. HOLISTIC CHILD DEVELOPMENT PROGRAMME

Holistic Child Development (HCD) programme is a newly emerging discipline within the past 5-6 years to promote Child Theology as its theological basis and protect the children. But it is ignored unconsciously or neglected deliberately in most of the theological institutions.

Reasons hindering the promotion of HCD programme

1. Churches are not realizing enough the importance of children in families, society and churches. Most of the Christian leaders treat children as students to learn from others rather than listening to what the children say to us about their views, socio-economic, cultural and psychological problems and expectations.

2. In theological education, study of children is either linked to the Feminist Theology or incorporated within the study of women and society or assigned to the Department of Christian Education. What is the understanding of children by the Department of Biblical Studies or in the history of Christianity or in the writings of great theologians namely, Augustine, Martin Luther, Calvin or Indian Christian theologians' or in the scriptures of various religions is not yet fully explored in seminaries except a few thesis on the social problems of children.

3. Procedural difficulties in approving any new course or a separate discipline by the Senate of Serampore as well as by the Board of ATA are a reality. Even if courses on HCD are offered as optional ones by seminaries, getting the approval for the courses is a problem.

4. No group either a particular denomination or a seminary or para-Church organization is devoting their full effort to develop child theology for HCD even though they are involved in taking care of children through their programs and projects such as managing orphanages, children homes and offering primary education and health schemes.

5. Creating child theology requires the involvement of children from various strata of society – rich, middle class, poor, upper caste, schedule caste/tribe and different religions and cultural traditions. Their perceptions, views, problems and expectations differ. So the question is about linking theoretical studies with practical requirement and giving credit to the involvement. This kind of HCD programmes

demand the teachers and academic office to do more preparation, monitoring and evaluation.

6.   Schools and institutions of churches are satisfied with giving formal education to children. They are not influenced to promote Child Theology and work for the holistic development of children. Nevertheless, some state governments provide free mid-day meals to children in schools but without dealing with other socio-economic and psychological problems they face.

Children at Risk – Issues and Reasons

Briefly repeated from chapter 1

Many of us are not aware that millions of children are at risk (CAR) in different parts of the world. In fact, no child whether rich or poor living in cities or villages, is safe today. Any child could be kidnapped for sexual abuse or child labour or for the sake of selling kidney to hospitals. Out of 400 million children at risk, more than 200 million children are in crisis (CIC) facing one or the other problem. According to one statistics India had 298 million children below the age of 14 out of 827 million in 1990. However, it has increased from 30 percent to 40 per cent in 2004 and estimated to be 400 million. Out of it, 100 million children between the ages of 5-14 are not in schools. They may be at home in domestic work or employed as child labour in carpet industry, fire works, auto-mobile workshops and in some dangerous jobs. More than 10 million children die each year because of poverty, mal-nutrition, ethnic conflicts and war in different parts of the world. It is estimated that 3,00,000 children under the age of 18 are in armed forces of the rebel groups in different regions of the world carrying guns and bombs and getting ready for suicide attacks at the cost of their lives. Many of them have not entered into schools to gain formal education except the training to use the guns and bombs. Thousands of children become orphans and left uncared since their parents die of HIV/AIDS or commit suicide or killed in accidents or ethnic conflicts. In the year 2007, nine million children in Africa celebrated their Mother's Day without their mothers who died of AIDS. Hundreds of female fetuses are aborted in various clinics in India. Every day some child is missing when going to or coming from his or her school or during great festivals or picnics and excursions. School education is becoming so burdensome and not giving cordial atmosphere that many children drop out of schools or run away from homes and become street children. Children from *devadhasi* families are forced to practice that system by some villagers. Sacrificing children for the sake of religious ritual happens even now in remote parts of India. Marrying a girl child to an elderly man goes on due to poverty or custom of the caste and village. Girls between the age of 11 to 18 from poor families in villages are bought for Rs.3000 and sold for Rs.50,000 in sex trade going on in big cities. Sexual abuse of children by the members of families, relatives and neighbours led many children to go through psychological trauma and social alienation.

The list of these issues and the problems faced by children are unlimited. The reasons are many and also complex demanding detailed analysis by experts. They can be pointed out here without discussing them in detail.

1.*Economic* reasons such as poverty, lack of medical facility and schools, unemployment, mal-nutrition, environmental degradation, illiteracy, globalization, high taxes on agriculture and alienation of land from communities and disparity in wages and scale of pay, widening gap between the rich and poor, have contributed to the problems of children.

2. *Sociologically*, the major factor is the structure and system of our society practicing patriarchy and gender discrimination. Another reason is the caste system practiced in India. Each child is born with a caste identity which discriminates children from their birth as high caste or low caste or dalits and untouchables. Paying dowry for the daughters to get married in the same caste and spending a huge amount for the wedding ceremony have paved the way for aborting female fetuses and practicing infanticide[3]. Alcoholism and drug addictions have broken families and thrown children on streets. Poor parenting, divorce and separation are affecting the social atmosphere at home that children cannot enjoy peace and progress.

3.Wrong *policies* of the government encouraging violence and conflicts between communities for cheap political gains and political movements recruiting children and training them for their ideologies (e.g. Islamic groups, RSS and

VHP, Naxalites, insurgent movements in North East India) have affected the population of children leaving them without much hope for their future.

4. *Religious teachings* encouraging the children to be sacrificed or married to elderly man, used as a medium for evil spirits, sorcery, thrown into the river or to be offered as a temple prostitute for the gods and goddesses have devalued the life of children. They are treated as a commodity for religious rituals and customs.

Both print and visual media have brought out these issues over the years in their programmes.[4] Churches have been working for the children particularly taking care of orphans and giving education and medical treatment through their schools and hospitals. UNO has required its member nations to accept the Child Rights Declaration and implement it.[5] NGOs both Christian and secular are working for the welfare of the children. However, Child Theology for HCD is developing recently in North America, Europe, India and South East Asia.[6]

III. CURRICULUM OF HCD – COMPONENTS, TEACHING AND LEARNING PROCESS

The nature and component of HCD curriculum have been discussed in the Global Academic Consultation on HCD held in Chiang Mai, Thailand from 13th-17th May 2007 and later in the Consultation held in Fuller Theological Seminary, Pasadena from 25th-28th March, 2008. The following components are important and should be reflected in the curriculum in total and not necessarily in each subject .

  Biblical Perspectives
  Theological basis
  Contextual dimension
  Ecclesiastical aspects
  Ministerial perspectives
  Missionoal dimension

The **general objectives** of the curriculum of HCD had been discussed in various consultations on CAR and HCD held in Bangalore (Sept .2-3rd 2005 and March 17-18th, 2006), Pune (Oct. 2007), Kolkata (24-26th Jan, 2007) and Global Alliance-South Asia Consultation on Curriculum and Resource Development (SAC-CARD) held in Bangalore from 11-14th Feb. 2009.

1.   To have the biblical perspectives on children and their development

2.   To study the status, role and problems of children in families, churches and society.

3.   To identify the reasons and oppressive forces and analyze the issues and develop strategies for the empowerment of children.

4.   To develop partnership and co-operation between Churches – Seminaries – NGOs – Missionary Organizations for exchanging of views, information and involvement at micro and macro-level.

5.   To get a verifiable result in caring, developing and empowering children as an outcome of theological education.

Already a few subjects have been created and offered in some seminaries. For example, 'Biblical Understanding of Children and Pastoral Perspectives', 'Foundations for HCD', 'Introduction to Child Theology', 'Family, Parenting and Child Development' are offered by some Bible colleges in India and South Asia. TAFTEE is incorporating the HCD aspects into their curriculum. Full-fledged HCD programme is now developed in India to offer MA, M.Min. M.Th and Ph. D in HCD to train pastors, lay leaders and staff of NGOs. In the global context, Malaysian Baptist Theological Seminary (Penang) is offering a fullfledged MA in HCD. AGST in Philippines is also offering a degree programme in HCD.

HCD in MA or M.Th or Ph.D can be offered as inter-disciplinary programme with the integration of theory and practice. The Department of HCD in a seminary can co-ordinate the team teaching of faculty members from two or three departments, monitor the practical involvement of those students with children and work out placement for their future ministry suited to the special interest of the students to work among the children of abused or HIV or prisoners or sex workers or broken homes or orphanages as pastors or social workers. Involvement as part of requirement in the curriculum of HCD strengthens the integration of learning theology and praxis. On the one side, it opens the eyes of students who come to the seminaries for theological education and touches their spirituality, perspective of humanity and enables them to move their churches and missions towards caring children at risk. On the other side, those practitioners coming from mission fields or projects of NGOs with first hand experience of working among children learn theological basis. Offering specialized courses with integration through Distance mode incorporating contact seminar classes periodically is the way forward to contextualize theological education and make the training more professional and relevant for churches and society.

Concluding Remarks

Since HCD progrmme is new and innovative, it has a long way to become full-fledged programmes in India. Listing of more courses, writing the syllabus, building the library resource and training the faculty members are tasks ahead of theological colleges that wish to offer HCD courses. All the seminaries, in a more realistic understanding, cannot offer fullfledged HCD programmes. However, all the seminaries can offer one or two Core subjects on Family, Parenting and Child Development under HCD programme to their B.Th, B.D/M.Div. students. Some seminaries and a few special institutes for HCD in different regions of India can plan and offer fullfledged MA, M.Th and Ph.D in HCD. Any innovative programme like HCD in India cannot be well established without net-working with churches, missions and NGOs such as Compassion, World Vision, KNH, Viva-net work and other para-church ministries going on among children. They provide field-opportunities for ministry as well as the feeder of personals for training and teaching. Accrediting and Affiliating agencies involved in theological education should come forward to extend their expertise in developing the curriculum and recognizing the programmes.

Endnotes

[1] A lengthy version of this paper was presented in OCI Consultation at UBS, Pune held from 3-7th Nov.08.

[2] Consultation held in Chiang Mai has listed 60 research topics in the field of HCD. The Curriculum Planning Committee of CFCD-India has listed more than 30 subjects at present. The process of CPC to list more subjects is going on.

[3] J.B. Jeyaraj, *Invisible Children-Infanticide, Feticide and Abortion* (Madurai: JIP, 2008).

[4] Refer to journals such as Economic and Political weekly (EPW), Frontline, India Today, Gender Studies, Manushi and various News Papers columns on children. Also websites and inter-net searches on Children.

[5] Refer to UN Charter on Child Rights

[6] Prof. Marcia Bunge in Valparaso University and scholars in Fuller Theological Seminary in USA, Dr. Keith White and Dr. Hadden Wilmer in UK, Dr. Dan Brewster, Dr. Menchit Wong, Dr. Sunny Tan, Dr. Rosalind Tan and Dr. Theresa Lua in South East Asia and scholars and practitioners in Christian Forum for Child Development (CFCD-India), Viva-India, Compassion, IMA, ATA and in the colleges of Senate of Serampore in India are developing Child Theology contextualizing it to their regional contexts. (Refer to their articles, reports, books and papers).

Questions for Further Discussion

(NOTE: The following questions are listed below for discussions in the class or bible study or seminars or training sessions. More questions can be added by the leader or teacher or pastor)

Chapter I

Biblical Perspectives on Children and Their Protection

1. Do we need to explore the biblical perspectives of children and their protection? Why? And How?

2. Discuss the theological dimension of children by studying various biblical texts. Can they be a basis for mission to and with children?

3. 'Understanding the heart of God for children is a must for us'-Explain with biblical texts and they way they can motivate us for the care of children today.

4. Compare a few law codes in the Old Testament dealing with the protection of children with the Indian laws on children. What are the changes needed today in our legal system and implementing the laws in our society?

5. Discuss the role of families and churches in protecting the children. Do we have 'Child Protection Policy' for our churches and schools? Have we made it known to parents, teachers and children?

Chapter II

Theology of Development and Transformation of Children

1. Does the Bible say anything about the development of individuals and society? –Explain Why and How?

2. What is Holistic Child Development according to Psychology and the Bible? Compare and contrast the key differences between the teachings of Psychology and the Bible.

3. How do you understand the concept of Shalom and the Kingdom of God in relation to children?

4. Discuss the need of co-operation of different Agents such as Churches, schools, NGOs and the Government for the development of children.

5. How can each of these agents contribute for the rights and empowerment of children?

Chapter III

Churches and Kingdom of God: Relationship and Development of Children

1. What is the difference between Quantity and Quality growth of a local church? How does each complement for the development of children?

2. Discuss the nature of the Church and the relationship between local churches and children.

3. What is the Kingdom of God and how do we make it to belong to children? – Explain.

4. How do you define 'Welcoming children' or 'receiving children' as Jesus said to his disciples and its implication for us? – Discuss

5. 'Unless you become like a little child, you cannot enter the Kingdom of God'? – Why? –Explain.

Chapter IV

Children in the Midst: Incarnation and Child Theology

1. Explain the key texts speaking about incarnation and relate them to the study of children.

2. Discuss in detail the key texts speaking about the 'child in the midst' of disciples (Matt.18:1-6).

3. Compare and contrast the ideas of 'God placing his child in the midst of people' and 'Jesus placing a child in the midst of his disciples'. Explain the meaning and purpose of these two actions.

4. What is Child Theology? How does the incarnation of Jesus provide Christological, sociological, political, ecclesiastical and missional basis to formulate a Child Theology?

5. What is Doing Theology? How can we implement Child Theology for the holistic development of children in a pluralistic community? Do we need a caste or tribe based Child Theology?-Discuss.

Chapter V

Invisible children: Infanticide, Foeticide and Abortion

1. How will you define the term 'invisible children'? Give some examples and state the reasons for considering them as invisible.

2. What are the reasons for the practice of male and female infanticide? Explain the way a child is killed by the family. How do they justify the practice of infanticide? Is there a religious or cultural reason to do it?

3. What are the reasons for the practice of foeticide? Explain the various methods used to do it. Who are the people involved in doing it? How do they justify this practice? What is the consequence on the mother of the child? –Discuss

4. Define 'abortion' in terms of medical science, legal and cultural practices. Discuss the reasons for the abortion. What are the consequences on the mother, father and members of the family for allowing abortion of a child?

5. What is the teaching of the Bible on abortion? Can Christians accept the practice of abortion? Discuss on what basis abortion can be done. How can a pastor educate his church on the issue of infanticide, foeticide and abortion?

Chapter VI

Children Rights to Education: Holistic Child Development Training for Parents and Trainers

1. Define the rights and responsibilities of parents and children. How much is your culture and social setting influence the rights and responsibilities of families?

2. Explain the educational system of schools in your location. How much is the school child-friendly to encourage all the children belonging to different caste, tribe, economic status and religious community to complete their school education? Discuss the merits and demerits.

3. What is the Constitutional provision for children to get their rights to education in your country? How does the Government implement this need?

4. What is the role of schools in training parents to encourage children for their holistic development? What sort of training the schools and churches can give for parents to raise up educated generation? How?

5. Are you aware of the Child Protection Policy of your church, school and community?

Chapter VII. Mission Agenda of Holistic Child Development

1. Explain the biblical basis for the mission of God. Relate the basis for the holistic development of children.

2. Ministry to children/by the children/with the children-Explain. Find out biblical and contextual examples for the above three categories.

3. Discuss the ecclesiastical responsibilities for the HCD.

4. Explore some case studies of liberating children from their problems and the way they were protected and development to enjoy welfare and justice.

5. How can the network or partnership among/between churches and organizations and NGOs be strengthened for the rights of children?

Chapter VIII

Raising up a New Generation: Vision and Mission

1. Do we need to raise up a new generation of children? Why? Discuss the reasons for the need of raising up a new generation.

2. Explain the concept of 'New Generation' from biblical perspective. Interpret texts in the OT and NT related to the idea of 'generation' and 'new generation'.

3. Discuss the role of parents in raising up a new generation in this modern context.

4. How can schools play a key role in shaping the character of the present generation of children to be a responsible citizen of the nation? What are the changes needed in their curriculum, teaching methods and commitment of teachers and management?

5. How can religious centers such as Churches, Temples, Mosques and Guruduwas raise up a new generation? What are the criteria for their basis to raise up a new generation? How can they measure their achievements?

Chapter IX

Holistic Child Development: Innovation in Theological Education

1. Discuss the different kinds of theological education or training going on in your region. Find out how many subjects are related to the study of children in the curriculum.

2. What are reasons for not including subjects to deal with the problems and prospects of children in the curriculum or training programmes.?

3. Evaluate the content of each subject related to the study of children and the value of such subjects for the mission to/with children.

4. Discuss the approaches or methodologies used by the teachers or trainers in teaching the subjects dealing with children in the seminaries or mission institutes or by NGOs.

5. Discuss the need of special institutes to offer HCD education in your region at Certificate/Diploma/Degree/Post-Graduate level to train pastors, teachers, social workers and lay leaders to train children parents and members of local community.

Research Topics

1. Select a few children of different age groups, caste or tribe or poor families and rich families and find out their view about children and God. If their views are contradictory to biblical teaching, how can we correct them?

2. Select schools of different level – viz. Government or Municipality or Panchayat school, Christian Mission schools, rich Private schools and schools run by temples or Mosques. Survey the status of children studying in these schools. What is the perspective of these children about God and children in other schools? Are our schools in the nation divided on class and caste orientation? Can schools foster better perspective of other children from poor, rural, tribal communities and relationship for equality and justice?

3. Evaluate the curriculum of Christian Education used by the churches. How much the curriculum and teaching methods develop children holistically? Can the Christian Education programme develop children with good values and the spirit of patriotism and commitment to nation building?

4. Select a few bible colleges and seminaries and evaluate their curriculum. How much their curriculum train the pastors to be transforming agents of children, families and communities? Are their teaching merely academic or spiritual to be professionals or to be practitioners and transformers of churches and society? What are the changes needed in our theological understanding of ministry and training?